THE NAKED TRUTH

It was bad enough when Sabrina opened the door to see Phillip, her husband, and Martine, his mistress, as naked as the day they were born.

It was even worse when Phillip showed no embarrassment but instead was angry at this interruption.

It was quite insufferable when this maddening man accused *her,* Sabrina, of acting like a common trollop in screaming recriminations at him—and reminded her that it was she who had insisted he have his complete freedom in return for giving her the protection of his name.

But what made it all so horrendously unforgivable was that he was undeniably right. . . .

AN HONORABLE OFFER

INDIGO MOON

by *Patricia Rice*

bestselling author of *Love Betrayed*

*Passion ruled her in the arms
of a Lord no lady should love
and no woman could resist*

Lady Aubree Berford was a beautiful young innocent, who was not likely to become the latest
conquest of the infamous Earl of Heathmont, the
most notorious rake in the realm. But as his
bride in what was supposed to be a marriage-in-
name-only, Aubree must struggle to stop him
from violating his pledge not to touch her . . .
and even harder to keep herself from wanting
him. . . .

AN
HONORABLE
OFFER

Catherine Coulter

A SIGNET BOOK

NEW AMERICAN LIBRARY

To My Sisters
Aniko, Ildiko, Leslie,
Ursula, and Zita

PUBLISHER'S NOTE

This book is a work of fiction. Names, characters, places, and incidents are either the product of the author's imagination or are used fictitiously, and any resemblance to actual persons, living or dead, events, or locales is entirely coincidental.

NAL BOOKS ARE AVAILABLE AT QUANTITY DISCOUNTS WHEN USED TO PROMOTE PRODUCTS OR SERVICES. FOR INFORMATION PLEASE WRITE TO PREMIUM MARKETING DIVISION, NEW AMERICAN LIBRARY, 1633 BROADWAY, NEW YORK, NEW YORK 10019.

SIGNET TRADEMARK REG. U.S. PAT. OFF. AND FOREIGN COUNTRIES
REGISTERED TRADEMARK—MARCA REGISTRADA
HECHO EN CHICAGO, U.S.A.

SIGNET, SIGNET CLASSIC, MENTOR, ONYX, PLUME, MERIDIAN AND NAL BOOKS are published by NAL PENGUIN INC.,
1633 Broadway, New York, New York 10019

First Printing, December, 1981

4 5 6 7 8 9 10 11 12

PRINTED IN THE UNITED STATES OF AMERICA

1

Each breath Sabrina took seemed more painful than the last. She clutched the palm of her gloved hand against her breast for warmth and drew to a stumbling halt against a large gnarled elm tree. She hugged its trunk and let the rough bark dig into her cheek. She savored for the moment the shelter it offered her from the biting cold December wind that swirled about her and whipped the naked branches overhead.

She gazed up at the bloated snow-laden clouds and knew that soon the storm would unleash its fury. She forced herself to look about. She had never before seen Eppingham Forest as a huge threatening expanse of dense trees and foliage, nearly impenetrable under the darkening sky.

She pushed herself away from the tree and forced her feet to move forward, in what she prayed was a southerly direction. She had been so certain of herself, even after her mare had sprained her leg, sure that she would find her way through the forest. She wondered now if she would ever find her way before the snow fell and blanketed any landmarks she might recognize.

A thorny bramble tore at her cloak and as she bent to pull herself free, the pain in her chest gripped her again, and she doubled over in a racking cough. Her eyes watered and tears fell in cold rivulets down her cheeks. She dashed her hand across her eyes, but when her vision cleared, it was Trevor's face, almost beautiful in its finely chiseled features, that rose before her. His pale green

eyes, slightly slanted and heavily hooded, mocked her.
She had been a fool to accompany him to the long portrait gallery, set away in gloomy isolation at the back of
the east wing of the hall. She shivered again, not from the
biting cold, but from the fear his memory brought her.

"Don't fight me, my little Sabrina. You're a coy minx
and I've been a patient man. Come now, admit that
you've wanted me."

The gilded edge of her great-grandfather's picture
frame cut into her shoulder blades. She could retreat no
farther.

"You forget yourself, Trevor. Since you are my
brother-in-law, I am willing to overlook your imper-
tinence." She wanted to sound strong and haughty, but
the set gleam in his eyes made her speech thick with fear.
"For God's sake, there is Elisabeth, your wife."

He laughed huskily and reached his hands toward her.

"Stop it, do you hear? Are you lost to all honor? How
can you treat Elisabeth so in her own home?"

"Her home, my little dove? When the old gentleman
dies, 'twill be my house and all who are in it shall call me
lord. You know that I would have preferred you, but it
was not to be. Do not withhold your favors simply because you are jealous of Elisabeth's good fortune. Be kind
to me, Sabrina, for I will give you pleasure you've only
imagined."

She sucked in her breath in disbelief as he leaned
against her and urgently caressed her shoulders. "I shall
scream, Trevor. The servants will obey me, not you."

"Scream yourself hoarse, Sabrina. When I make love, I
do not do it in the hearing of ignorant servants. Ah, I feel
you trembling, my love."

His face was so close to hers she could see the small
drops of perspiration on his lips. She had always thought
his hands too soft and white, his fingers too beringed, yet
when he closed them about her throat, she felt the
strength of him. Her fingers clutched about his, but she
could not pull herself free.

His fingers tightened about her neck and his face

blurred above her. He suddenly released her and she parted her lips to suck in precious air. She felt his mouth against hers and his tongue thrusting hungrily between her lips. For an instant she could not believe what he was doing and held herself rigid. She gagged on his tongue, and instinctively clamped down on it with her teeth.

"You little bitch!" he snarled, furious. He drew back and slapped her hard on one cheek and then the other.

The force of the blows sent her reeling back against the portrait. "You're naught but a vicious and cruel beast, Trevor!"

Her insults seemed to please him. The dark mottled red faded from his face and he laughed. "I like a wench with spirit, Sabrina. A fine, aristocratic young lady you are. I wonder when I take you, as I most assuredly will, if your virgin's blood will flow blue or red."

It hit her with full force that he intended to rape her. She heard herself babbling almost incoherently. "I . . . I will tell Grandfather what you are, Trevor. He will have you killed!"

"You will tell the old gentleman not a thing, little dove. If you do, be assured that I shall assist his rotting old body to find its final resting place. Now, my dear, enough of this nonsense." He paused a moment and gazed negligently about him. "I think it amusing to take you here, in full view of your illustrious ancestors. Do you not think it fitting, Sabrina, that the upstart grandnephew take his rightful place? Such an honor for you to be bedded by the future Earl of Monmouth."

"Lecherous bastard! That you could even be related to the Eversleighs sickens me!"

What a pleasure you are, my dear," he said in a delighted voice, his eyes sweeping her body. "So much more spirit than your Milquetoast sister Elisabeth."

Sabrina shuddered and tried to inch away, but he dug his fingers into her shoulders, pinning her against the portrait. His pale eyes narrowed suddenly and before she could react, he grasped the neck of her gown and pulled it downward. The muslin bodice shredded in his hands. Her mind went blank with fear when he lowered his gaze to her breasts, heaving against the white chemise. Her body willed her to protect herself and she lunged suddenly forward and struggled against him with a frenzied strength she did not know she possessed.

He grasped a flailing arm and twisted it painfully behind her back. A cry tore from her mouth as he tightened his grip, as if delighting in causing her pain. With his other hand, he grasped the laced edge of her chemise and tore it down to her waist. His eyes were glazed with lust as he gazed at her breasts. "God, you're a beauty. Stop fighting me, Sabrina, and I will teach you passion." He pressed his hand roughly against her breast and squeezed it cruelly.

"Stop it!" she screamed, trying yet again to wrench away from him.

"You must learn obedience to your lord, my dear. Pain and pleasure, many times they are the same side of the coin. Whis is uppermost in your woman's sluttish soul, Sabrina?"

"You're despicable, mad!"

His hand left her breast and he clutched at her belly, probing harshly at her through her gown.

"No!" she screamed, sickened with revulsion.

He gave a loud creak of laughter, like an animal's shout of victory. He cupped her hips tightly in his hands, lifted her from her feet, and toppled her onto the hard wooden floor. She felt his lean body slam down on top of her and his male hardness pressing against her belly. She writhed against him with all her strength, but could not free herself.

Suddenly a hand slipped free of his hold and she struck him full in the face with her fist. She felt the touch of sticky blood on her fingers.

His features contorted into a mask of fury and he slapped her, again and again, until she saw nothing except explosions of white pain.

Suddenly, he stiffened above her and she saw his eyes narrow and take on an unseeing, glazed look. He slapped her again, cursing her loudly. She heard him utter a strange, animal-like groan. "Damn you, you little bitch," he growled, and rolled away from her.

Through a haze of shock and pain, Sabrina saw that he was lying on his back beside her, his breathing erratic, panting. There was a wide stain soaking through his breeches.

She jumped to her feet and clutched her torn gown over her breasts. "You beast, you filthy beast," she cried. "I shall kill you myself, do you hear? If ever you try to touch me again, I shall kill you!"

He gazed up at her and touched his cut lip, his noble features once again beautiful in their repose. "You . . . overexcited me, Sabrina, this time. Pain and pleasure, little dove, beautifully and irrevocably intertwined. I shall have you, and no one shall stop me, least of all you. Don't lock your door against me, else I shall tip the balance to pain."

Choking back a sob, Sabrina turned and fled from the portrait gallery, the low heels of her slippers click-clacking like a frightful drumbeat in her ears.

She heard the cat-soft footsteps of a footman and huddled into a small embrasure until he passed her. She gained her bedchamber and with trembling fingers quickly twisted the key in the lock. Stepping to a long mirror beside a walnut armoire, she touched her fingers to her ravaged face. She gazed dumbly at her puffy eyes, still wet with her tears, and her swollen, flushed cheeks. She stared at herself in silence, raging against her own impotence, her helplessness against him.

She remembered when he had first arrived from Italy but a month and a half before, so winsome in his charm, almost boyishly eager to win approval, particularly from Elisabeth. She thought about the first time she had noticed his hands, soft and white, like a woman's. Grandfather had growled under his breath that Trevor was naught but a pampered, vain fop.

Grandfather. Sabrina turned away from the mirror and sat, shoulders slumped, upon her bed. He was so ill. If she told him that Trevor had tried to rape her, after but two weeks of marriage to Elisabeth, he would go into a rage. She swallowed back a sob. Only her grandfather stood between her and her cousin, and he was too old and too sick. Sabrina rose with sudden decision. She would go to Elisabeth. Together, they would decide what was to be done. She quickly dashed cold water on her face to lessen the flushed swelling.

She found her sister in her bedchamber, seated at her small writing desk, penning letters, Sabrina thought, to the wedding guests.

"Leave us, Mary," she said shortly to the maid.

Elisabeth raised pale blue eyes questioningly to her sister, but said nothing until the maid had closed the door. She laid down her pen and out of habit smoothed a wisp of pale hair back into its knot at the nape of her neck. "What is the meaning of your dramatic entrance, Bree?"

"Elisabeth, I must speak with you. I—I know that this will come as a shock to you, but you must help me. We must help each other. It's Trevor, Elisabeth—he just tried to rape me."

Elisabeth arched a pale blond brow and glanced over at the clock on the mantelpiece. "Really, Sabrina, it is scarce after two o'clock in the afternoon."

Sabrina gazed dumbly at her sister, unwilling to believe the flippant mockery in her voice. She rushed forward and laid an urgent hand on Elisabeth's sleeve. "You must listen to me, Elisabeth! It would make no difference to Trevor if it was day or night! He asked me to show him the portrait gallery, and once there . . . he is vicious and cruel, Elisabeth! He even threatened to harm Grandfather if I told him what he tried to do. You must help me decide what we must do."

Elisabeth shook off her sister's hand, as if her touch was distasteful to her. "I forbid you, Sabrina, to speak any more such wanton nonsense. You speak of my husband and our cousin. Does it mean so little to you that he will be the Earl of Monmouth after Grandfather's death?"

Sabrina took an involuntary step backward. "Elisabeth, have you not heard me? It is not wanton nonsense. You must believe me, Trevor has no honor. He is a lecher,

Elisabeth, and unworthy of you. Please, what are we to do?"

Elisabeth sat back in the delicate French chair and tapped her fingertips softly and rhythmically together. "I gather you are still a virgin, Bree?"

Sabrina stared wide-eyed at her sister's calm, impassive features.

"Well, are you?"

A dull flush mounted over Sabrina's cheeks. She knew that if her cousin's body had not played him false, she would not be. "Yes, Elisabeth, I am."

Elisabeth's thick lashes nearly closed over her narrowed eyes. "So, my dear sister, you teased Trevor, and being a man and weak of flesh, as they all are, he gladly accompanied you to the gallery. You then ran away from him when you realized he had every intention of taking your wanton teasing seriously."

Sabrina gasped aloud. "For God's sake, Elisabeth, you cannot believe what you are saying! You make it sound as though I purposefully tried to seduce your husband! I tell you, he is vain and cruel, a strutting evil man who cares not one whit about any of us! Please, Elisabeth, you must help me, help yourself!"

Elisabeth stood abruptly, towering over her sister, and flattened the palms of her hands on the desk top. "Now you will listen to me, you pampered little wretch! For years, even before our parents died, I have watched you twist Grandfather around to your every whim, wheedle your way into his affections so that he had no love left for me. Oh yes, Grandfather allowed me a season in London with Aunt Barresford, hoping that I would find a husband so he would be rid of me. But I always knew that my place was here, even though at every turn you have tried to usurp my position and my authority as the eldest. No more, Sabrina. I am Trevor's wife, and when that miserable old man dies, I shall be the Countess of Monmouth. On that day, my dear sister, I shall be the undisputed mistress here and you will be nothing more than I wish you to be!"

Sabrina drew back at the naked hatred she saw on her

sister's face. Dimly she realized that the cold aloofness Elisabeth had always shown masked a bitter, twisted loneliness. But that she was the cause of Elisabeth's unhappiness left her appalled. She struggled to understand her sister. "Elisabeth . . . surely you are overwrought. You cannot mean that you married Trevor only so that you would be the Countess of Monmouth."

The bleak five years since her eighteenth birthday and her one season in London stretched out endlessly in Elisabeth's mind. Five years watching this precocious child grow into womanhood. She said with deadly calm, "I have done exactly what I intended to do, and you, Sabrina, never had, and never will have, anything to say in the matter."

Sabrina felt a knot of fear clog her throat. "Elisabeth," she pleaded, her voice hoarse, "Trevor threatened to come to me again, even to my own room! He hurt me, Elisabeth . . . he is not natural!"

"Shut up!"

Sabrina stared at her sister's set face. "I had never thought that you so disliked me, Elisabeth," she said finally, striving to sort through all the venomous words her sister had spit at her. "I have never done anything to harm you. I did not know that my loving Grandfather made him care for you less. Indeed, I feel that you must be wrong. Do not turn away from me, Elisabeth. You are my sister and I seek only to protect you and me from that terrible man."

"Get out, Sabrina! I will hear no more of your lies!"

Sabrina drew herself up to her full height. "If you will not heed my words, then I must go to Grandfather." She turned on her heel and walked quickly to the door.

Elisabeth's voice rang out sharply. "If you have the audacity to carry your filth to Grandfather, I shall tell him that in your jealousy, you threw yourself at Trevor and that he repulsed you! Think, sister! Think of your shredded honor! You can expect no quarter from me!"

Sabrina felt suddenly like a hated stranger in her own home. She stood uncertainly at the door, staring bleakly back at her sister.

Elisabeth pursed her thin lips and said with studied preciseness, "No, Grandfather would not believe you. You know, of course, what Trevor would say. Go ahead, Sabrina, go to him. See how quickly he loses his doting affection for you. Mayhap such a vile story would topple him into his grave. Would you like Grandfather's death on your hands?"

Sabrina shook her head stupidly back and forth, unable to frame words.

"You know, Sabrina," Elisabeth continued, carefully watching her sister, "there is really nothing left for you here. If indeed you are so concerned about my husband's attentions toward you, perhaps it would be better if you left." She saw wrenching fear in her sister's vivid eyes and turned abruptly away from her. "Leave me," she said harshly, "your presence sickens me."

Sabrina licked away a tear that had fallen down her cheek onto her upper lip. She tried to get a grip on herself, to force herself to bury for the moment at least the terrible memories of that afternoon. She pressed her hand against her bodice and felt hope at the thought of the three pounds tucked safely inside her chemise. It would be enough to buy a stage ticket to London, to her Aunt Barresford.

She pushed back a heavy lock of hair that had come loose over her forehead, and looked about her. Surely she had walked in the right direction. Were the thick trees not beginning to thin? It could not be too much farther to Borhamwood and the warmth and safety of the Raven Inn.

She felt the searing pain in her chest again, and doubled over, hugging herself tightly. She could hear her own raspy breathing and admitted to herself for the first time that she was ill. She had escaped from Trevor, but to what end? To die alone and lost in this accursed forest? "I don't want to die," she cried out into the bitter whistling wind. In a frenzy, she scrambled through the brambles, each tree becoming a goal to reach and surpass. She felt a surge of hope, for she was certain that the trees were thinning ahead of her. A treacherous root wound its way through the soft moss floor of the forest, and though her eyes saw it, her mind was too clouded to give her feet warning. She hurtled forward and sprawled face downward on the frozen ground. She was stunned by the force of her fall and lay still. She felt curiously warmed by the thick moss that softened the fierce shafts of cold air that swirled about above her.

I will lie here but a little longer, her mind whispered. I am safe from Trevor. It is so very warm. Yes, just a little longer, until I am stronger.

2

Phillip Edmund Mercerault, Viscount Derencourt, drew up his bay mare, Tosha, gazed about him at the forbidding wilderness, and cursed long and fluently. Damn Charles anyway! The man was a sapskull and incapable of providing an accurate direction to anything, save perhaps Bond Street. Not only had he seen no sign for a village called Borhamwood, there had not even been a farmhouse at which he could stop and beg a cup of coffee to warm himself. He had been a bloody fool to wave his valet, Dambler, off with his carriage and luggage. Now he was cold and hungry and had only two changes of clothes in the leather bag strapped to his saddle. Hunting and pre-Christmas festivities at Moreland. Moreland be-damned! he swore glumly.

He patted Tosha's glossy neck and gently dug his heels into the sides of her belly. He assumed a heartening tone and said to his horse, "Come on, Tosha, if we stay here much longer, they'll find us thawing out in the spring."

He wondered, his forehead furrowing in a frown, if he was indeed riding toward the north, for the unremitting dense forest gave him no clue. Tosha suddenly snorted, and he saw to his left a cottage nestled in a small hollow, carved out, it seemed to him, from the midst of the forest itself. He wheeled Tosha about, the thought of hot coffee scalding his lips dampening his anger at Charles.

On closer inspection, he saw that it was not a cottage, but a two-storied red brick hunting box, its facade covered with ivy trim that climbed to the roof. He swung off

Tosha's back in front of the columned entrance, stamped his cold feet, and thwacked the knocker loudly.

He grunted in disgust when there was no response to his knock. The place appeared quite empty. "The owners had the sense to leave this dismal forest until spring," he muttered to himself. "Tosha," he continued to his mare as he swung back into the saddle, "I promise you an extra bucket of oats if you get me to Moreland so that I may thrash Charles."

Phillip groped with one gloved hand through the rich layer of his greatcoat to the watch in his waistcoat pocket. It was nearly eleven o'clock in the morning. He gazed apprehensively up at the gray sky and turned Tosha about again toward the narrow, rutted path.

Despite his fur-lined greatcoat, the swirling wind whipped against him, chilling him to his very bones. He shivered and lowered his head close to his mare's neck.

What had begun as a carefree excursion to roam about the countryside on his own was rapidly becoming a deuced uncomfortable encounter with the winter elements of Yorkshire. He thought now that there was nothing he would rather see more than Dambler's dour countenance, his thin mouth drawn down at the corners in a perpetual look of mourning. At least his valet would have a precious cup of coffee in one bony hand.

A snowflake dropped on the bridge of his nose. He pulled his greatcoat more closely about his throat, ducked his head closer to Tosha's neck, and urged her on. At a fork in the path, Phillip raised his disgruntled face again toward the quiet sky. He had absolutely no notion of which direction to take. He drew a guinea from his waistcoat pocket, flipped it, and with a shrug, turned Tosha to the path at his left.

Despite his discomfort, he found himself grinning at the thought of what his friends would have said had anyone even hinted the week before that Viscount Derencourt would be lost in a forest in Yorkshire.

The snowfall became suddenly thicker, and Tosha, who disliked being uncomfortable as much as her master, snorted and quickened her pace.

The viscount forced away further speculations about his grim present circumstances and thought about Martine, his languid, sensuous mistress. When he had told her that he was traveling to the north for a round of Christmas parties and would be gone from London for some time, she had roused herself, propping herself up on her elbows to gain his attention, and given a lazy laugh. *"Ah, mon grand chou, tu préfères les elements d'hiver à moi!"* He grinned, much of the opinion that he would most willingly part with the bulk of his worldly goods if he could at this moment be warm and naked in her large bed, entwined in her shapely arms.

The snow was driving down in earnest now and the viscount drew up Tosha once again in an effort to get his bearings. It was the thin blanket of white that caused his eyes to rest upon a large splash of dark blue. He narrowed his eyes against the white glare and wiped the rivulets of melted snow from his face.

"What the devil," he muttered, and wheeled Tosha off the path into the forest. He drew her up and gazed down in consternation at a dark blue velvet cloak that covered a motionless female form.

"Good God! A woman!" He jumped off Tosha's back and knelt down beside the still figure. He gently turned her over and stared down at a young girl's face. She was as pale as the white snow around her and her lips were nearly blue with cold. Two narrow scratches slashed down her cheek, the blood congealed with dirt and snow. A thick tress of black hair had escaped the hood of her cloak and fell in wet strands over her forehead.

The viscount stripped off a leather glove and slipped his hand inside the cloak to her chest. She was alive, but her breathing was labored, and he could not rouse her. He had seen many cases of severe exposure three winters ago, in Poland, after the French retreat from Russia, and knew that the result was more often than not a slow numbing death. He quickly scooped her up in his arms, pulling his greatcoat about her as best he could. She was featherlight, despite her soaked clothing.

He realized that he could not continue on, even if he

were alone, for the pelting snow was fast becoming a blizzard. The hunting box was the only answer. Even if the caretaker of the place did not return, it would at the very least allow them shelter.

He pressed her tightly against his chest in an effort to warm her, and wheeled Tosha back toward the hunting box. "Life becomes complicated," he murmured between his mare's twitching ears.

Phillip dismounted in front of a small stable next to the hunting box and quickly led Tosha inside, carrying the girl in the crook of his right arm. He laid her gently down on a pile of hay, quickly removed Tosha's saddle and bridle and covered her with a thick horse blanket.

The heavy oak front door of the hunting box was locked tightly, just as the viscount had expected it would be. His boots crunched in the light blanket of snow as he walked quickly to the back of the house. He came upon another door, this one less sturdy. He took a step back, lifted his right leg, and sent his boot crashing through the door. Clutching the unconscious girl against his chest, he walked into a small kitchen.

He shoved the broken door closed and pulled a small table against it to keep out the raging wind. The kitchen had a rather homey air, he thought, with many small personal items strewn about on the table and counters, a sure sign, he hoped, that the place was not abandoned during the winter months. A neat stack of logs climbed halfway up the wall next to the fireplace and although he did not take time to look into the pantry, he felt fairly certain that there would be sufficient food to keep them from starving.

He carried her quickly from the kitchen, down a narrow corridor that led to the center of the house. He gazed only cursorily into a small dining room, and across the hall, into a parlor. All the furnishings were covered in ghostly white holland covers.

Phillip felt the cold from her wet clothing and hurried up the staircase that wound up in circular fashion to the floor above, taking the steps two at a time.

He found a large bedchamber toward the end of the upstairs corridor, carried her to the daised bed in the center of the room, and whipped back the holland cover. He laid her down and with brisk efficiency removed her sodden cloak. The gown beneath the cloak was equally wet, and as he unfastened the long row of hooks down the bodice, his practiced eye noted the quality and style of the gown. She was no farmer's daughter, that was certain. He frowned at the sight of her boots. They were riding boots, not made for trekking about in a forest. He quickly stripped off her petticoat and shift and rolled down her stockings. With hardly a glance at her body, he bundled her under the covers and drew the musty sheets to her chin. He gathered up the thick masses of raven hair, as wet as her clothing had been, and spread them into a black halo on the pillow, away from her face.

He gently placed his hands against the forehead and cheeks. She was cold to the touch, yet he knew that when he had warmed her, the fever would come and very probably snuff out her life. Just as it had killed Lucius, he thought angrily, his mind laying bare the raw memory. Lucius, his French half-brother, who had willingly followed the doomed emperor into the untamed wilds of Russia, a strong man, a rugged man, so unlike this slip of a girl. As he gazed down at her still figure, he saw for an instant Lucius's ravaged face, deeply etched from the weeks of hunger and the driving winter wind and snow.

Almost fiercely, Phillip pressed the covers hard against her, molding them to the contours of her body. He forced himself to shake off the painful memories that occasionally still haunted his dreams. He gazed again, briefly, at the small pale face and the curved lips that were still blue-tinged with cold. He had failed to save Lucius, but he was damned if he was going to let her die.

He stacked his arms with blankets from the linen closet and layered them over her, then took himself downstairs to the kitchen to fetch logs for a fire. The indolent, rather negligent air for which he was known among his acquaintances fell away from him as if it had never existed.

He laid a huge fire in the fireplace and fanned the embers until flames roared up the blackened chimney. He glanced once again at his patient, saw that there was no change in her, and went to the stables to see to Tosha and to retrieve his baggage.

He shaded his eyes from the driving snow as he walked the short distance between the house and the stable. It struck him forcibly that it was unlikely that the servants who cared for the hunting box would be able to return, at least so long as the blizzard lasted.

As he walked into the stable, he was greeted with a low whinny from Tosha. He saw, with no little relief, a bin overflowing with hay. At least, he thought, he would not have to concern himself about his horse. He patted Tosha's glossy neck, picked up his bag, and made his way quickly back to the house.

He felt cheered at the cozy warmth of the bedchamber. As he unpacked his two changes of clothing and laid them carefully over a chair, it occurred to him that he should put her in some sort of nightgown. He pulled the holland cover off a short, squat armoire and rifled through the drawers. They were filled with men's clothes, and all of them too small for him, he thought ruefully as he lifted them out for inspection. Beneath some underthings, he found two old and well worn velvet dressing gowns.

He sat down beside her and pressed his hands again to her forehead and cheeks. It seemed to him that her skin had warmed to the touch and her lips were a more natural pink color. But she remained unconscious. He gently probed her head through the masses of black hair, but he could find no betraying lump. Gently, he eased the pile of blankets down below her breasts and pressed his cheek against her. Her breathing was labored and he heard a wet crackling sound. He tensed, remembering the same sound from Lucius's tortured lungs. He stripped the blankets from her body and quickly felt each of her limbs. There were no broken bones. She stirred, bringing her arms weakly over her breasts, and shivered violently. He pulled her arms from her body and quickly slipped her into one of the dressing gowns. He smiled slightly at the smallness of her, for the dressing gown covered her nearly twice over. He sashed it at her waist, pulled the blankets up to her chin again, and gently slapped her cheeks.

She mumbled unintelligible sounds, and turned her face away from him. "Come on," he urged, shaking her, "it is time for you to face the world, and me." He remembered all too well the men whom the cold had kept from consciousness and drawn deeper away from life. "Dammit, do as I tell you," he shouted at her.

He clasped her shoulders in his hands and shook her. She whimpered softly, and tried to bring her hands up to strike him away. But she did not have the strength to move the mounds of blankets.

"Open your eyes and look at me," he commanded, still shaking her.

Sabrina heard his voice as if from a great distance and forced her eyes to open. She became aware of a man leaning over her and felt sudden terror. She cried out, "No, please no, Trevor, let me go! Let me go!"

Phillip stared down into large violet eyes, slanted ever so slightly and fringed with thick black lashes. He saw the fear in them and said gently, lowering his face close to hers, "I am not Trevor and I will not hurt you."

She blinked rapidly several times. The man's voice was unknown to her. She strained to clear her mind and her vision. Her eyes became nearly black in her concentration. "You are not Trevor," she said in a raspy voice.

"No, I am not and you have nothing to fear from me."

She suddenly felt the immense weight of the covers and struggled to free herself. "Please," she whimpered softly, "it hurts so dreadfully. I cannot breathe."

Phillip knew that even if he pulled the blankets from her chest, it would not lessen her pain. He compromised and eased back some of them. "It will not help, even if I pull you free of all of the blankets. Do you understand me?"

She continued to struggle, and Phillip caught up her hands in his own and held her tightly. "Nay, little one, I must keep you warm. I know it is painful for you to breathe, but you mustn't fight me." He remembered his long-ago words to Lucius and spoke them aloud. "Take slow deep breaths. I will try to help you."

She nodded almost imperceptibly and closed her eyes.

He took himself once again to the linen closet, grabbed several towels, and set them near the grate. Some minutes later, he lifted the top towel gingerly, for it was nearly too hot to touch, and carried it to the bed.

As he pulled back the covers and opened the dressing gown to bare her chest, he said gently, "This will hurt you for just a moment, but it will let you breathe more easily." She gasped as he laid the hot towel over her breasts and impotently tried to strike it away.

He held her hands and drew the dressing gown and blankets over her. She whimpered in pain and he saw tears wet her lashes.

He did not release her hands. "I am sorry," he said softly, "but it must be done." He tried to distract her.

"What is your name?"

She drew a grating breath and whispered, "Bree."

"Brie is a French cheese. Surely your parents cannot have had so bizarre a sense of humor."

She smiled weakly. "Bree is my nickname, 'tis short for Sabrina."

"That is certainly more palatable than a French cheese. My name is Phillip."

"Phillip," she repeated vaguely. She was surprised that the pain in her chest seemed to be lessening as the heat of the towel sent dizzying warmth deep into her body.

She gazed up at the face above her, a handsome youngish face with regular features. She found herself staring into his eyes, compelling hazel eyes that, she thought, were almost too beautiful to belong to a man. She wondered fleetingly who he was and why she was with him, but the questions slipped away from her.

Phillip saw the intensity of her gaze and wondered what she was thinking. She tried to pull her hands free of his and he let them slip out of his grasp. Tentatively, she brought her hand toward his face. He continued to gaze down at her, his expression unchanging. "You are not like Trevor," she said foolishly. What little strength she had failed her and her hand fell weakly to her side.

"No, Bree, I am not." He gathered her slender hands once again into his and looked down a moment at the tapering fingers. She had wanted to touch his face, for what reason he did not know. Perhaps, he thought, she wanted to assure herself that he was not this man Trevor.

A shadow of pain crossed Sabrina's face and she turned her head away from him on the pillow, not wanting him to think her cowardly and weak. But she could not prevent the racking cough that made her body arch forward with its force.

Phillip rose hurriedly and fetched another hot towel. She shuddered as he laid it over her breasts. He covered her again and rose to look for medicine, anything that would ease her pain. In a small room down the corridor, he found a cache of bandages, ointments, instruments, and laudanum, as he had expected to find in a hunting box. He measured a few drops of laudanum into a glass of water and walked back to Sabrina's bedchamber.

He slipped his arm beneath her head and brought her upright. "Here, Bree, it will lessen the pain."

Although he forced her to sip slowly, the liquid sent her into a paroxysm of coughing. He held her firmly until she regained her breath and placed the glass again to her lips. She managed to swallow the remainder of the laudanum between short, convulsive breaths. Phillip gently eased her back down and she lay quietly, waiting for the pain to leave her.

Phillip stood studying her, letting his eyes rove over the slender contours of her body, and felt a strong tug of protectiveness toward her. She can be no more than eighteen years old, he thought, a young lady of quality and in all likelihood a virgin, for there was no wedding band on her left hand. He felt anger at the man Trevor, who seemed to be responsible for her plight.

He smoothed back a curling lock of raven hair that had fallen over her brow. She seemed to have fallen asleep, her thick lashes lying quietly against her white cheeks. She is really quite lovely, he thought, almost inconsequentially.

Phillip left the bedchamber door open so that he could hear her if she awakened, and walked downstairs to the kitchen. He remembered somewhat ruefully now how he had bunkered around campfires, as had his fellow officers in Spain, roasting birds and rabbits to survive. He had learned to make soup from the remains, had even watched his men bake flat bread in the ashes. But damn, that was more than four years ago. Since that time, it had never occurred to him to wonder where his next meal would come from. He thought of the exquisite repasts prepared for him by his French chef, Dupin, in London, and resolved to give the fellow a higher wage upon his return.

He walked resolutely to a small, cold pantry he had noticed earlier off the kitchen. He was pleased and relieved that the owner of this hunting box certainly knew how to keep it stocked. A haunch of smoked ham hung, beautifully cured, from a hook in the ceiling; there was a bin of flour, sugar and salt, onions, carrots, dried peas, and even a partially filled barrel of apples, shrunken and dried.

Phillip Edmund Mercerault, Viscount Derencourt, donned a large white apron and set himself to the task of making soup. He sliced vegetables, cut up a slab of ham into small pieces, and tossed the lot into a pot with the dried peas. He gazed about him for water, realized that it would not magically appear, and took himself outside to fill a large pot with snow. Some minutes later, he stood next to a newly built-up fire in the grate, gazing down at his pot of soup. "You're not such a useless frippery fellow after all," he said aloud. He stripped off his apron, rinsed the evidence of his cookery from his hands, and strode back upstairs.

He walked quietly to the bedside and looked down at Sabrina. Her eyes were closed and her breathing so raspy that he did not have to bend over her to hear it. He gently touched his hand to her cheek and found her cool to the touch.

Sabrina felt fingers, featherlight, against her cheek and forced her eyes to open. She could make out a man's face above her and for an instant felt a stab of fear. Her memory righted itself and she whispered, "Phillip."

"Yes, Sabrina," she heard him say in a deep, reassuring voice.

For a moment, she thought it strange that he should know her name. She remembered in wispy snatches her flight from Monmouth Hall, her horse twisting her leg in the treacherous undergrowth of the forest, and the bitter, unrelenting cold. "I am so cold," she rasped out. She frowned, trying to understand. "I am not in the forest."

"No, you are not. You are safe with me now. Lie still, Bree, and I will help you."

How did he know her nickname, she wondered as she tried to snuggle deeper under the blankets.

Phillip retrieved another towel from the grate, this one so very hot that he had to toss it several times into the air so that she would be able to bear its heat. She sucked in her breath as he placed it gently over her.

"There, you should feel like a burned slice of toast in a very few minutes."

"I feel more like a hollow loaf of bread," she said shakily. She felt the scalding heat and forced herself to lie quietly. His fingers touched her hair and she heard him say, "Try not to move your head, your hair is still damp."

She gave him a travesty of a smile, and whispered, "I don't think that any part of me could move."

He patted her shoulder. "Try to sleep now, Bree. I shall be here if you need me." She had closed her eyes and he expected no reply. Phillip walked to the long narrow windows and pulled back the draperies. He could see nothing save swirling snow splattering against the windowpanes. A crooked smile passed over his face. The fates and Charles's wretched directions had certainly conspired to alter his life, at least for the present.

The aged Earl of Monmouth sat hunched forward in his chair gazing with ill-disguised contempt at his elder granddaughter, Elisabeth. He shifted his eyes momentarily toward his grandnephew and heir, Trevor Eversleigh, but his impassive handsome features betrayed nothing. Though the earl's body was painfully crooked with gout, his voice rang out sharply. " 'Tis two days now, two days without a clue, without a sign of Sabrina. You know very well, Elisabeth, that she would not leave her home without some powerful reason to motivate her." He pulled a crumpled piece of paper from his dressing gown pocket and waved it at Elisabeth. "As for the letter she left me—it tells me nothing. Dash it all, girl, what does she mean that she can no longer remain here and must go to her Aunt Barresford in London?" He thought of Sabrina's mare, her legs scratched from brambles, the left foreleg lame, returned yesterday to the Hall, and felt his blood run cold. "Enough of your frumpery tales about her depressed spirits! I want the truth from you, girl. Now, if you please!"

Elisabeth stood tall above the earl, her figure almost wraithlike in its slenderness, and nervously shifted her weight to her other foot. What was she to say to this doddering old man who was the undisputed master, and did not even allow her to sit in his presence? Under her grandfather's piercing gaze, she felt what little color she normally had fade into a deathly pallor. She tugged uncertainly at a wispy strand of pale blond hair that had worked its way loose from its modest bun.

"Perhaps, my lord," Trevor said gently, moving closer to her side, "Elisabeth does not wish to cause you more pain." He clutched one of her limp hands in his and squeezed it. "Come, my dear, we must not further dissemble. You cannot protect your little sister forever."

Elisabeth's eyes widened at her husband's words and she gave her head a tiny shake.

"Well, girl, don't stand there like a stupid cow! Out with it! If you know something about Sabrina's leaving, I will hear it now, by God!"

His harshness emboldened Elisabeth to speak out in a low, precise voice. "As Trevor says, Grandfather, I am loathe to cause you pain. But since you insist upon hearing the truth . . ." She shrugged her narrow shoulders and continued more quickly. "If you must know, Bree was jealous of me . . . and Trevor. She wanted him for herself." She stopped abruptly and felt herself grow cold at the growl that came from her grandfather's throat.

"My love," Trevor said softly, "his lordship must know the full of it. Tell him, I beg of you." Elisabeth felt his fingers tighten their grip on her hand and it required all her effort to keep from wincing in pain.

She drew a deep breath. "She tried to . . . throw herself at Trevor, Grandfather, to seduce him so that in his honor, had he taken hers, he would have been compromised in your eyes, mayhap even compelled to leave his home and me."

"What a bloody farrago of nonsense! Drivel, girl!"

"Nay, Grandfather, I speak the truth. Indeed, I saw her. She asked Trevor to accompany her to the portrait gallery, to see Grandmother Camilla's portrait. When they were alone, she flaunted herself, tried to make Trevor make love to her."

Elisabeth faltered, but Trevor continued smoothly, his green eyes limpid in their honesty. "I told her, my lord, that although I held her in great esteem, I would not betray Elisabeth. She flew into a rage and threatened to tell you that I had made . . . advances toward her. Elisabeth happened to be standing near and saw the whole."

The old earl dropped his gaze to his twisted fingers. The silence in the library was broken only by the occasional crackling of burning logs in the fireplace. A spasm of pain furrowed the old man's brow and Elisabeth took a quick step toward him.

"Stay where you are, girl," the earl snarled, his eyes snapping. "So you are telling me that Bree fled her home with naught but a meaningless letter to me, because of your noble rejection of her, Eversleigh?"

Trevor said calmly, "I would assume so, my lord. Perhaps she felt . . . mortified at her behavior and dreaded the whole being told. My lord, she should have realized that as a gentleman I would not have let a word of what happened pass my lips. As for Elisabeth, I am quite certain that she has already forgiven her sister."

His fingers tightened again on Elisabeth's hand and she said quickly, "Trevor is right, Grandfather. Bree knows how much I love her."

"Aye, 'tis certain of that I am," the earl said, ferocious irony in his voice. He gazed through the long French windows at the end of the library at the blizzard, still in its full fury. And Sabrina had not reached Borhamwood to take the stage to London. He felt a spasm of grief grip him, such as he had not felt since his wife, Camilla, died. Sabrina was so very like Camilla, her eyes as deep a violet, her coloring vivid and unforgettable. Not for an instant did he doubt her. Her sense of honor was as strong and unbending as was his own. He felt impotent rage sweep through him. Sabrina might be dead and he was forced to endure Elisabeth and Trevor's betrayal of her. Without looking again at his granddaughter or his heir, the earl said coldly, "Send Jesperson to me. If there is any report on Sabrina, you will tell me immediately." He waved a hand in abrupt dismissal.

"You may be certain that we will, my lord," Trevor said smoothly. Still grasping Elisabeth's hand, he led her from the library. Once he had pulled the doors closed, he turned to his wife. "Are you not all of twenty-three years of age, my dear?"

At her startled nod, he continued in a silky, mocking voice, "And little Sabrina is but eighteen. You had a full five years, my love, to win the old gentleman's regard before she entered the world. How miserably you failed."

"She is gone . . . mayhap forever."

"Perhaps even beyond earthly cares by this time."

Elisabeth's lips tightened. "If she had not been such a whining little fool, running to me for protection. She expected me to denounce you."

"Come, Elisabeth, you have always hated Sabrina. That she proved herself to be a teasing little wanton should please you."

"You and I both know that it is not true," she said softly, her eyes fastened intently upon his face.

"Even though I have been your husband for but two weeks now, my dear, know that I expect loyalty and obedience from you."

Elisabeth's voice grew softer still. "I choose to give you my loyalty because it is in my interest to do so. But as the future Countess of Monmouth, believe me, Trevor, that I shall not allow you to sully the Eversleigh name."

Trevor regarded his passionless bride and wondered if

anyone would ever hear her moan with desire. Since their wedding night, he had treated her with unflagging gentleness, forcing himself to curb his demands. There would be a better time to show her that he was her master, in all things. For the moment, it rather amused him to see her try to control him. She did not even realize that it was the shadow of the old earl that held him in check and not any warnings from her. After the old man died, he would do precisely as he pleased.

He gave Elisabeth his most engaging smile and said with honeyed sweetness, "Alas, my dearest wife, men are sometimes weak. You need have no further worry—'tis you I love and desire above all women."

Elisabeth let his words pass, because she did not think they merited an answer. She stared down at the great emerald wedding ring on her third finger. It was something of which she should be proud, a symbol of what she had long thought she would never have in life. Yet, it still felt alien to her, as alien as it had almost two months ago when the earl had summarily called her to the library, placed the ring in her outstretched hand, and announced baldly, "You are to be married, Elisabeth. The Eversleigh emerald is yours. I trust you will like the fellow, for he will be the Earl of Monmouth after my death."

She had stared at him, wide-eyed, her mouth unbecomingly agape.

"My cousin, sir, Trevor?" she managed finally to ask.

"Of course, my girl, do you think the title would go to a stranger?"

But Trevor Eversleigh was a stranger. Elisabeth had met him only twice in her life, when he visited from his home in Italy. She remembered a slender young man with light green eyes and straw-colored hair, his broad forehead and straight nose classical in their beauty. But somehow, he had seemed soft to her, his apparel rather too precise, his fingers covered with too many rings.

"No, no, of course not, Grandfather," Elisabeth said hastily. "He is coming here?"

"Certainly, how else could you wed with him?" He expected no answer, and waved Elisabeth peremptorily toward a chair opposite him. "Sit down, and I will tell you the whole of it."

The earl looked down at his hands a moment, then began. "As you know, Elisabeth, Trevor is the grandson of my younger brother. You will not remember Trevor's father, Vincent, for he besmirched the Eversleigh name and fled to the continent with a divorced woman, a harlot. I will not sully your ears with tales of his mother's despicable behavior in Italy. Suffice it to say that she contracted the pox some three months ago and died a wretched death. It was then that your cousin wrote me. I do not intend to hold the doings of Trevor's antecedents against him, for he is, after all, my heir and the future Earl of Monmouth. I grow old, Elisabeth. I want Trevor Eversleigh here, at Monmouth Hall, so that he may learn what will be required of him as the future earl. You might as well know too that it is my right and choice to bestow the Eversleigh wealth where I wish. I have told Trevor that the wealth would be his if he agreed to take you for his wife. His reply, of course, shows his good sense. He will, of a certainty, live here with you, at least until my death."

Elisabeth said uncertainly, "But I cannot remember that cousin Trevor even liked me, Grandfather."

"Stuff and nonsense! It's been a full six years since you've seen each other. He is nearly twenty-eight now, a man grown, and you, I might add, are growing no younger with the passing summers. No romantic, childish drivel from you, Elisabeth. He will treat you well enough, trust me for that."

"Yes, Grandfather," Elisabeth said, nodding obediently.

"He will be arriving next week. Your banns will be read then."

The earl turned away from her, as if she were no longer in the room. "You may go now, Elisabeth, to contemplate your good fortune. Send Sabrina to me."

As she walked from the library, Elisabeth had found herself smiling. Whatever her uncertainties about her future husband, she felt elated at the prospect of being married. She had long thought herself on the shelf, her season in London with her aunt, Lady Barresford, having resulted in only two offers for her hand, both from gentlemen with an obvious eye to her dowry. At long last she would be freed from whispered snide comments about her inevitable spinsterhood, freed from unflattering comparisons between herself and Sabrina. And above all, she thought, her pale eyes shining, she would be the Countess of Monmouth.

Elisabeth felt Trevor's fingers caressing her shoulders and flashed him a confident smile. She wondered, almost dispassionately, if her younger sister was dead.

"I fear for Bree's safety," she said aloud to Trevor, trying to disregard his hand, which was caressing her shoulder and moving toward her breast. Her words had their desired effect and he released her abruptly.

"Yes, so do I," he said softly. "It is really quite a pity, quite a pity."

She started at the pensive tone in his voice and felt a stab of anger. "Perhaps" she said in a tightly controlled voice, "she has found shelter."

"Yes," he said slowly. "Perhaps she will soon be returned to us."

"If she does return, I assure you, Trevor, that she will not long remain."

Phillip pulled off his cravat, tossed it on the settee, and sank down wearily into a chair beside Sabrina's bed. He frowned distastefully at the soup he had brought for her, but forced himself to eat the stringy vegetables and the too-salty ham pieces. He set the empty bowl down, leaned back heavily, and closed his eyes. He wondered how long it would be before Charles became worried at his absence. Would he send men out to search for him? A rueful smile flitted over his mouth. It was doubtful, yes, quite doubtful. He imagined that a round of ribald jokes was very likely circulating among the gentlemen of his acquaintance at Moreland, each in turn, he thought, laying wagers on his imagined amorous encounter in the wilds of

Yorkshire with some comely female. What a pity it was that he was not living up to their gleeful imaginings.

He gazed at Sabrina, who was sleeping fitfully, and found himself wondering about her family. The few words she had spoken were in a soft cultured voice, with no heavy Yorkshire accent. Although he realized he was rather an ass for doing it, he pictured a cold, domineering stepmother and a weak, absent father. How else, he wondered, shaking his head, could such a thing happen to a young, well-nurtured girl?

"Well, my dear," he said to the silent Sabrina as he rose and laid the palm of his hand against her forehead, "I shall find out about you soon enough." In his next breath, he cursed softly. Her skin was hot and dry to the touch. The fever he had so dreaded was upon her.

Grim lines deepened about his mouth as she tossed fitfully under the mounds of blankets. Suddenly, she opened her eyes and struggled frantically against the covers. She looked blindly past him and cried out, "No, you cannot, Grandfather, no! My poor Diablo. No!"

Phillip grabbed her shoulders and pressed her back. She gazed up at him, her eyes glazed and unseeing, and brought up her hands to pound against his chest. "Let me go, do you hear? Let me go!"

She sobbed pitifully, choking on her own tears. He scooped her up and rocked her gently in his arms. "Hush, Bree," he said softly, smoothing back the tangled black hair from her forehead. "You are safe now, I promise you."

She quieted and he thought that she would sink back into sleep. But she reared back in his arms and tried to pull away from him. " 'Tis so very hot. Why do we have the fire when it is so very hot?"

He forced a glass of water to her lips and she downed the cool liquid in great, avid gulps. "Open the window, Mary, please open the window!"

Phillip cursed again, this time for his own lack of foresight. There was only one way he knew to bring down her fever. He reluctantly released her and hurried to the small room where he had found the supply of medicines and bandages to fetch a bottle of alcohol.

Sabrina felt that she was suffocating from the waves of burning heat that seemed to come from within her. She heard a man's voice, vague and far away from her. "Lie still, Bree. I will help you."

She felt wet cloth against her face and tried to strike it away. She again heard a man's voice, clearer this time. "You must lie still." She frowned in an effort to understand, but her tenuous hold on reason crumbled at the effort. She suddenly felt cool air on her body and a smoothing damp cloth that seemed to cover all of her. She arched her back against it, relishing its coolness. She felt hands clasp her about the waist, turning her over. She struggled mindlessly until she felt the damp cloth moving purposefully up and down her back, and over her hips, cooling all of her.

Phillip bathed her with the alcohol several times an hour throughout the afternoon, and into the evening. A weary smile lit his eyes when he touched his hands to her cheeks. For the time being, at least, he had broken the fever. He thought for a moment that he saw an answering smile before she closed her eyes in sleep.

Phillip wearily shucked off his clothes, pulled one of the blankets from Sabrina's bed, and stretched out in a large chair near the fireplace. He listened to the night wind howling outside and the swirling gusts of snow slamming against the windowpanes. It was a comforting sound that relaxed his tired muscles and soothed his mind. He was not concerned about hearing Sabrina if she awoke during the night, for he was a light sleeper, his years on the Peninsula having taught him that men who released themselves completely into sleep often never awoke in the morning. The French had deployed small bands of soldiers, disguised as peasants, to slip into English camps and dispatch as many of its members as possible. He would never forget the deep gurgling death sound that had erupted from the throat of his sergeant, a campaign-hardened old soldier from Devonshire. Phillip had caught his assassin and choked the life from the man with his

bare hands, but of course, it had been too late for his sergeant. He felt again the wave of nausea and fury that had
consumed him as he had stood helplessly watching the
man die.

You're becoming a morbid fool, he told himself, and
leaned over to pinch out the flame from the one candle at
his elbow. He gazed for a moment at his large, shapely
hands, with their elegantly manicured nails. They were
the hands of a gentleman, a Corinthian, a man whose
pleasures and pastimes gave no clue of any preoccupation
with the memory of the bloody violence that had occurred
on the Peninsula.

He pinched the candle wick, sighed deeply, and settled
back into the chair. He thought it curious that this one
sick girl had stirred the embers of his past, making him
relive scenes he had believed long buried within him, or
forgotten.

Miss Teresa Elliott frowned down into her glass of
sparkling champagne. "Really, Charles," she complained
aloud in a disgruntled voice to regain her host's wandering attention, "you must have some idea where his lordship could be! Did you not say that you yourself provided
Phillip with directions to Moreland?"

"Yes, I believe that I have mentioned that fact."

She ignored the irony in his voice and continued, "Are
you not concerned that Phillip has not yet arrived? After
all, this wretched snowstorm . . . perhaps he is hurt, lying
helpless somewhere."

Charles gazed at Miss Elliott's undeniably alluring face
and thought for perhaps the third time that it was quite a
pity that such beauty should be wasted on a strident, pet-
ulant woman.

"I fail to understand the total want of feeling you are
displaying, Charles," Miss Elliott said after some moments, snapping down her glass of champagne onto a side
table. "Did you not say that Phillip's valet is here? What
does he have to say in the matter? Surely you have questioned him."

"I begin to believe, Teresa," Charles said sweetly, "that

the champagne is befuddling your memory. Yes, of course I have spoken at length with Dambler. The telling has not changed during the course of the day."

She waved dismissal with a slender hand. "Bah! What a story! The idea that his lordship would send his valet ahead because he wanted to explore the countryside. And alone, of all things! Really, Charles, you know that servants are not to be trusted. Should you not question the fellow more closely?"

Charles motioned to a footman to refill Miss Elliott's glass. Dambler's story that the viscount wanted to roam about Yorkshire seemed not at all unusual to him. On several occasions in the past, Charles had thought Phillip an unaccountable man. But it was wildly unlikely that the viscount could be lost in the blizzard. Phillip was not the type of man to lose himself anywhere, unless, of course, he wished it. He felt Teresa's fingers tugging relentlessly at his sleeve.

"Surely you intend to send out a search party in the morning."

Charles regarded her thoughtfully and concluded that the gathering frown on her forehead could be fully as unpleasant as the snowstorm raging outside. He adopted his placating voice, one he had discovered long ago to be most efficacious with his overly sensitive mother. "Now, Teresa, you know full well that any men I sent out from Moreland would find themselves lost within feet of the front gate. I have no choice but to wait until the weather clears a bit. If Phillip hasn't arrived by then, most assuredly I shall myself lead the search."

He wished he could tell her flatly to stop making a cake of herself. A ghost of a smile flitted over Charles's lips. He thought it quite likely that at this very moment, Phillip was quite at his ease in some inn or in a nearby residence, downing warm ale and seducing the prettiest wench about. Since Phillip had returned some seven years before, a ball in his shoulder, from the battle of Ciudad Rodrigo, he had adopted the attitude that discomfort of any sort was to be avoided at all costs. He repeated his thoughts, in a much censored form, to Miss Elliott.

"Do not forget, Teresa, that Phillip was a soldier for many years. Even if he did find himself caught unawares in the blizzard, he would have had the good sense not to continue on his way to Moreland. I am certain that he is well protected from the elements . . . and undoubtedly regretting his absence from you."

He saw Miss Elliott preen at his hastily added comment, and sought silent forgiveness from the absent viscount. He was delighted when her attention was claimed by Edgar Plummer, a marvelous guest in Charles's opinion. Mr. Plummer bowed his slight frame over her hand and charmingly begged her to indulge the assembled company at the pianoforte. Charles sighed with relief when Miss Elliott, after coyly refusing this request for some minutes, finally acquiesced and followed Mr. Plummer to the pianoforte at the end of the long drawing room.

"Now we're in for it! More of her melancholy French ballads—dedicated no doubt, to poor Phillip!"

"Hush, Margaret," Charles said softly to his younger sister, who had seated herself next to him on the red brocade settee. "At last the lady is well occupied. Remind me to buy a Christmas present for Edgar. Dashed decent fellow he is."

"Was she bothering you again about Phillip?"

"Of course. Methinks Miss Elliott has a marital eye set upon our Phillip. Fortunately, I had the good sense not to tell her that the viscount is likely relieving his tedium during the storm in the arms of some Yorkshire beauty."

"Charles!" Margaret screeched, feigning shock. "You really should not say such things . . . even though I am now a married lady."

Charles grinned, taking in his younger sister's sparkling brown eyes and the pouting fullness of her mouth. She had added weight since her marriage to Sir Hugh Drakemore some six months earlier. She looked alluringly soft, the roundness of her breasts apparent above the décolletage of her satin evening gown. "A married lady you may be, my dear sister, but I know that you have been awake to every suit since you turned fifteen."

The engaging smile left Margaret's lips and she turned

her brown eyes, now slightly narrowed, toward a fine display of Dresden pieces in a buhl cabinet. "You know, Charlie," she said slowly, "I fancied myself much in love with Phillip . . . until I met Hugh, that is. I set all sorts of girlish traps for him, but he always treated me like you do—with affection to be sure, but rather like a small puppy underfoot." She turned to Charles and continued in a saddened voice, "Phillip turned thirty last summer. I have often wondered why he has never married. I know for a fact how many lovely debutantes would gladly accept him."

Charles had been well aware of his sister's infatuation with Phillip, and had wisely held silent counsel in the matter. He saw changes in her now, brought about, he supposed, by his brother-in-law, Sir Hugh Drakemore, a steady, moderate gentleman some years older than Margaret. He read deep caring for Phillip in her eyes, and asked her abruptly, "You have met the Countess of Bufford?"

Margaret cocked her head to one side, her soft brown curls bobbing inquiringly. "Of course. She is a leader among the ton. Mother dislikes her intensely, but she has told me to always give the countess due deference. I must say, Charlie, that I feel sorry for Lord Bufford. He is like an amiable hound following after his mistress . . . waiting for her to toss him a bone."

"Inelegantly phrased, but, I suppose, accurate enough. She was a debutante some ten years ago, and quickly earned herself the title of the Ice Maiden. She was endowed with both splendid beauty and wealth, and her instant success followed naturally from both of these facts together. Phillip was a young captain in the hussars, in London that spring because his father, the late viscount, had just died. Phillip was young, inexperienced in the ways of such women as Elaine, and raw with grief from the death of his father."

Margaret's eyes widened and she gasped. "You don't mean that Phillip fell in love with her?"

Charles shrugged his shoulders. "I cannot be certain of exactly what it was he felt for Elaine, but it was undeni-

ably certain that he wanted her. Is that love? Ah, look,
Edgar is pleading with Miss Elliott to continue her
concert. Cross your fingers that he will succeed."

"I don't care if he succeeds or not, Charlie," Margaret
said, her voice impatient. "Come, tell me what happened."

Charles eyed his sister thoughtfully, wondering why he
had brought up the matter now, after so many years. He
said slowly, "Very well, Margaret, but you must promise
to keep this knowledge safely under your chestnut hair.
Most people know a little of what occurred, but not the
whole of it."

"I promise, Charlie."

"Phillip asked Elaine to marry him and she agreed.
The date was set for the following April, for no marriage
could take place during Phillip's year of mourning for his
father. It is too long ago for you to recall it, but during
the fall of eighteen-oh-five there were many violent skir-
mishes on the Peninsula. Phillip felt it his duty to rejoin
his regiment, over Elaine's objections. I sometimes wonder," Charles mused aloud, "how we all could have been
so wrong. A bloody pack of fools we were! Phillip returned to London on leave in early February to resign his
commission and set Mercerault Ashby in order for its new
mistress. He had changed somewhat, I can remember
thinking that, as if he had been catapulted too quickly
into manhood."

"Do not think me a ninny, Charlie, but I have thought
that Phillip's eyes are a mirror to his soul. I have seen
laughter in his eyes when there was none about his
mouth, and, sadness too, I think."

"Not only are you a ninny, my dear sister, you have
also been reading too many romantic novels."

"Very well, I shall cease my insightful comments on
Phillip's *beaux yeux*. Continue with your story."

"I shall never forget the night he came to my lodgings
on Half Moon Street, vilely drunk, his face so white and
set that I thought he had been at odds with the devil himself." Charles spoke more slowly as he remembered Phillip's young face, his lips twisted in bitter humiliation, his

hazel eyes mirroring his disillusion. He heard his voice, cold as ice.

"Elaine wants to wed now, Charlie, not in April as we had planned."

Charles had replied cautiously, "Is it that she missed you more than you had believed? Surely this is a good sign."

A harsh laugh broke from Phillip's throat. "Miss me! God, that is a rare joke! Give me a glass of brandy, Charles, and be quick about it!"

Silently, Charles moved to the sideboard, poured brandy from the crystal decanter, and handed it to his friend. Phillip tipped the brandy down his throat and, with a growl of fury, hurled the empty glass toward the grate, where it smashed into myriad fragments of glass.

"Dear God, Phillip, what has happened?"

The viscount raised his eyes and said in a voice so flat and soft that Charles had to lean close to make out his words, "Elaine—my Ice Maiden—is pregnant, my friend. Rest assured that I am not the father."

Charles reeled back on his heels. "But who?" he asked helplessly.

"Exactly my question to dear Elaine, which, of course, she tearfully refused to answer. It was not particularly noble of me, but I waited, like a sniffing Bow Street Runner, then followed her. There is no doubt in my mind that the father of her child is her wastrel cousin, Roger." Phillip paused a moment, his eyes turning hard. "Of course he will never know the sex of his child, for I am going to kill him."

Charles sucked in his breath. Of a certainty he had seen Elaine much in her cousin's company, but he was, after all, part of her family. To the eyes of the polite world, there had been nothing questionable about her behavior.

"What do you intend to do about Elaine?"

"That panting little bitch?" His shoulders shook in laughing self-mockery. "If she is an ice maiden, Charles, I ask you, what is every other lady? Well, my friend, I'll tell you what they are—sluts who have no honor, who will part their thighs to the closest male of their acquaintance. I thank God that I have seen the truth in time to escape their clutches."

Charles shook the viscount's shoulders. "You're drunk as a wheelbarrow, Phillip, and you don't know what you're saying! Come to bed. We'll decide what is to be done on the morrow, when you've a clear head and your wits about you."

"No, Charles. What must be done will be done now, tonight. I am off to kill that cur, Roger. You will act as my second?"

"But Phillip——"

Phillip cut him off, his voice harsh. "I require an answer from you, Charles."

"But the scandal, Phillip. Have you thought of what this would do to your mother? To Elaine's family? My God, man, you are the Viscount Derencourt!"

Phillip regarded Charles for a brief moment, then said softly, "If I do not have my honor, Charles, I have nothing. Most likely, all of society will damn me to hell." He rose and shrugged into his greatcoat. "Are you coming, Charles?"

There was a grim, faraway look in her brother's eyes and Margaret impatiently shook his sleeve. "What happened, Charlie? You've trusted me thus far, please, you must tell me the rest of it."

"Needless to say, I accompanied Phillip to Roger Travers's lodging. Both he and his valet were gone. I remember that his housekeeper, a nervous little scarecrow of a woman, showed Phillip a note written by Roger saying that he had left on an extended visit to the continent. As you know, Margaret, there was no scandal. As for Elaine, obviously, she rid herself of the child. It is my opinion that she must have harmed herself irrevocably, for she has never borne Bufford an heir. Phillip left immediately for the Peninsula. It was Elaine who inserted a retraction of their engagement in the *Gazette*. The following June, she married Bufford. The rest, my dear Margaret, you know."

"How could she have served Phillip such a blow!" Margaret exclaimed angrily.

Charles took his sister's small hand into his. "I know that you will guard this secret. Phillip would be most displeased if he knew that I had told you."

"Is it because of that faithless bitch that he has never married?"

Charles was silent for several moments, gazing toward Teresa, who was still charmingly displayed at the pianoforte. "Perhaps such an experience would shape the lives of some men, embitter them, make them hate and distrust women. But not Phillip. He is much too perceptive a man to allow Elaine's despicable behavior to jade his view of the entire female sex."

"But then, why has he not married?"

Charles grinned. "Such a tenacious little bulldog you are, Margaret! I would that you contrive to remember that I am of Phillip's age, and I am not married. Let us just say that I, for one, am destined to be a bachelor. As for Phillip . . ." He shrugged. "Phillip, my dear, is a very careful man."

A martial gleam narrowed Margaret's eyes. "That wretched woman! I tell you, Charlie, Phillip has not married because of that dreadful experience."

"Like all ladies, my dear, you cannot be content unless a gentleman has a deep, twisted secret in his past that has kept him from the altar. Do believe me that the Phillip of ten years ago is most assuredly not the Phillip of today."

Charles's attention was drawn to the sound of Miss Elliott's petulantly raised voice. "No, I have no wish to play whist," he heard her say to the dowager Countess of Mowbray. "The Viscount Derencourt is my partner and I shall wait for him before I play."

"Another ice maiden, I think," Margaret said softly to her brother. "You may be certain that I shall be discreet, Charlie," she added as she rose. "Now, my dear, 'tis off I am to partner the countess in whist."

3

"Please, oh, please, build up the fire. It is so very cold!"

Phillip bundled Sabrina's shivering body more tightly against him, although he was already wretchedly uncomfortable and overly warm. Her face was buried in the hollow of his throat and he could feel the pain each rasping breath brought her. A few errant strands of her hair tickled him under his nose, and he moved his head slightly on the pillow. She moaned softly at his movement and he felt her hands clutch at him, as if she were seeking to bury herself in the warmth of his body. He felt sudden desire for her, and cursed himself roundly. "You're a rutting bounder," he muttered to himself, and forced his mind to other things. How different it had been when he held Lucius against him, as now he held Sabrina, letting his body's heat flow into his shivering limbs. Unlike Lucius, she was nearly engulfed by his body, every part of her warmed by him.

He turned his thoughts from his long dead half-brother to the raging storm outside the windows. A blizzard in December. He made a silent vow to keep his feet firmly planted in London during future winters. A slight smile crossed his lips and he dropped a light kiss on Sabrina's forehead. He was a complaining fool. He had never been much a believer in fate, reckoning that man was his own master, until chance or his own stupidity changed his life. His finding Sabrina had been chance, and he wondered how much further his finding her would change her life, and whether she would change his.

He awoke the next morning sweating and stiff. He felt like giving a shout of victory when he realized that Sabrina was also sweating. He gently eased himself away from her and she rolled into a small ball, her sleep unbroken. He stood quietly, listening to her quiet, deep breaths.

"This time I've won," he said aloud to the silent room. He stood a moment longer, watching the gentle rise and fall of her breasts. He felt absurdly happy, and quite pleased with himself. The chill in the room made him cease his self-congratulations and he took himself off to build up the fire.

As Sabrina slept on into the morning, Phillip heated buckets of water on the grate in the kitchen and dumped them into a copper bathtub. He looked longingly into the steaming tub, threw off his clothes, and lowered his large body into the hot water. After he had scrubbed himself thoroughly, savoring the feeling of cleanliness, he distastefully eyed the pile of clothes next to the tub. Without a second thought, he dumped the clothes into the water and washed them as best he could. He grinned ruefully, thinking of the look on Dambler's face when he saw his master's fine white lawn shirt hopelessly wrinkled, the ruffles about the neck and wrists hanging limply. He thought about ironing, but quickly decided that enough was enough.

He hung his clothes to dry in the kitchen, dressed himself in his only remaining change of apparel, and walked back upstairs to Sabrina's bedchamber.

She still slept, curled up on her side away from him. Her brow was cool, but her dressing gown was still damp with perspiration. To spare Sabrina embarrassment and himself discomfort, he hoped that she would not awaken until after he had changed her.

Phillip quickly eased off the dressing gown, resolutely ignoring the stirring in his loins at the touch of her body. He did not, however, prevent himself from admiring the round softness of her breasts, her curving, white waist and belly, and the slender shapeliness of her legs.

She moaned softly in her sleep and tried to draw her legs up toward her chest, trapping his hand momentarily against her belly as she moved. He gently removed his hand and pulled the dressing gown about her.

Phillip straightened over her and looked down at her quiet face. He felt a deep concern for her and yet he did not even know her. She could very well be another virago like Elaine, he grunted to himself.

The two loaves of bread that the viscount eased from the old iron oven brought a crooked grin to his lips. They were rather flat and burned about the edges, and reminded him of the quarry stones his workers had hauled from the sandstone pit near Mercerault Ashby, his Essex home, to repair the ancient watchtower wall. He waved his hand over the bread to cool it, and gingerly broke off a corner to taste his handiwork. The bread tasted rather like quarry stones, he thought with a grimace. He consoled himself with the thought that it was nonetheless edible and nourishing.

After assuring himself that Sabrina still slept, Phillip shrugged on his greatcoat and took himself to the stables to see to Tosha. Snowflakes still swirled about him, but the howling wind had abated considerably. He looked about at the white frozen landscape, now serene and peaceful, and breathed in the clear, cold air.

Snowdrifts nearly as high as his waist pressed against the sides of the house and stables, looking for all the world, he thought with a contented smile, like the scallops of white frosting on one of Dupin's masterfully constructed cakes. He gazed cursorily toward the path that wound its way to the front of the house, like a giant, sleeping snake. No one would be traversing that road for at least several days.

Tosha welcomed him with a bored whinny and rubbed her velvety nose against his gloved hand. "If we are here much longer," he told her, "you will be too fat for a gallop."

Phillip filled the bin with more hay, scooped up a bucketful of snow that would soon melt in the warmth of the stable into fresh water, and walked slowly back to the house. He raised his head at the sound of the reedy chirping of a lone sparrow and gazed into the snow-laden branches. "If you have any sense, my little friend, you will beg shelter from a woodpecker." He shook his head and smiled. Damn, if Sabrina did not soon regain her wits, he would be conversing with the furniture.

He had nearly finished righting the havoc he had created in the kitchen when he heard a soft, thumping sound from overhead. He tore off the white apron in an instant and bounded upstairs, taking the carpeted steps two at a time.

He pushed open the partially closed bedchamber door and stopped in his tracks. Sabrina stood next to the bed, clutching the bedpost for support, the dressing gown he had wrapped about her hanging loosely on her slender frame, the hem trailing about her like a voluminous green cloak.

He took a quick step forward, his concern for her making his voice abrupt. "What the devil are you doing out of bed?"

She threw her hand up in front of her, startled, and took a jerky step backward. Her feet caught in the dressing gown and she fell clumsily against the small table beside the bed.

He caught her under her arms before she could crash to the floor.

"Take your hands off me!" she cried, and tried vainly to pull herself free of him.

He smiled at the cold hauteur in her voice. Although he knew her body intimately, he realized that he was practically a stranger to her. It was doubtful that she even remembered the few short minutes they had spoken together before the fever had overcome her. He sought first to reassure her.

"I will not hurt you, Sabrina. Do you not remember who I am?"

She shook her head at him mutely, and he read fear in her eyes.

"Come, Sabrina, you must get back into bed. I promise you that you have nothing to fear from me." She stiffened in his arms as he carefully lifted her back onto the bed.

She stared up at him, her large violet eyes unblinking and questioning.

He sat down beside her and out of habit, laid his hand against her forehead. "The fever is gone," he said matter-of-factly. "You will get well again, but it will take some time. No dashing about for you just yet, Sabrina." He gently drew the covers back over her.

"You know my name," she said slowly, her large eyes still fixed intently upon his face.

"Yes. And I know that your nickname is Bree, very much like my favorite French cheese. My name is Phillip."

Her smooth white brow furrowed in concentration. "Phillip," she repeated vaguely, her voice low and hoarse. "Where am I?"

He smiled down at her ruefully. "That, my dear Sabrina, I cannot tell you, for I have no idea myself exactly where we are. I am a stranger to this particular part of Yorkshire."

"If you are a stranger, then what are you doing here . . . my lord?"

"My lord? Now how would you know that I was a lord, a merchant, or otherwise?"

Her eyes fell to his left hand and he let his gaze follow hers.

"I have never known a merchant, or otherwise, to wear a signet ring."

Phillip looked a moment longer at the heavy ruby ring, passed from son to son in the Mercerault family for nearly one hundred years. "You are most observant, Sabrina. If you will allow me to introduce myself to you, I am Phillip Mercerault, Viscount Derencourt."

Phillip thought he saw a flash of recognition in her eyes, but she lowered her heavy black lashes before he could be certain. "May I know more of your name than just Sabrina?"

She hesitated perceptibly before she said carefully, "My name is Eversleigh, Sabrina Eversleigh."

"That is a start." As he spoke, he realized that the name of Eversleigh was not completely unknown to him.

He cudgeled his memory for a moment, then gave it up. Sabrina's eyes were tightly closed.

"Sabrina," he said softly, "do not go back to sleep just yet, you must eat first." He turned at the doorway and said over his shoulder, "You must stay in bed. Next time I might not be so lucky as to catch you before you fall."

Phillip returned to the bedchamber some minutes later, balancing a tray on his arm. "Luncheon is served, my lady. Come, let me ease you higher on the pillow."

She opened her eyes and gazed up at him steadily. "I do not have a signet ring, my lord."

"No, that is true." His eyes flickered briefly over her bare slender fingers. "Nor, Sabrina, do you have a wedding ring." Her eyes widened and he thought he saw a flicker of fear. He quickly retrenched. "Enough of rings, and no more lords and ladies." He clasped her under her arms and eased her to a sitting position, sat down beside her, and vigorously stirred the soup to cool it.

"A recipe from his majesty's own kitchens," he said with a grin, and placed a spoonful of broth into her mouth.

She downed nearly half the bowl before shaking her head. "It is truly delicious, Phillip, but I cannot hold one bite more. Wherever did you find it?"

"You bruise my sensibilities, Bree. If you must know, I am not entirely a worthless fellow, and the recipe is my own."

"A viscount does not cook," she said succinctly.

"If a viscount happens to spend some years on the Peninsula, I assure you that he learns quickly how to keep body and soul together. When you are better, I fear you will realize what a travesty of a soup it really is."

A shadow crossed her face. "My father was killed at the battle of Ciudad Rodrigo."

Eversleigh. Perhaps that was why her name sounded so familiar to him. "I am sorry," he said gently. "Before I let you return to your slumbers," he continued hurriedly, not wishing her to dwell on sad memories, "you will be so kind as to greet my bread as royally and enthusiastically as my soup."

She opened her eyes wide and watched intently as he broke off a small chunk. She laughed hoarsely and it cheered him.

"It looks for all the world like a turtle."

"You mock my chef's creation, madam?"

Her smile deepened and two dimples appeared on either side of her mouth. "Oh no, sir, I have always been most fond of turtles—usually, of course, as pets."

"You are impertinent, Sabrina." While she chewed on the bread, he added, "I had thought my poor bread resembled more the quarry stones near to my home than a turtle."

She swallowed a bit and said with a serious expression, "It is by far the most superior viscount's bread I have ever tasted."

"Quite an accolade, but I think I must do more with the yeast in my next batch."

She smiled again, but weakly, and leaned her head back against the fluffed pillow. She stiffened when he laid the palm of his hand against her cheeks.

"No fever," he said shortly, by way of explanation.

"How long have I been here . . . with you?"

"Two and a half days. I do not know how long you were wandering about in that damnable forest before I found you."

"It is Eppingham Forest."

"Ah. Now I know that you are an Eversleigh and that this forbidding place is called Eppingham Forest."

"What is the day today?"

"It is Wednesday, I believe."

Wednesday. She turned her face away, not wanting him to see her anguish. She had left Monmouth Hall on Sunday. It seemed an eternity to her. She thought of the note she had left her grandfather and blinked back a tear. He would know now that she had not reached Borhamwood. By now he might think her dead.

Sensing her pain, Phillip said gently, "We will speak later of why you left your home, Bree. It is quite likely that your family is at this very moment searching for you.

The blizzard has nearly blown itself out." He closed his hand over hers. "Do not worry, my dear, all will be well. Undoubtedly, my friends are out in force scrubbing about your Eppingham Forest for me as well."

Sabrina could only nod weakly, not certain what he had said to her. She felt weary, incapable of thought. She gazed up at him for a long moment, and heard herself say, "Your eyes . . . you have such beautiful eyes. It seems so long ago, yet I remember wanting to see you frown or smile so that I could read your eyes, so that I would know what kind of a man you were."

"My eyes would not tell you that, Sabrina," he murmured softly. "Sleep now. All will be well, I promise you."

She did not reply. Phillip sat quietly beside her until he was certain that she slept. So I have beautiful eyes, have I, Sabrina, he thought, smiling crookedly. He rose quietly and walked to the window, staring out over the white landscape. Where had he heard the name Eversleigh before?

"Well, girl, don't stand there gawking! Have you any news for me?"

Elisabeth stood before the earl, her eyes downcast, her fingers nervously plucking at the folds of her gown. "No, I am sorry, Grandfather. All of our men have been searching since the blizzard lightened this morning, but as yet, there is no word."

"Trevor is searching with the men?"

"He began the search, Grandfather," she said cautiously, raising her eyes.

"Just what does that mean?"

"Trevor is greatly affected by our severe weather. He was forced to return to the hall a short while ago. He is in his bedchamber, warming himself."

The earl slewed his head about and stared silently for several moments through the bowed library windows onto the frigid white landscape. "Bree is no fool," he said softly, more to himself than to Elisabeth.

No, 'twas always I who was the fool, she thought, bitterness twisting in her belly, never the earl's precious Sabrina. "But I did not run away," she said aloud, "disgracing myself and my family."

The earl's grizzled gray brows drew sharply together. He said acidly, his gaze flitting contemptuously over her, "Bree is no wanton, Elisabeth, even though it suits your uncaring nature to insist upon it. Your spite does you no credit. Sabrina throw herself at that poppinjay, Trevor? The notion is ludicrous!" He saw Elisabeth blanch, but doubted he could bully her into telling him the truth. He had believed, foolishly perhaps, that Elisabeth's dislike of her sister would lessen once he had secured her a husband, and not just any husband, but the future Earl of Monmouth. He had made certain that she would marry before Sabrina, even going so far as to deny a powerful nobleman Sabrina's hand until after Elisabeth was safely wedded. He shook his head, knowing that he was not being entirely honest with himself. No, he had wanted above all things to keep Sabrina with him for as long as possible. If only Clarendon had wanted Elisabeth instead of Sabrina. But of course, he had been drawn to Sabrina the moment he had met her. He forced his eyes back to Elisabeth's pale face. "Well, have you nothing to say?" he demanded, not really knowing what he expected to hear from her.

Elisabeth saw the earl's cold blue eyes resting upon her and forced herself to remember that she was the future Countess of Monmouth. This old man would soon have no more power over her. He would be buried and forgotten, at least by her. "Why is it, sir, if Bree decided to leave Monmouth Hall—for whatever motive—that she did not come and discuss her plans with you? You have said yourself that her letter told you nothing. Does that fact not imply her guilt . . . and shame in this entire wretched matter?"

She saw that she had shaken him. He appeared to shrink visibly in his chair, and his fierce blue eyes dimmed. Ah yes, she thought, your precious Sabrina, who had always shared her fancies and problems with her doting grandfather—gone with only a meaningless letter to you.

The earl drew a deep breath. "I shall never believe the story you and your husband have tried to foist on me, Elisabeth. And now, my girl, you will get out!"

She sucked in her breath, turned on her heel, and walked quickly from the library, without a backward glance. As she made her way across the flagstoned entrance hall, she wondered what would happen to her and Trevor if Sabrina was not consumed by the blizzard.

"Lady Elisabeth."

She turned abruptly, her hand on the balustrade. "Yes, Ribble?"

"Forgive me, my lady, but the Marquis of Arysdale has come to call on Lady Sabrina. He is in the drawing room. I—I did not tell his grace that Lady Sabrina is not . . . here."

Elisabeth's mouth suddenly went dry and she licked her lips nervously. Good God, Richard Clarendon, here! She saw that Ribble was watching her and forced an impassive smile to her face. "I will see him, Ribble." She felt both frightened and excited at the prospect of seeing Richard, the man she had fallen in love with when she was fifteen and he, twenty-two. She had given him every encouragement over the years, had even blatantly talked of her dowry to him, one befitting an heir to the Duke of Portsmouth. When his young wife had died over two years ago, she still held to her slender hopes. She remembered the shock of betrayal she had felt when but six months ago, she had overheard him tell the earl that it was Sabrina he wanted. Her humiliation was made all the worse by the fact that neither of them seemed to care that she was within earshot.

The earl had said jovially, "My little Bree will at least turn you into a very restrained rake, my boy. Such nonsense would never be to her liking, so make up your mind to mend your ways, for I'll not push the girl into a marriage that would bring her unhappiness."

"Sabrina is young, sir," Richard had said suavely, "a spirited, charmingly unbroken little filly. As my wife, my lord, you can be assured that she will never desire for anything more than I can give her. And that, sir, includes other gentlemen."

"So, Richard, you think that your charms and . . . prowess will satisfy my granddaughter, do you?"

"Lady Elisabeth."

She shook herself free of the memory and turned irritably to the butler. "Yes, Ribble?"

"If I may inquire, my lady. Lady Sabrina . . . is there any word of her?"

Elisabeth knew that servants had their ways of discovering things. Surely this old fool of a butler knew that Sabrina had disgraced herself. Yet, he had the temerity to approach her, the now undisputed mistress of Monmouth Hall, to inquire after Sabrina.

"I fear, Ribble," she said coldly, "that my sister could not have survived the blizzard. The men are still searching, as you know, but soon his lordship will realize the futility of it and call them back. Her body will undoubtedly be recovered when the snow melts."

She saw a spasm of grief pass over the old man's wizened brow.

"It is of course a great tragedy," she continued more coldly still, moving away from him, "and a loss to all of us. You may follow me to the drawing room now, Ribble."

Ribble silently opened the double doors to the drawing room and Elisabeth swept into the room.

She greeted him with forced brightness, her hands outstretched. "Richard, why ever are you in Yorkshire, now of all times? I vow that London must be more pleasant a place than Yorkshire at this time of year."

The Marquis of Arysdale straightened from his negligent pose against the mantelpiece and gracefully raised Elisabeth's hand to his lips. "A pleasure to see you, Elisabeth. Marriage appears to agree with you. I only regret that I was unable to attend your wedding."

Elisabeth felt herself respond to the light kiss on her palm, and a slight blush rose to her pale cheeks. Richard was a notorious rake, she had long known it, but she had never cared. Now that she was married and knew well what men wanted of women's bodies, she wondered how different lovemaking would be if Richard were her husband. The stain of red deepened on her cheeks as she pictured Richard's large muscular body naked beside her.

"Where is Sabrina, Elisabeth?"

She lowered her gaze from the marquis and said in a credibly shaking voice, "I pray you to sit down, Richard. The news I have for you is not pleasant."

"What the devil do you mean by that?" The lazy animal grace disappeared.

"Please, Richard," she begged softly, and waved to a blue brocade settee.

"Where is Sabrina?" the marquis asked grimly as he took his seat unwillingly beside her.

How she would have liked to destroy his affection for Sabrina, to tell him how she had disgraced herself, but she knew that she could not. Richard was unpredictable. It was possible that he would go into a rage, perhaps even kill Trevor. "Sabrina has . . . vanished," she said. She lowered her head and waited in silence.

"Sabrina is not a witch. I have never seen her with a broomstick! What the deuce do you mean, she's vanished?"

"It is just as I said, Richard," she managed in a quivering voice. "She fled the Hall last Sunday, before the blizzard. She left Grandfather a vague letter telling him that she intended to go to Aunt Barresford in London. But, of course, we have heard nothing. We fear that she could not have survived."

The marquis bolted to his feet and stared hard down at her, his dark eyes glittering dangerously. "Damnation, Elisabeth, what is this farrago of nonsense? Sabrina knew that I was coming to visit her . . . indeed, there is no doubt in my mind that she knew the reason for my coming."

Elisabeth trembled, relishing the power he had just given her so innocently. "Perhaps, Richard," she said softly, her eyes liquid with commiseration, "you have just provided us with the reason for her running away."

"That's a damned lie, Elisabeth, and well you know it!" He turned on his heel and strode angrily toward the door.

Elisabeth flew to her feet. "Where are you going, Richard?"

He said over his shoulder, not even turning to face her, "To see the earl. It appears that I will never get a sensible account from you."

Sabrina was running down a long, narrow room. People were staring down at her, yet they made no move to help her. She whirled about in her flight at the sound of footsteps closing behind her. Trevor was coming toward her and she saw undisguised lust in his eyes. Something sharp dug into her back and she cried out as she turned. The people's eyes were watching her, uncaring and cold. She screamed as a hand clutched her shoulder.

"Sabrina! Wake up!"

Her terror held her a moment longer from consciousness.

"Wake up! You're having a nightmare!"

Her eyes flew open and she stared up at Phillip's face. She gave a broken cry of relief and threw her arms about his chest.

"The faces . . . there were so many faces and none of them would help me."

Phillip held her tightly against him, smoothing tangled curls back from her forehead. "It was a nightmare, Sabrina. You have nothing to fear. What faces did you see?"

She drew a deep, shuddering breath and leaned back in the circle of his arms to look up into his face. "The faces . . . . they must have been the portraits in the gallery. So many of them . . . all dead, they could not help me."

"You fled to the portrait gallery to escape from Trevor?"

"Yes . . . no," she said, her voice defiant as she gained a hold on herself.

"Who are you, Sabrina? And who is Trevor?"

Even though a part of her wanted to tell him the truth, she knew that she could not. So long as Trevor and Elisabeth stood together at Monmouth Hall, she could never return, nor had she any wish to. She could well imagine Phillip's reaction were she to pour the whole sordid story into his ears. He would take her back and undoubtedly force a confrontation with Trevor. No, she would not allow it. She had made her plans and as soon as she gained her strength back, she would leave Yorkshire and go to her Aunt Barresford. She forced herself to draw away from Phillip.

"I have told you. My name is Sabrina Eversleigh. Trevor is someone who is of no concern to you."

"I beg to differ with you, Bree, everything about you is of concern to me. But I do not at all loathe a little mystery. I have both patience and time on my side."

She reared up suddenly on her elbows. "My money . . . where is my money?"

"You refer to the three pounds and some-odd shillings I found in your bodice?"

Embarrassed color flew to her cheeks. "Yes," she whispered.

He rose from her bed and said gently, "Obviously there is no gambling hell about where I could dissipate your money. Your three pounds are quite safe, I assure you. Since you are awake, I must insist that you eat some more of my soup. You would not wish to return home looking like a wraith."

She felt hated tears fill her eyes. "My home is in London. And it is to London that I must go when I am well again."

"What a clanker, Bree. You will tell me now, I suppose, that you were simply out for a nice winter's stroll and got lost in your Eppingham Forest."

She flinched at his sarcastic tone, but managed to retain her calm. "I was here visiting acquaintances of my family. I live with my aunt in London. Please, Phillip, you must help me return to her."

"What is your aunt's name?"

Sabrina bit her lower lip and turned her face away. "She is married to a . . . London merchant and lives in the city. Her name would mean nothing to you."

"You are an orphan then?"

She had never thought of herself as such, even though both of her parents had died when she was very young. She nodded and was silent.

"God, but you're stubborn! How can you expect me to get you back to your . . . aunt, if you will not tell me who she is?"

"I will return on the stage. That was where I was going when my horse went lame. I did not realize that it would snow."

The viscount threw up his hands. "Enough, Sabrina. If you continue with these unbelievable tales when you are better, I shall take my hand to your bottom."

If she did not look so pitiably weak, the withering, haughty look that she shot him would have been one of the most effective he had ever seen. He was forced to chuckle. "Spare me, my lady. Allow me to fetch your soup now."

"Don't call me that!"

"Why, Sabrina? Even though you do not have a signet ring, I am not altogether ignorant of the ways of ladies of quality."

She shook her head back and forth on the pillow and fell into a spasm of coughing. Phillip leaned over and clasped her against him, gently rubbing her back until the raspy coughs subsided.

"I feel so wretched," she muttered.

"I know." He pressed her gently back down and covered her. "No more grand inquisition, at least for now."

Phillip paused and gazed briefly back at Sabrina before leaving the bedchamber. Lord, she was stubborn!

"Your visit is poorly timed, Clarendon. It would have been better for all of us had you come a week earlier."

"I could get nothing from Elisabeth, my lord. Perhaps you will tell me where Sabrina has gone so that I may go fetch her."

"Stop glowering like Satan himself, Richard! Sit down, my boy, I have enough idiots in my own household without adding you to their numbers."

The marquis curbed his temper and lowered his lean

body into a leather chair facing the earl. He looked closely at the crippled old man and for the first time felt a stab of alarm. He had aged years since the last time he had seen him. His eyes seemed sunken in his face and his shoulders drooped pitiably.

"What has happened, my lord?"

"She is gone, Clarendon, with but a note to me. My men are scouring the area within a twelve-mile circle, but as yet there is no sign of her."

The marquis said impatiently, "Yes, Elisabeth told me of the letter. She said that Sabrina has gone to her Aunt Barresford, in London."

The earl's voice was flat, almost emotionless. "No one of Sabrina's description has left from the posting house in Borhamwood. She is well known in the village, and no one has seen her."

"Then she is staying with friends near to here."

"I am sorry, Richard, but no."

The marquis bounded from his chair like a suddenly unfettered animal and strode back and forth in front of the earl. "Damnation, this is ridiculous!" he said hoarsely. He leaned over the earl's chair and placed a hand on each arm. "Why, sir, why?"

"What did Elisabeth tell you?"

"Elisabeth?" The marquis shrugged irritably. "Only some nonsense about Sabrina running away because I was coming to see her."

A travesty of a smile crossed the earl's thin lips. "It appears that Elisabeth is playing off all her stories. In a way, my boy, I wish I could believe that, but you must know the truth of it—to the best of my knowledge, Sabrina did not remember that you were coming. You have been singularly unsuitor-like these past months, Clarendon, for a man who professes to care for my granddaughter."

Richard drew back, his dark eyes narrowing. "If you will recall, my lord, I agreed to leave Sabrina be until she had turned eighteen. Her birthday was two weeks ago. It would appear that you have not much encouraged my suit with her."

To the marquis's surprise and complete discomfiture, a lone tear fell from the earl's eye and fell crookedly down his wizened cheek.

"Don't you understand what I have been telling you, Richard? She is gone and very likely dead. Her horse returned, lame, and we have had no sign of her. The blizzard lasted two days—no one could have survived it!"

The marquis curbed a shaft of fear that tore through his body and said with a certainty that he was not sure he felt, "Sabrina is young, my lord, but no fool. She is safe, somewhere, she must be! Dammit, why did she leave in the first place?"

The earl forced himself to think about his nephew and heir. Trevor Eversleigh would not make much of an earl, but at least he was an Eversleigh and the line would not die out. He knew that if he told Clarendon the story Elisabeth and Trevor had foisted upon him, the marquis would likely kill Trevor without a second thought.

"I'll not have you yelling at me, Clarendon," the earl said finally. "I am sorry, but I do not know."

At the incredulous look on the marquis' face, the earl added, "The grief is more mine than yours, my boy. I have lost my granddaughter."

"I do not accept your answers, old man," the marquis said coldly. "Sabrina is not dead."

The earl turned his bony hand palm up in a helpless gesture.

The marquis strode quickly to the door. His hand was on the doorknob when he turned suddenly. "Where is your nephew, my lord? I would like to meet the fellow."

The earl managed to keep his eyes from meeting Richard's. "Trevor is in his room, nursing a chill. He was leading the search when he was overcome by the cold."

The marquis snorted derisively.

Mouthing Elisabeth's words, the earl said, "Trevor lived all of his life in Italy, and he is unused to the harshness of our winters."

"Will you send for the fellow, my lord, or shall I visit him in his sick room?"

The earl saw there was no hope for it, and nodded

slowly. "Fetch us both a glass of sherry, Richard. I will see if he is well enough to see you." He raised his hand and tugged on the gold-tasseled bell cord.

Trevor leaned over the side of his bed and pulled open his dressing gown. The maid, Mary, lay on her back, her white legs parted, her breathing heavy with desire. "Please, sir," she panted, stretching out her arms to bring him down upon her.

Trevor slowly slid his fingers along the inside of her thighs, until they closed over her. She moaned softly as he caressed her, and pushed her hips upward toward him.

"Such a slut you are, my girl," he said in a husky voice. He felt her tremble and quickly straddled her, guiding himself deep inside her. She tried to clasp her arms about him to bring his mouth down to hers, but he struck them down. He pushed her skirts higher and brutally dug his fingers into her soft buttocks.

She cried out. He thrust deeper and she moaned, her hips writhing beneath him. "Yes, my little harlot," he whispered, "you adore the pain, do you not? The pain and pleasure together. . . ."

Trevor brought his hand up and closed it over a white breast. He kneaded her as he moved within her, and smiled as he felt her stiffen beneath him. He twisted her nipple cruelly, and thrust himself deep within her. Even as she moaned her pain, her body plummeted her into tearing pleasure.

Trevor felt his own body tense and as he released his seed within her, he gave a shout of satisfaction. "My little whore," he crooned, laying his face next to her slack mouth. He rolled off her suddenly and cursed. Damn Sabrina! She was a slut like the rest of them, yet she had denied him. Now she was dead and he would never have her. He gazed at Mary, who was lolling shamelessly before him. Cheap bitch, he snarled at her under his breath.

There was a knock on the bedchamber door. Mary's eyes flew open to look at him in consternation.

"Cover yourself," he hissed. He rose from the bed,

straightened the covers, and pulled his dressing gown closed.

"Who is it?" he called out in a querulous voice.

"It is Jesperson, sir. His lordship wishes to speak with you in the library."

"A moment, my man. I must dress. Send me my valet." He turned to the disheveled maid and said curtly, "You might as well do something useful while you are here." He pointed to the chamber pot. "Empty it, my girl. I will call you when I want you again."

"But sir——"

"Enough! My valet will come in at any moment. Get out now, girl."

"Yes, sir," Mary said, her voice soft and reproachful. As she picked up the chamber pot, she gazed at him from the corner of her eye. He had shucked off his dressing gown and stood naked by the fireplace. His body was not as beautifully formed as his face. He appeared so soft and white, almost like a woman. And yet she knew she would return willingly enough when he called for her again. The pain in her breasts and buttocks still remained, but it seemed only to heighten the memory of the aching pleasure he had given her. She shook her head at herself as she sidled from the room. She was surprised and somewhat discomfitted at her reaction. Master Eversleigh was a strange, demanding gentleman. She thought smugly of her tight-lipped, prim mistress and wondered if the master had ever managed to make that glacial lady cry out with passion.

When Trevor gracefully entered the library, his apparel was immaculate.

"Ah, here you are, Trevor. This is the Marquis of Arysdale. Richard, my nephew, Trevor Eversleigh."

Trevor stretched out his beringed fingers and winced as the dark, powerfully built man mangled them in a strong, harsh handshake.

"Your grace," he said softly, "an honor." He turned an emerald ring on his finger, away from the bitten skin that had been crushed by the marquis's large hand.

The marquis saw this gesture, took in Trevor's fobbed,

precise clothing, and instinctively drew back. God, he thought, disgusted, the man is a vain coxcomb.

"Trevor, the marquis is here because of Sabrina. He is most concerned, just as we are, about her disappearance."

"Most upsetting, your grace, most upsetting." Trevor drew a lace handkerchief from his waistcoat pocket and daubed it to his forehead.

"I am to marry Sabrina, sir," the marquis said between gritted teeth, "and am looking for a logical explanation for her leaving."

A furious pulse beat in Trevor's neck. "I fear, your grace," he said with a slight lisp, "that I cannot be of assistance to you. Of course, my sister-in-law's precipitous departure has come as a great shock."

The marquis turned away, unable to hide his contempt, and quickly drew on his gloves. "I will not trouble you further," he said to the earl.

"What do you intend to do, Richard?"

"Scour the damned county for Sabrina, my lord. Good day, sir," he said to Trevor, and strode from the library.

Trevor looked at the earl. "You did not tell me that Sabrina was to wed that man."

"She had not accepted him as yet," the earl replied tonelessly.

"I see," Trevor said softly. He began slowly and precisely to turn the gold fob this way and that on his waistcoat. "Such a brute of a fellow he is."

"He is a man. Go back and nurse your cold, Trevor, I wish to think."

A slight sneer indented the corners of Trevor's mouth. "I believe, my lord, that my cold has been sufficiently attended to. I shall speak with my poor Elisabeth now."

The earl's voice halted him at the door.

"I would suggest, nephew, that *your* reason for Sabrina's running away not reach the marquis's ears. He is not an understanding man and I vow he would kill you with his bare hands."

Trevor shuddered delicately. "Such large hands he has," he murmured, and left the library.

4

". . . and without so much as flinching or batting an eyelid, Nell ordered him to drop his trousers. Then she marched him in front of her back to camp, naked as the day he was born, and said to the colonel. 'The lout tried to rape me, sir! I trust that you will see him hanged!' She handed the colonel the pistol and pulled the papers the fellow had stolen from her bodice. 'If attacking a defenseless woman is not enough cause, sir,' she said, 'I trust these documents detailing the English strategy will settle the matter.' The colonel looked at Nell, then at the naked fellow, and dropped his monocle."

"Phillip, you must stop making me laugh! It makes my chest hurt! Sergeant Nell, 'tis a marvelous name."

"Yes, and a more courageous woman I've yet to meet. I believe she is the madam of a very fancy bordello in Brussels now."

"Good heavens! Evidently, Sergeant Nell must have approved of what she saw."

"A little decorum, if you please, Bree."

"If you want me to be a simpering chit, Phillip, you must not tell me such spicy stories."

Phillip leaned forward and tweaked her chin between his thumb and forefinger. She said wistfully, "So many adventures you have had. I have done naught but ride horses, attend boring parties, and scold lazy ser——" She clipped off her words and stared at him stonily.

He said smoothly, "How very enterprising of you, Bree,

to be a bruising horsewoman in London, particularly in the business districts."

"Hyde Park is not the only place to ride, Phillip, and besides, my uncle is a very well-to-do merchant. I can ride any place I wish."

He cocked a disbelieving brow. At her haughty stare, he shrugged and grinned down at her. "Did you know that Wellington is famed for his masterful retreats?"

"But Wellington is England's most victorious general! It is said that he is incapable of losing a battle."

"Precisely, my dear. As a student of his, I have learned when to retreat in order to win the final victory."

"Very well, Phillip, this time I shall grant you the final word, but that is all."

He grinned at her. "And you, Bree, are quite well enough now to have a proper bath." He picked up the thick black braid that hung lifeless and dull over her shoulder. "Your hair, too. What do you say?"

"I would like that. I am beginning to feel quite crawly."

"Don't be insulting. I have nursed you most thoroughly."

She flushed and turned her face away.

He rose and said with a hint of impatience, "Don't be missish, Sabrina. Would you prefer that I had left you in the snow?"

"I am sorry, Phillip," she said in such a humble voice that he stared down at her in amazement. "You have been so very good to me."

"Nonsense, Bree," he said gruffly, and left the bed-chamber.

When he returned, two large buckets filled with hot water slung over his arms, Sabrina was sitting up in bed, gazing at him with an expectant expression on her face. He was obliged to chuckle.

"Please don't dive into the tub until I've filled it."

"You have soap?"

He poured the water into the large copper tub and straightened to face her. "I do wish you would stop doubting my abilities as a scavenger . . . as well as this finely stocked house." She merely smiled and he took himself off to fetch more water.

After he had filled the tub, he turned and paused a moment, watching her unbraid her hair. "I don't suppose you know who the owner of this hunting box is?"

"Why——" She broke off, bit her lower lip, and glared at him. "Of course I don't know. I have told you that I live in London."

"Yes, certainly. How very stupid of me to have forgotten." He grinned, ignoring the mulish set of her mouth, and pulled back the covers. "Come, Sabrina, your bath awaits."

She tucked the dressing gown tightly about her and swung her feet over the side of the bed. He held out his arms, but she paid him no heed. She stood up and almost immediately fell against him. "I feel as weak as water," she muttered against his chest. "Please help me to the tub, Phillip, then you may leave."

"I shall at least carry out the first part of my lady's command," he said, and swung her up into his arms. He eased her down at the side of the tub. She looked up at him stonily. "I shall be fine, now, thank you."

"I have no intention of nursing you back to health only to have you drown in a bathtub." He held her up with one arm and began to unknot the sash at her waist.

"Please, Phillip, I can take care of myself," she gasped, trying to push his hand away.

He frowned over the top of her head and released her abruptly. "Very well. I shall go see to my horse."

She grasped the edge of the tub and did not move until he had left the room. She cursed herself roundly for the absurd weakness she felt and after several abortive attempts, finally succeeded in untying the sash. She shrugged out of the dressing gown, letting it fall in a heap about her feet. She gazed stupidly at the tub. Its edge seemed to her to be an insurmountable height off the floor. She gritted her teeth and concentrated all her energies on climbing over the side. Her fingers suddenly slipped on the edge of the tub, and she cried out as she fell backward onto the floor. She felt near to tears in her vexation and lay quietly a moment, trying anew to marshall her strength.

Two strong arms clasped her about the waist and raised her to her feet. "No!" she choked, mortified.

"Hush, my dear," Phillip said sternly, and lifted her into the tub.

The warm water swirled up about her chin as he released her. Her eyes flew to his face in consternation. Her expression was so comic in its dismay that he was hard pressed not to grin.

He said matter-of-factly as he rolled up his sleeves, "I'll wash your hair. You, I trust, can manage to wash the rest of you." As she held herself stiff for some moments longer, he added with some impatience, "Taking young virgins is hardly to my liking, I assure you, Sabrina." He did not wait for her to reply before setting about scooping handfuls of warm water over her hair.

He pointedly ignored her furtive movements as she washed herself while keeping herself hidden from his view. He found that he rather enjoyed scrubbing her long thick hair.

"Close your eyes, Bree, and I'll wash your face."

She opened her mouth to flatly refuse this command and got a mouthful of soapy lather for her effort. He laughed at the indignant expression in her eyes, the only part of her face that wasn't white with suds.

"Hold your breath, under you go," he said, and pushed her head into the bathwater without further ado. She came up, sputtering for breath.

"Really, Phillip. . . ."

He merely chuckled and wiped off her face.

When all the soap was finally rinsed from her hair, he fashioned a towel about her head, turban-style. He thought briefly about how he could save her further embarrassment, but saw from the evident exhaustion on her face that there was no hope for it. He pulled her upright and swung her out of the tub, splashing liberal amounts of water on both himself and the floor.

She did not have the strength to protest his treatment and clung to him weakly as he towelled her dry. She sud-

denly became aware of his closeness, of her own nakedness and the strength of his arms as she held fast to him.
He turned her slightly to dry the front of her, and instead
of flushing with embarrassment, she found that she was
gazing steadily up into his face. She trembled as the towel
traveled over her belly.

Phillip felt her fingers clutching at his arms and smiled
reassuringly down at her. He met her eyes when he felt
her tremble, and found their expression unreadable. He
felt a rush of desire for her, and cursed himself silently
for being a cad. Without looking at her again, he bundled
her up in the dressing gown and carried her to a chair
next to the fire.

"It is time for your servant to carry out another duty."
He turned away from her before she could reply and
pulled the blankets and sheets from the bed.

Sabrina regarded him for a long moment from the corner of her eye, drawn to the hard leanness of his body.
She wondered about the strange, yet distinctly pleasurable
sensation she had felt when he had touched her, so very
different from the revulsion she had experienced at Trevor's hands. She shook her head, bemused, and regarded
him warily when he came back to brush out her wet hair.

Sabrina slept through the afternoon and awoke near
sunset. She lay quietly for some minutes, savoring the feel
of the clean sheets. She raised her hand to her hair, carefully arranged about her head. The black waves shim-
mered through her fingers, soft and nearly dry. She
smiled, remembering Phillip's good-natured grumbling as
he had brushed through the wet tangles.

Her lingering cough brought her struggling up to her
elbows to catch her breath. She was not at all surprised to
hear Phillip's booted footsteps on the stairs.

"Drink this, Bree, it will soothe your throat."

She looked up at him through watery eyes. He held a
cup to her lips and she gingerly sipped strong, hot tea.

She lay back against the pillow and gazed up at him. "I
think she must have been quite mad," she muttered
vaguely, after some moments.

Phillip placed the teacup on the night table and sat on

the bed beside her. In an unconscious gesture, he smoothed a thick tress of black hair from her forehead.

"Who was quite mad, Bree?"

"The girl you were once engaged to," she said without hesitation. Absurdly, she realized that if she were sitting primly across from him in the drawing room at Monmouth Hall, such a thought would never have found its way into words.

"Good grief! Whatever made you think of her?"

She felt rather foolish for having said such a thing but also cheered by his obvious indifference to the lady. When she had casually asked him if he was married, his reply had been abrupt and unencouraging.

"I presume you are referring to Elaine?" he prodded gently.

She nodded, mutely, aware that she had been impertinent, intruding into an area that was none of her concern.

"And just why do you think her mad?"

She gazed intently at him for a long moment, then said with an impish smile that brought forth her dimples, "With you about, Phillip, she would have been able to make so many economies. She would hardly have required more than one servant!"

"Just because I am an unusually resourceful man, Bree, and able to cope quite well with your vagaries, I will thank you not to cast me irrevocably into the role of a major domo."

She strove for an indignant expression. "What, pray tell, are my multitude of vagaries, sir?"

"Let us begin with your woeful lack of trust in me. I think I must have bored you to tears with the anecdotes that have spanned my thirty years. Yet you, Sabrina, have told me not one whit about yourself. Except, of course," he added in a precise voice, "a royal number of clankers."

She bit her lower lip and gazed down at the green coverlet that was bunched about her.

He saw that she had retreated from him yet again. "You must know," he continued, his voice turning hard, "that the servants that care for this house will be able to return any day now. The weather has turned warmer and the snow is melting rapidly. If I am to help you return safely to your family—wherever they may live—you will have to make a clean breast of it. Was Diablo your horse, Sabrina? Did your grandfather shoot him?"

His abrupt question achieved its desired effect. She gazed at him in startled confusion. "How—how did you know about Diablo? I was but ten years old. My sister took him without my knowing of it and crammed him over a fence." A furrow of remembered pain crossed her brow. "He broke his leg and had to be shot. But how——"

"You were delirious in your fever and cried out about him."

She began to feel alarmed. "Did I speak of anything else?"

"Trevor."

"Yes, Trevor," she repeated dully, and turned away.

Phillip rose and looked down at her. "Dammit, Bree, you must stop being so private with me. No matter what happened, I can help you, if you'll but tell me the truth."

"My truth has nothing to do with you, Phillip." At the angry flaring of his brows, she added with decision, "Starting tomorrow morning, you need never see me again. I shall be quite well and request only that you take me to Borhamwood so that I may take the stage to London."

"I cannot do that, Sabrina," he said in a surprisingly gentle voice. "You know very well that I cannot assist you to escape from your family and put you on a common stage to go heaven knows where."

She saw that he was inflexible and held her tongue. Perhaps, she admitted to herself after he had left her to prepare her dinner, it was unfair of her to try to convince him to assist her to get to London.

Phillip appeared quiet and thoughtful during the evening and Sabrina was aware of his eyes upon her, worried and questioning. For a moment, she felt uncertain. She thought about the chaos that would likely await her at Monmouth Hall and resolutely remained silent. In an effort to distract him, she said, "You told me you were visiting friends here in Yorkshire."

"Yes," he replied shortly, realizing that if she lived in the area, it was likely that she knew Charles Askbridge.

"Whom were you to visit, Phillip?"

Phillip pulled his attention from his filthy hessians and forced his voice to matter-of-factness. "A friend of yours—Sir Charles Askbridge."

Charlie! She cursed herself silently. What a fool she had been to even inquire. She drew a deep breath, aware that Phillip was watching her closely. "The name, I think, is somewhat familiar to me."

"As you well know, Bree, his Yorkshire home is called Moreland. Even though the directions he provided me were execrable, I would wager that Moreland is not too far distant from here."

Indeed, she thought, Moreland is no more than nine miles distant. How very close he had been to his destination. She shrugged and pretended to study her fingernails.

"I wager you are also acquainted with his sister, Margaret."

She shook her head and stared at him with a vacant expression. There was an uncomfortable silence for some moments. Sabrina assumed what she hoped was a guileless expression and asked, "Why were you by yourself, Phillip? Most unusual for a viscount, I should say."

"Very well, you close-mouthed chit, since you know my life history, I might as well add the final details. I would imagine that you are aware of the rounds of Christmas parties held outside of London at this time of year." She looked at him blankly, and he said sourly, "You should have been an actress and trod the boards, Bree. In any case, Charles invited me to Moreland and gave me directions that led me to this isolated place. I had sent my valet ahead, whilst I looked about the countryside. So you see, Sabrina, it is probable that both Charles and your family are out now looking for us." He added significantly, "It cannot be longer than a day now, two at the most."

She knew that he was right, but held her counsel, for

an idea had burgeoned in her mind. She gave a convincing yawn and stretched. "Your delicious soup has made me quite tired," she said mendaciously and snuggled down under the covers.

"Thank God I was never burdened with a sister," he said, and raised his eyes heavenward. "There is a world waiting outside this room, Sabrina. I would that you think about that." He leaned over and patted her on the cheek. "Good night, Bree."

"Good night, Phillip," she said softly, and closed her eyes.

Phillip blew out the candle and walked from her room to a bedchamber down the hall. Since she no longer needed his constant attention during the night, he had begun the previous night to sleep in another room, in a lumpy, musty bed that was at least more comfortable than the cramped chair in Sabrina's room.

Sabrina lay quietly in the darkened room reviewing her plan. With the snow melting, her grandfather—no matter what he thought of her now—would have an army of men searching for her. Even if Grandfather believes me dead, he will search, she thought. She could envision a battleground at Monmouth Hall if she were found and returned to him. He was too old and too sick for that. She knew that there would be no way to keep the truth from him— Elisabeth's betrayal of her and Trevor's vile treatment of her—it would all come out. She could not bring such bitter disillusion to her grandfather. She knew of a certainty now that she could not bring herself to ever again live in the same house with her sister and Trevor, even if Trevor's lecherous behavior toward her were stopped.

She forced her thoughts from her erstwhile home, back to her plan. It seemed to her the essence of simplicity. That she was still pitifully weak from her illness, she resolutely ignored. She would write Phillip a note, apologizing for her abrupt departure on his horse, and provide him directions to Borhamwood, where she would stable Tosha and take the stage to London. She would also pen a letter to her grandfather, reassuring him that she was safe and that she still intended to go to her Aunt Barresford.

She slipped quietly from her bed, lit the candle on the night table, and padded on bare feet to the small desk near the fireplace. She found a pen and several scraps of paper and quickly wrote the lines she had rehearsed. She felt a curious sadness when she ended ". . . please forgive me, Phillip, but I cannot stay here any longer. I thank you for saving my life. Now, I must take care of myself." Her fingers paused, and then she quickly added, "I shall never forget you. —Bree." Her letter to her grandfather took some time longer for her to compose, for it distressed her to cause him further pain. It is the only way, she told herself resolutely, and folded the paper.

She found her gown and cloak, rumpled but dry, hanging in the armoire. She did not see her undergarments. She shrugged at this mild inconvenience, tugged off the dressing gown, and pulled on her dress. She felt her strength ebbing quickly, but she knew that time was against her. She picked up the three pounds that Phillip had laid in a neat stack atop the table, and stuffed them into the pocket of her cloak.

Her boots made not a sound as she crept down the stairs, with both hands on the railing. By the time she reached the outside kitchen door, she was trembling from weakness.

The door latch clicked back with a loud grating sound that made her turn quickly and gaze back into the house. She reassured herself that there was no sound from above stairs, pulled the door open, and quickly slipped outside.

She paused a moment in the cold moonless night and leaned heavily against an elm tree. She thought of Phillip, of his gentleness and kindness to her, and felt a lurching ache deep within her. She had known him for only a short time and yet it seemed quite natural for him to be with her. She resolutely pushed away from the elm tree and found that she was weaving shakily back and forth. She forced her feet to move slowly toward the stable.

She unlatched the stable door and stepped into the dim interior. Tosha craned her neck about at this untimely intrusion and neighed softly.

"Hush, Tosha," Sabrina whispered, and moved slowly

to the bay mare's head. "What a beauty you are," she crooned, stroking the silky mane. Tosha eyed the stranger uncertainly, but allowed herself to be stroked.

Sabrina gazed longingly at the saddle, but realized that she would never have the strength to haul it up on Tosha's broad back. She slipped the bridle off a hook near Tosha's stall and tugged the mare's head down to slip it on.

Once she had fastened the bridle in place, she looked about for something she could stand on, and spotted an empty box lying in the corner of the stable. She felt beads of perspiration standing on her forehead by the time she had hauled it beside the mare's back.

"Please hold still," she begged, gazing uncertainly at Tosha's twitching ears.

After several aborted attempts, she managed to throw herself, stomach down, onto the horse's back. She lay there, her feet dangling, rather like a heavy sack of grain, she thought, until she had enough strength to haul herself upright.

She grasped the reins in her hands and cluck-clucked softly. Tosha did not move. She dug her heels lightly into the mare's sides and flicked the reins again.

"I regret to tell you, Sabrina, that my horse allows only me to ride her."

She whipped about at the sound of Phillip's amused voice and saw him leaning negligently against the stable door, his arms folded over his chest.

She opened her mouth and closed it again. "You!" she finally managed to gasp in disbelief. "I was so quiet . . . how . . . ."

He did not shift from his position. "You of all people should realize that I am a light sleeper. It saved my life on several occasions on the Peninsula. Now, perhaps, it has saved yours also."

Sabrina drew herself stiffly upright and said in her most uncompromising voice, "If Tosha will not allow me to ride her, then I shall simply have to walk to Borhamwood. I know that you cannot help me, indeed, I shall not ask you to. Who I am and what I want to do are none of your affair. I do thank you for your kindness, Phillip, but now I must leave."

She slid clumsily off Tosha's back. When her feet touched the ground, she had to hold onto the mare's mane for a few moments to steady herself. As Phillip still said nothing, she was emboldened to believe that he had accepted her words. Although the thought of trudging through Eppingham forest in the middle of the night gave her considerable pause, she had no intention of relenting. She took a few unsteady steps toward him and gazed up at him fleetingly to see if he would move from in front of the stable door.

He straightened and she found herself staring at the middle buttons of his white shirt. She unwillingly raised her eyes to his face.

"Come back to bed, Sabrina, before you make yourself sick again."

"No," she declared stoutly, and raised her nose in the air.

"Most haughty, my lady, but your attempts at sangfroid leave me quite unmoved." Still, he made no move to touch her. "Do you care so little for your life to attempt a midnight walk through the forest? I do not doubt that there are wolves about."

"I will walk in the road," she said, her expression stony.

"You will walk nowhere, Bree," he said softly. He held out his hand. "Come, my little one."

"I am not your little one," she snapped. "I have made up my mind, Phillip. Please move aside, I would leave now."

He sighed deeply, as would a sorely-tried parent at a stubborn child. He found he admired her display of bravado, misplaced though it was.

"Would you please remove Tosha's bridle?"

Sabrina blinked at this request, and without a word turned about and unfastened the bridle and slipped it from Tosha's head. She tugged on the mare's mane and walked her back into the stall.

"I should have hidden your clothes," he said in a pensive voice as she walked slowly from the stall toward him.

She ignored him and pulled her cloak more closely about her face. "Good-bye, Phillip," she said, and took a wobbly step past him. She felt his fingers tighten about her arm.

"Damn you, let me go! You have no say whatsoever about my actions, and I will not be bullied!"

"Surely your grandfather would not approve of such unladylike language."

As his grip did not loosen, she quickly lowered her head and sank her teeth into the back of his hand.

"You little witch!" He released her, but she got no farther than the stable door. He grabbed her about the waist and tossed her over his shoulder, ignoring her cry of fury. She rained blows upon his back, but they appeared to have no effect on him. Her strength gone, she could do nothing but lie limply. She felt impotent tears sting her eyes.

Once in her bedchamber, Phillip eased her down to her feet and held her tightly against him for a moment.

"Please, Phillip," she whispered, her face buried in his white shirt, "let me go."

"No, Sabrina," he said gently, the warmth of his breath touching her forehead. "I will not allow you to kill yourself, for that is very likely what your mad scheme would lead to, and I have told you why I cannot take you to London. Such an act would be outrageous folly, and little better than kidnapping." He shook her slightly so that she looked up at him. "I will stand by you, Sabrina, and that is a promise." He did not know what his confidently spoken words might entail, but surprisingly, he had meant what he said. He only wished she would believe that he would not abandon her.

He became suddenly brisk, aware that she was trembling. "Can you undress yourself?"

"Yes," she muttered indignantly, but she found that she was sagging against him, her arms hanging limply at her sides.

"I will help you." She wanted to strike his hands away

when he prodded at the small clasps on her gown, but she could not.

Phillip pulled the gown over her head, scooped her up in his arms, and sat her down on the edge of the bed. He reached quickly for the dressing gown that she had dropped unceremoniously on the floor in her hurry to escape and as he tossed her gown aside, he saw spots of blood on it. He felt an instant of panic.

"My God, what have you done to yourself!" He whipped about to look at her. She was staring down at herself stupidly.

"Lie down and let me look at you. However did you hurt your——"

"No!" she shrieked, and grabbed a blanket to cover herself.

Appalled, he gazed at her as she cringed away from him. "But, you are bleeding . . ." he began, only to shut his mouth as realization of her predicament broke through to him.

"Thank God *that* is all that is the matter," he said, relief in his voice.

"Get out!" she cried.

He stood quietly gazing down at her for several moments. Her long raven hair spilled down her back and over her white shoulders. Her head was lowered and she clutched the blanket over her breasts. He said gently, "I will fetch you what is necessary."

She merely dropped her head lower, mortified. He would have liked to chide her, to assure her there was no cause for such embarrassment, but decided it was best to say nothing.

He returned to the bedchamber some minutes later and silently handed her strips of white linen. "Shall I get you some hot water so that you can bathe?"

She nodded mutely, still refusing to meet his eyes. "Sabrina," he began, a touch of impatience in his voice.

She raised her head and cut him off. "Thank you. Please go now."

He was relieved at the calmness of her voice. After he

had placed a bucket of warm water by her bed, he said, "You will call me if there is anything you need?"

Again she nodded, and not knowing what else he could do to help her, he turned and left her room.

Sleep eluded Sabrina until near to dawn the next morning. She felt impotent and helpless. Her plan had failed ignominiously and she was left with nothing but a dreadful sense of the inevitable. She wrapped her arms about her stomach to ease her discomfort and finally fell into an exhausted sleep.

Phillip took in her pale, drawn face the next morning, and the dark smudges under her eyes. He set her breakfast tray on the table beside her and helped her to sit up. "I have brought you good strong tea and toast. It should make you feel more the thing."

"I feel quite the thing!" she nearly shouted at him. "I would thank you to mind your own affairs!" She looked at him stonily and he said finally, with a touch of asperity, "Being a woman is naught to be ashamed of. You are acting as though I were the devil himself, with the sole aim of causing you embarrassment."

As she did not reply, he said only, "Eat your breakfast. I have many chores to perform and will see you later."

He left her to herself for two hours. After he had bathed and shaved, he returned to her bedchamber and lightly tapped on the door.

He heard a muffled, unwilling, "Come in."

She looked to him not one whit better than she had two hours before. "You cannot sleep, Bree?" He walked over to her and sat on the side of the bed. He smiled at her gently and touched his hand to her pale cheek. "Perhaps a hot bath would make you feel better."

She flung up her hand and struck his chest with her fist, furious at his woeful lack of sensitivity. He clasped her fist in his large hand and bore it back down to her side.

"You did not allow me to finish," he said, recovering quickly. "Since a hot bath is out of the question and you are obviously in need of rest, I will give you some laudanum. There are a few drops left, sufficient, I think, to ease your discomfort."

"Yes, please," she replied in a choked voice.

Phillip shook the few remaining drops of laudanum into a glass of water and handed it to her. She downed the entire contents without taking a breath and leaned back against her pillow, waiting hopefully for oblivion.

Philip moved quietly about the bedchamber, straightening the disorder from the night before. He bent down and added several more logs to the sputtering embers, and kicked them with the toe of his boot to spread out the flames. He turned slightly and gazed toward the bed from the corner of his eye. To his dismay, Sabrina lay wideeyed, staring blankly ahead of her.

He pulled the large chair closer to the fireplace and walked to her bed. "You're exhausted and must rest," he said. "Come. I will help you." He gathered her into his arms, blankets and all, and carried her to the chair. He eased himself down, and drew her close against his chest. She gazed up at him for one long moment and closed her eyes. A small sigh escaped her lips and she turned her face inward against his shoulder.

Phillip laced his fingers under her back to hold her steady, and leaned his head back against the chair top. It was some time before he felt the tenseness leave her body and heard her breathing steadily in sleep.

One moment Phillip was sleeping, the next he was alert, his eyes fastened to the half-open door. He heard soft bootsteps on the stairs. He was on the point of dumping Sabrina onto the floor and flinging himself toward the door when a very familiar face appeared.

He stared at Charles Askbridge.

Charles opened his mouth and closed it. His confounded gaze took in Phillip sitting in a large leather chair holding a motionless female in his arms.

"My God!"

"Be quiet, Charles, I do not wish you to awaken her."

Charles obliged, unable in any case to find suitable words to express his bewilderment. He walked quietly toward Phillip and looked down into the half-hidden face of Sabrina Eversleigh. "My God," he said again, his voice barely above a whisper.

Sabrina stirred at the sound, but was too deep in sleep to be roused.

Phillip shook his head at Charles, and carefully rose. He carried Sabrina back to her bed and gently eased her down. He turned to the still open-mouthed Charles and motioned him from the room.

Phillip gazed down once more at her sleeping form and, satisfied that she would not soon awaken, followed Charles from the room.

He was silent until they had reached the bottom of the stairs. "Well, Charles," he said, turning to his friend, "this is a surprise. Do you often break into houses and creep up stairs?"

"Break into houses!" Charles turned a baleful eye toward the viscount. "Hellfire, Phillip, this is my house!"

Phillip felt a mixture of relief and amusement. "The devil you say. Well, old boy, since the absentee landlord has decided to inspect his property, I suppose it would be impertinent of me to boot him out. Do step into your cozy front parlor and I shall serve you up a glass of sherry."

"Phillip, damn you, what the devil are you doing here—and with Sabrina Eversleigh? Good God, man, the entire county is out scouring the forest for the both of you."

"So you know my patient, do you, Charles?" He placed a full glass of sherry into his friend's outstretched hand.

"To your health, Charles," he said, and clicked his glass.

Charles downed the sherry in one long gulp.

"I do wish that you would dispose of that pistol, my friend. I do think it would be a pity if you were to shoot me in the leg with it."

Charles looked dumbly down at the pistol hanging out at an odd angle from his waistcoat pocket. Gingerly, he drew it out and laid it on top of a table. "I wondered if perhaps my intruder could be you," he said inconsequentially.

"You were quite correct. But as you can see, my motives are of the purest."

Charles thought of the ashen-faced Stimson, who along with his wife, was the caretaker of his hunting box. A reluctant grin came to his face. "Poor Stimson—he and his wife keep this place in good order for me during the winter months—he was trembling with fear when he came to see me this morning at Moreland. He said that rogues had taken over the house, and thought he should inform me immediately."

"I think I prefer intruder to rogue."

Charles dropped himself into a holland-covered chair. "How long have you had Sabrina here?"

"Five days now," Phillip replied calmly. "By the way, Charles, just exactly who is she anyway?"

Charles raised incredulous eyes to the viscount's face. "You don't know?"

"No, she has most stubbornly refused to tell me."

"Well, Phillip, you've passed the line this time! By God, man, I had not thought your tastes ran to young, innocent virgins—and this one is not only young and innocent, she is also the Earl of Monmouth's granddaughter!"

"The deuce you say! Why that little minx! Incidently, my friend," Phillip added in a quiet voice, "I did not seduce anyone. I was following your impossible directions to Moreland when I found her close to the edge of the forest, unconscious and suffering from severe exposure. Luckily for her, I remembered passing this place and brought her here, just as the blizzard began. So she is the earl's granddaughter, you say."

Charles groaned and rose to fetch himself another glass of sherry.

"Who is the man called Trevor?" he asked, turning a pensive glance to his agitated friend.

"Trevor? Oh, you mean Trevor Eversleigh, the earl's nephew and heir. He recently wed Elisabeth—Sabrina's older sister—not above a month ago. Quite a lot of flash and ceremony. Bree seemed to be quite all right then."

"Bree? You know her that well, Charles?"

"Known her all her life. Monmouth Hall lies only

about ten miles to the west of Moreland." A look of alarm suddenly passed over Charles's face. "You say she has been quite ill. Will she be all right, Phillip?"

"Yes. She is now merely weak. In a week or so, she should be quite fit." Phillip turned suddenly toward the door. "Follow me, if you please, Charles, my bread should have sufficiently raised itself by this time for baking."

"Your what?"

Phillip merely grinned and left the room. For want of anything better to do, Charles followed him to the kitchen, a room that to the best of his memory he had never entered.

"I am lord and master here," Phillip said, waving his arm about the kitchen. He smiled ruefully as he tested the dough. "If my meager experience serves me, my yeast needs more time to work its magic. Do sit down, Charles," he added smiling, "I am at present tied to my kitchen."

For the first time, Charles took in the viscount's appearance. His white shirt, though clean enough, was wrinkled, as were his fawn-colored breeches. His hessians brought a look of distaste to Charles's face. "Wait until Dambler sees you!" he exclaimed.

"Dambler is with you then. Excellent. I trust you have kept him from overly fretting about my absence."

"No, he is out at this very moment searching for you with my other men. Both you and Sabrina Eversleigh, I might add." He shook his head, in private amusement. "If you must know, Teresa Elliott has been driving me distracted with her infernal tongue. She was trying to shove me out into the blizzard to search for you. At least you no longer have to worry about that young lady leg-shackling you. What a shrew!"

"I assure you, Charles," Phillip said dryly, "that I have never had any intention of wedding Miss Elliott."

"Well, even if she did not bedazzle you with her beauty—which I cannot deny is near to overpowering—it is now out of the question."

"Charles, what the devil are you talking about? If my

faulty memory has not failed me, I recall having taken her for only one ride in the park. That certainly should not give any lady hopes of marriage."

"Evidently, Teresa places sufficiently high confidence in herself to think she would bring Beau Mercerault about. But as I said, Phillip, she is no longer in the picture. You have jumped from the pan into the flames."

"I begin to think that the glass of sherry has addled your wits, Askbridge. Would you care for a cup of strong coffee? As well as chef, I have also become butler."

"Bree Eversleigh is a charming girl," Charles continued, disregarding his friend's strange humor, "near to eighteen, if I am not mistaken." He mentally ticked off the years in his mind. "Yes, she is two years younger than my sister, Margaret," he said finally.

"I had thought her to be about that age," Phillip concurred, well used to Charles's circuituous routes about a subject.

"I suppose it would be best if I seconded you to the altar, old boy. I am certain the old earl would like to keep things as hushed up as possible."

It suddenly struck Phillip with blighting force what Charles was talking about. He said with dampening precision, "You must have windmills in your brain. It is ridiculous that Sabrina and I should wed. My God, man, I have known her less than a week."

"That's the point, Phillip," Charles continued doggedly. "Your reputation with the ladies is not exactly a well-kept secret. You have kept a young unmarried girl with you for nearly a week. She is hopelessly compromised. I doubt that even Richard Clarendon would want her now."

Richard! Good God, that was why the name Eversleigh had sounded so familiar to him. Richard had mentioned to him one night in the midst of a game of piquet, that he was going to wed a young girl from Yorkshire. Now here was Charles playing at an unbelievable propriety, demanding that he, Phillip, wed the chit.

"Richard Clarendon," Phillip repeated slowly, aloud.

"Yes. When he realizes that she has been with you, as great a rakehell as himself, he will probably be inclined to shoot the both of you! Like a madman he's been, nearly killed one of his horses in the snow, searching for Sabrina."

But Richard could not love Sabrina, Phillip thought, else why would he have continued in his dissipated pleasures? He racked his memory, trying to recall Richard's exact words. They had been in a gaming hell just off Millsom Street, both men having left their mistresses but an hour before. Richard was slightly in his cups and the brandy had begun to curl pleasantly in Phillip's stomach as well. "I have found me a wife," Richard said, gazing into the flame of a candle at his elbow. Phillip, thinking he was jesting, laughed and refilled his glass. "She's a delightful girl," Richard continued, still looking into the candle flame, "though I must needs wait some six more months for her. Old Eversleigh made me promise to let the girl reach her eighteenth birthday before declaring myself."

Phillip drew back in some surprise. "You have buried one wife, Richard, and have your heir. You have told me many times that you would never again embark on such a confining, perilous course."

Richard grunted and downed another glass of brandy. "I want her," he said thickly. "She's vivid as life itself. You know," he continued, raising his eyes to Phillip's face, "she is the only comely female I know who has not used all her wiles to trap me. She is curiously unaware of passion, indeed, appears to be sublimely unaware of her effect on men. Yes," he finished, closing the topic, "I want her."

Phillip became aware that Charles was speaking. "I am sorry, what did you say, Charles?"

"I asked you what you intend to do."

Phillip regarded him with some surprise. "Why I shall return her to her family, of course." He suddenly thought of Trevor. "You say, Charles, that Trevor is married to Sabrina's sister?"

"Yes. If you ask me, the whole thing was a bribe. Elisabeth is not a particularly lovable woman."

"Does Sabrina have an aunt in London?"

"Lady Anisa Barresford. You have been to several of her soirees, have you not? The tall dark lady who has a decided squint."

Sabrina's merchant aunt! He nodded absently. Obviously she had intended to flee to her aunt for protection. At least Charles had added sufficient facts so that he would be able to force the whole truth from her. Then, he thought, he would decide exactly what was to be done.

"You still refuse to admit to having compromised her?"

"Dammit, Charles, she has been quite ill. I have cared for her as if she were my own flesh and blood. I cannot believe that saving the girl's life would cast me into the mold of the ravaging villain."

"If it helps, I believe you. But no one else will, let me assure you. She will be ostracized as a wanton, the moment it is discovered that she was with Beau Mercerault."

"My reputation is so very damning, Charles?"

"Yes. You, of course, would emerge unscathed from this episode, but Sabrina?" He shrugged.

Phillip felt a surge of anger course through him. It was true that he had felt desire for her, but he had in no way taken advantage of her. Their intimacy had been forced upon her by her illness. He thought fleetingly of Martine, his mistress. By God, if only he had stayed in London, exquisitely occupied in her arms, none of this ridiculousness would ever have occurred. He calmed his sense of injustice. Sabrina had happened to him and he would be a bounder to leave her sullied in the eyes of the world. "I don't suppose," he said bleakly, "that there is any way of keeping the entire affair hushed up?"

"No, not with the entire county alerted to both your and Sabrina's disappearance. It must come out."

Phillip rose and began pounding mercilessly at the dough. He looked down at the white flour on his hands and smiled despite himself. He repeated softly to Charles the same words he had spoken to Sabrina. "I have done quite well by her, you know."

"Evidently you have, but now, my friend, you must do much more."

Phillip cursed fluently.

Charles appeared unruffled at the colorful string of invectives. "It is the right thing to do, Phillip, the honorable thing."

"Honor bedamned," he growled, and sent his fist again into the dough.

"One cannot bedamn honor," Charles said stoutly.

Elaine bedamned my honor, Phillip thought with sudden bitter memory. His mind raced over the past ten years, years that he had spent by himself, concerned with only his pleasures. He said slowly, "I suppose that you are right. Someone must see to her. I have the distinct impression that left to her own devices, she would fall from one scrape into another. At least I can hold her on a tight rein."

To Phillip's surprise, Charles threw back his hand and laughed heartily.

"Explain your unwanted display of mirth, if you please, Charles."

"You are quite right about Bree and her scrapes. Lord, when I remember the mischief she was always leading poor Margaret into." He cocked an amused brow. "You have known her for less than a week, Phillip. And she has been quite ill at that. Beware, my friend!"

Phillip thought about her outrageous attempt to escape from him the night before. "She will obey me, I shall see to it." He formed the dough into two loaves and slid them into the oven.

"You will join me for lunch, I trust, Charles. We must decide what is to be done. When Sabrina wakes up, I shall inform her."

5

But Charles did not remain for lunch, the two men having decided that Sabrina's grandfather should be informed at once and the search halted. Phillip prepared a tray for Sabrina and made his way upstairs to her bedchamber.

He found that he was rather looking forward to her reaction when he told her that he knew who she was. At last he could break through that stubborn, silent barrier she had erected. He decided that he did not at all dislike her stubbornness, certainly not a bad quality in a wife—if controlled, he amended to himself. Now that he had accepted the fact that he would wed her, he thought she would suit him quite nicely. She was undeniably lovely, both in face and figure, and her quickness of wit pleased him. Although he had known her but five days, he realized that he did care about her sufficiently to embark upon married life without too many qualms as to its success. She would enjoy the protection of his name and all the advantages his station in life could afford her. He thought her intelligent and spirited, a combination that should make her adjustment to town life not at all bothersome, particularly to him. He would, of course, have to make it clear to her, sooner or later, that although he would be her husband, he had no intention of dismantling his comfortable habits. She would have to understand that he was simply not ready to become a monogamous mate, for he treasured his freedom highly.

"I knew that it was viscount's bread that I smelled. I could eat an entire loaf, I think."

Phillip smiled at her with new eyes, and set the tray down on the bed. "Your lunch, Sabrina."

She fed herself with great relish and he grinned at her sudden gluttony. "Since you are so thin now, Bree, I shall not chide you about stuffing your face with food. However, I draw the line at a fat wife."

She dropped the rumpled napkin onto the tray and gazed up at him, stupified. "It is not summer, my lord, so I cannot assume that you have been too long in the sun. I have no taste for inane jests. Explain yourself."

"As you will, Lady Sabrina."

"I told you that I did not care to be called that, Phillip!"

"Very well, my dear. I will allow you to have your way for a while longer." He sat down beside her and took her hand into his. "Sabrina, will you marry me?"

"Marry you," she repeated blankly, her violet eyes widening.

"Yes, my dear. We have, after all, known each other all of five days now. And, of course, I do know you in some ways much better than you know me. Still," he added, his eyes twinkling, "I believe that you will come to appreciate me in those ways as much as I admire you."

Sabrina pulled her hand free of his. "Really, Phillip, I must believe that you have been dipping liberally into the sherry! Surely, you are jesting!"

"I am perfectly serious, Bree, and I'll thank you not to accuse me of drunkenness. A man of thirty years does not jest about such a serious business as marriage, I assure you. Now, Sabrina Eversleigh, will you marry me?"

She gazed at him intently, cudgeling her mind to understand him. She shook her head slowly, her eyes never leaving his face. "No, my lord, I will not marry you. You are obviously trying to protect me, but I assure you that it is not necessary."

"Is it that you prefer Richard Clarendon, Sabrina?"

She looked at him blankly. "Richard? Of course I do not prefer him. Indeed, I scarce know him, save that he visited us rather frequently during the summer. Good God, Phillip," she added, finally struck by the implication of his question, "how the devil do you know about Richard Clarendon?"

"Charles Askbridge has been here. 'Twas he who mentioned Clarendon and made me remember why it was that the name Eversleigh was so familiar to me. You see, Bree, Richard told me himself, some five months ago in London, that he wanted you, that he was waiting only until you reached your eighteenth birthday." He added by the way of explanation, "I mentioned Clarendon to you to see if you cherished any tender feelings toward him. I am pleased that you do not."

Sabrina waved away his words with her hands. "Charles—here?"

"Yes, Bree. He came most stealthily to see if his hunting box had been taken over by villains and rogues, as his caretaker had told him. Although he was not overly surprised to see me, indeed, expected as much, his shock at seeing you was memorable, particularly since you were lying blissfully asleep in my arms. In short, Sabrina, Charles is off to tell your grandfather that you are all right and to fetch a carriage so that we can go back to Monmouth Hall."

Her faced drained of color. "Oh no, Phillip—I cannot go back there!"

"Why, Sabrina? Come, my dear, 'tis time that you tell me exactly what happened."

She splayed her hands in front of her, unwilling even now to tell him of her shame.

"Have you still not learned that you can trust me, Sabrina? You must tell me the truth now, if I am to protect you. I know that Trevor Eversleigh is your grandfather's grandnephew and heir and that he is married to your sister, Elisabeth. You may now continue."

She looked away from him a moment and realized that there was no hope for it. She said slowly, unaware that her memories were making her tremble, "Trevor tried to rape me."

She stared beyond his left shoulder, unwilling, he thought, to face him. "I thought as much, Bree. Now, tell me the rest of it."

She continued in a low voice, "I had thought initially that Trevor was a well enough man and was pleased that Elisabeth was finally to marry. But none of us saw beyond his handsome face and pleasing manners. He is vicious and cruel. He seems to delight in inflicting pain. He trapped me in the picture gallery, away from the family and the servants. He would have succeeded in raping me had he not become overly excited, and thus for the time being, unable."

She fell silent and Phillip nodded gently, "You then ran away?"

She shook her head. "No, I went to my sister and told her what Trevor tried to do to me. She believed me, you know, but refused to take my part. She told me that if I went to Grandfather, she would swear that it was I who tried to seduce her husband. It was then that I realized that I could no longer remain at Monmouth Hall with Elisabeth and Trevor, with my grandfather thrown willy-nilly amongst the three of us." She raised bleak eyes to his face. "It was stupid of me, I suppose, not to return to the Hall after my horse went lame. I got lost and became ill in the cold. You found me."

"As I told you, Sabrina, when you return to the Hall, it will not be alone. You will be with me, under my protection. If you will consent to be my wife, I will have you out of that ménage within the week."

"You have been most kind to me, my lord, and now you owe me nothing. I would ask only that you escort me to London, to my Aunt Barresford. It is the best solution."

Phillip drew back, nonplussed at her refusal. Although he did not wish to, he realized that he had to tell her of the seriousness of her situation. "No, Sabrina, it is no solution at all. Although you are not aware of it, you have spent nearly a week with a most dissolute profligate, Beau Mercerault. Even if I were to take you to London, to your aunt, your reputation would be in shreds. The best solution, the only solution, Bree, is that you marry me, and quickly." He waited to see understanding of her predicament dawn on her face.

He drew back in consternation when she said calmly, "It is most generous of you to wish to sacrifice yourself, Phillip, but I will not allow it. Methinks Charles has been playing propriety. I have no intention of having you saddle yourself with me—indeed, I would have no honor if I were to allow you to do so. Again, my lord, my answer is no."

"You are acting the fool, Sabrina, and I will not have it. Dammit, don't you realize what has happened?" He added in a hard voice, "Even if you wanted Clarendon, let me tell you that it is doubtful that he would still want you."

She made no effort to control her burgeoning anger at his words. "How dare you! You ridiculous men most comfortably create and maintain two sides of the coin! The one side for you brave, honorable specimens, and the other for hapless women, whom you despise or protect depending on your whims at the moment. I tell you, I refuse to be bandied about amongst you. You may take yourself to the devil, my lord!"

Phillip thought inconsequentially that he should not have fed her before making his offer. He was not particularly angry at her, for he saw some truth in what she said. He paused a moment, eyeing her heaving breasts with some interest, and proceeded in what he hoped was a reasonable tone of voice. "I should not have thrown Clarendon up at you, but I wanted you to understand that your life could not be as you left it. I submit that it would be most wise of you to accept me as your husband."

She shook her head wearily. "Let us part friends, Phillip. I will not marry where there is no love."

He had been a fool, he thought ruefully, to admire her stubbornness. He decided upon a more drastic approach. "Perhaps," he said softly, his voice a caress, "I should take you now. It is certainly what everyone will believe, once it's known that you've been with me. Believe me, Sabrina, I do not mind that you are, at the moment, at your most womanly."

"You filthy bastard!" She rolled away clumsily to the

other side of the bed and yanked the covers tightly up to her chin.

He cursed himself silently, realizing that he had pushed her too hard. He saw that she was shaking, but made no move toward her. "I'm sorry, Bree. You are quite right, I acted the bastard. But I am not at all such a bad fellow, really. We will, I am certain, manage to rub along quite well together." He added in an almost apologetic voice, "You really have no choice in the matter, my dear. You see, I had no idea that you would react in such a violent manner. Charles and I decided that it would be best if he informed your grandfather even now that you and I would wed. When you next see your family, it will be as my betrothed."

"I will see you in hell first, Phillip. I am not a fallen woman, and I refuse to encourage anyone in thinking that by marrying you."

He looked down at her, at a loss for words. He did not think of himself as being conceited or puffed up with his own consequence, but he did know his own worth. Indeed, it had been with great dexterity that he had managed for the past ten years to keep his bachelorhood intact. Now here was an obstinate chit of a girl, one whose life he had saved, flinging his honorable offer in his face. He realized that he could not very well abduct her and force her to the altar. Damnation, what the hell was he supposed to do now?

He looked toward the window at the sound of horses and a carriage drawing up in front of the hunting box. Sabrina whipped around at the sound.

"Well, Sabrina?" He turned, his brow raised.

She shook her head mutely.

He turned and without a backward glance strode from the room.

He met Charles at the front door and saw that the carriage drawn up outside had no earl's crest on its door.

"It is my carriage," Charles said, as if reading his thoughts. "Come into the parlor, Phillip, we have a new and very different problem to deal with now."

Phillip shut his mouth on an oath and followed Charles into the parlor. "Well?" he demanded finally, after watching Charles take several sharp turns about the room.

"The Earl of Monmouth has had a stroke and is at the moment quite ill. The physician will allow no one to see him. He assured me that he would tell the earl that Sabrina was safe and well, but he feared that the old man would not even understand."

"Damn! This means that Trevor Eversleigh is now temporary master."

"Trevor and Elisabeth. It would interest you to know that Elisabeth had already called in the men from their search for Sabrina. As revolting as you may find it, it is my opinion that both she and Trevor were quite chagrined to find out that Sabrina is still alive." He shook his head, as if unable to believe what had happened. "Elisabeth was never a particularly likeable girl, but now I find her hardened, lost to all natural affection for her sister."

"Still, Charles, why is it your carriage that you bring?"

"There is more, Phillip. When I told Elisabeth that Sabrina was safe, she inquired rather urgently, I thought, what Sabrina had told me about her running away. I told her that I did not know the details, but that Sabrina had likely spoken to you. I saw her glance meaningfully at her husband. Then the both of them hastened to tell me that Sabrina had left the Hall because she had tried to seduce Trevor and he had rebuffed her. They were surprised that she had left, but thought it was because she was too ashamed to stay." Charles ran a distracted hand through his hair. "I doubt not that they will soon be telling everyone in Yorkshire their version of this wretched affair. In any case," he continued, "Elisabeth then coldly informed me in that frigid way of hers that she would find it difficult to forgive her sister for her perfidy. She did offer to take her back, but I realized I could not allow it."

"To hell with both of them! Surely no one would believe such drivel! Sabrina finally told me, after much prodding, that Trevor tried to rape her and her dear sister took his side against her. And that, Charles, was why she ran away. I tell you, I have only known Sabrina for five days now, but I know that she is speaking the truth."

"If it will make either of us feel any better, I must doubt that the gentry hereabouts will believe the tales that Elisabeth and Trevor will be spreading. Sabrina is well known and much liked in these parts."

"That will be little consolation, I fear." Phillip paused a moment, and said softly. "On the heels of your joyless news, I must add that Sabrina has refused to wed me. I am not to be allowed to sacrifice myself, in her words. When I remonstrated with her, she turned on me like a veritable tigress."

Charles whipped up his head in amazement. "You're telling me that she won't have you? Good God, Phillip, I find it difficult to credit!"

Phillip shrugged. "I can't very well beat her, you know. You want to take her to Moreland?"

"Yes. The only problem is that most of my guests are still there. Margaret will be delighted to see Sabrina, of course, and will most likely insist on taking over the care of her. Despite your efficiency, Phillip, once back in civilization, you must relinquish your charge."

Phillip nodded. After a long moment, he said, "I must go to her. It will be difficult to break all of this to her."

"There is no need."

Both men whipped about. Sabrina stood in the doorway, her hair streaming about her shoulders and down her back, the overlarge dressing gown pulled tightly about her, held by his fisted hands. Her eyes were huge and dark in her pale face.

"My poor girl," Phillip began, taking a quick step toward her, his hands outstretched.

"It is pleasant to see you again, Charles," she said in a low, strained voice, disregarding Phillip.

A pale wraith that was very unlike the sparkling, laughing Sabrina stared at him. Charles said shakily, "Sabrina, you are ill."

"Will Grandfather recover, Charlie?"

Charles raised his hands in front of him in a hopeless gesture. "The physician is unsure, Sabrina."

Sabrina felt the room spin unpleasantly about her. She fell where she stood, the dressing gown flaring out about her like an unfurling green fan.

6

Phillip gazed over the sloping west lawn of Moreland, watching the gray afternoon shadows lengthen into night. He turned at the sound of Richard Clarendon's angry voice.

"Damnation," Clarendon growled, the small lines of dissipation at the corners of his dark eyes deepening as the frown on his forehead grew more pronounced. "What a bloody mess! I've a good mind to go put a bullet through that filthy bounder right now."

"Unfortunately," Phillip said dryly, "the old earl is in no shape to refute what Elisabeth and Trevor have said. Very simply, Richard, it is their word against Sabrina's. And since she ran away, in the eyes of an objective man, such an action would point to her guilt rather than away from it."

"Don't be such a cold bastard, Phillip," Richard said in a harsh voice.

"Let me finish, Richard. The fact remains that Sabrina was not raped. I cannot believe that Sabrina, or the old earl for that matter, would want the only male relative in the Eversleigh line to be dispatched to hell before providing an heir. And I cannot think it worth it for the Marquis of Arysdale to have to flee to the continent to avoid the king's justice for the likes of Trevor Eversleigh."

The marquis banged his fist down upon the mahogany desk in impotent frustration.

Charles stepped forward and handed Phillip and Richard each a glass of brandy. "Come, Richard, Phillip is right, you know. Killing Sabrina's brother-in-law would help neither of you. At least she is alive, thanks to Phillip."

Phillip shot Charles a darkening glance. Richard had been momentarily sidetracked, having just heard about Elisabeth's and Trevor's behavior. But Phillip knew it was only a matter of time before the marquis would recall that Beau Mercerault had had Sabrina with him for five days.

He had no chance to ponder Richard's attitude, for at that moment the library door was flung open and Teresa Elliott rushed into the room.

"Phillip!" she cried, her voice a mixture of relief and reproach. She caught up the skirt of her silk gown and ran gracefully toward him.

He caught her hands and held her away from him. She was overly made up, he thought, her lips too red and the rouge she wore calling too much attention to the bright spots on her cheeks.

"But you must be quite fagged," she said, raising her blue eyes to his face, "taking care of that girl for five days."

Phillip stiffened and released her hands. He inquired, an edge to his voice, "May I ask, Teresa, how it is that you know what I was doing for the past five days?"

She pursed her lips into a beguiling pout and shrugged her rounded shoulders. "It was obvious for all to see, my lord." She gave a tinkling laugh, hoping to amuse him out of his strange mood. "You know what servants are . . . indeed, I have been hearing the oddest stories. Is it true that Charles had to bring her here to Moreland?"

"I wonder at your listening to servants' gossip, Teresa," Phillip said shortly, knowing full well that the matter was no doubt being discussed with great relish among both gentry and servants. "Are you acquainted with Richard Clarendon, the Marquis of Arysdale? Richard, Miss Elliott."

She turned with feline grace toward the marquis and extended a slender white hand. "Such a pleasure, your grace," she murmured softly, her eyes taking in his athletic body and his devilishly handsome face. She had seen him upon several occasions in London, but had never been allowed to meet him, her mama having warned her in no uncertain terms that a man with such a rakehell reputation, even though he was a marquis, could never be made to come up to scratch. She felt a warm glow suffuse her cheeks as he gazed down at her, his dark eyes narrowed, the expression on his tanned face abstracted. She smiled to herself, knowing that her beauty normally had such an effect on most gentlemen. The marquis appeared to be no exception.

"Honored, Miss Elliott," he said only, and turned abruptly away.

Charles, who was well acquainted with Teresa's opinion of herself, saw her eyes glittering dangerously at the marquis' obvious lack of interest, and hastened to say, "My dear Teresa, you have come upon us at what I am afraid is a most inopportune time. We would not wish to bore you with matters of business. May we be allowed to enjoy your company at dinner?"

"We will see you later, Teresa," Phillip said, not bothering with Charles's roundabout expressions.

Miss Elliott looked for a moment irresolute and rather put out. Seeing that the marquis's attention had not wavered from the fireplace, she forced herself to pin a complacent smile on her lips.

"As you will, gentlemen. I suppose you are much occupied with what to do with that wretched girl."

"I repeat, Teresa," Phillip said, his expression stony, "that you should not listen to servants' gossip."

Teresa's curiosity was piqued, but she recognized that to press the viscount further would not place her in a favorable light. "As you will, my lord," she said in a submissive voice. She dropped a graceful curtsy and left the library.

"Yet another calculating bitch," Phillip said under his breath.

Richard Clarendon continued to gaze meditatively into the fireplace, his attention seemingly upon the licking tongues of orange flame. As much as he disliked to acknowledge it, he knew that the viscount was correct in his assessment. Killing Trevor Eversleigh would solve naught. He turned his thoughts to the days and nights Sabrina had spent with Phillip. He reasoned to himself that he had never known Phillip's tastes to run to innocent young virgins, particularly young ladies of quality. But Sabrina was so vibrant, so animated, so very different from any other young lady of noble birth that had come to Richard's practiced attention, or, he reasoned, to Phillip's. Just the thought that Phillip had seen her naked, had touched her body, made him grit his teeth. Damn, she had never even allowed him to kiss her hand—indeed, had quite innocently laughed when he had made the attempt. He could still see her wide violet eyes fastened in high good humor on his face, and hear her tinkling laughter when she had told him not to play the gallant, for it was such a bore. He could not help but wonder if she had intrigued Phillip just as she had him.

He turned away from the fireplace, his black brows drawn nearly together as he looked toward Phillip. "Did you lay a hand on her?"

"Of course," Phillip said in his calm voice. "She nearly died, Richard. Would you that I had left her where she lay?"

"You know very well what I mean," Richard snapped.

Phillip gazed at his friend for a long moment, weighing his words. "When Charles found us, he convinced me that I should offer for her, as five days spent alone with me, regardless of the circumstances, would ruin her reputation. She turned me down flat, Richard, as, I am convinced, she will do to you, if you've still a mind to have her. However," he continued, looking straight into his friend's dark eyes, "I intend once she is better to push her again to accept me as her husband."

"If you have not damaged her, then I shall take her to wife."

Phillip winced slightly. "You will discover that she will not have you, Richard." He thought that if the situation resolved itself and she became his wife, what had happened to her would not at all be such a bad thing. Although he did not love her, he had come to like her and respect her mightily. He would, he concluded, treat her much better than Richard would. To his mind, Clarendon merely wanted Sabrina to wile away his boredom for a time. He could see the marquis setting her up as a new mother for his young son, whilst he resumed his profligate pleasures in London.

"Bree is a most feted young lady," Charles said. "Should I join the fray and also offer myself as the sacrificial husband?"

"Put a hatch on it, Charles," the marquis growled. "I would see her. Has that damned physician come down yet from her room?"

"I shall inquire," Charles said stiffly, and pulled the bell cord.

Sabrina lay quietly, for she did not want Margaret to know that she was awake. She felt the soft satin of her own nightgown against her body. How kind of Elisabeth, she thought with bitter irony, to send her clothing to Moreland.

She felt awash with misery at her own helplessness. She had to regain her strength soon so that she could go to her grandfather, assure herself that he would be all right, and convince him that it would be better for all of them if she went to London. It occurred to her that she would now have to apply to Trevor for her inheritance from her mother, the ten thousand pounds that was hers upon her eighteenth birthday. It belonged to her, and even Trevor could not prevent the solicitors from turning the funds over to her. How very disappointing for him that I did not conveniently die, she thought. A sob broke from her throat.

"Bree, my love, you are awake. How do you feel?"

Sabrina raised glazed eyes to Margaret's face. "Painfully alive," she whispered.

Margaret misunderstood her. "Oh, my dear, let me fetch Dr. Simmons. I believe he is still downstairs."

Sabrina held Margaret's hand in a weak grasp. "No, Margaret. It is not my body that feels pain. It is most kind of you and Charles to accept me at Moreland. I shall be strong again, quite soon, and take my leave of you."

She wondered dispassionately what her Aunt Barresford's reaction would be when she arrived on her doorstep. She did not believe that, with her ten thousand pounds, her aunt would be terribly disgruntled at her sudden appearance.

"You will stay here as long as you please, Bree," Margaret protested. "Even at this moment, Charlie is busily dispensing our guests. Indeed, I will not have to leave you. My husband, Hugh, will be arriving from London in two days and we will all celebrate Christmas together. And of course, there is Phillip and the Marquis of Arysdale. He, Charles, and Phillip were closeted together in the library for the longest time!"

"Richard Clarendon is here?"

"Why yes, Bree. He was searching for you like all the other men."

Sabrina quickly digested this bit of information and felt a surge of anger. Undoubtedly, the gentlemen were discussing what was to be done with her. And now, Richard Clarendon must needs be part of it. She wondered if they weren't perhaps gambling, the loser to take her off everyone's hands. Sabrina Eversleigh, neatly wrapped up like a Christmas gift and dispensed with quickly, to the most unlucky of them.

"Is there yet any news of my grandfather, Margaret?"

"No, my love, his condition remains the same." Margaret suddenly became brisk. "Now, Bree, you mustn't fall into a fit of doldrums. You are alive and we are all together. Your grandfather will recover, you will see." Silently, she wondered what was to become of her friend if she continued to refuse Phillip as a husband. She realized with a start that she was shaking her head in amazement that any lady would refuse the Viscount Derencourt. Particularly considering, she thought, a blush tingeing her cheeks, that they had been alone together for five days. Surely, Sabrina must have come to at least like the viscount.

There came a light tap on the bedroom door. Sabrina clutched wildly at Margaret's hand.

"Please, I don't wish to see anyone!"

Margaret patted her hand, a worried frown settling on her face. "But what if it is Phillip, Bree——"

"No, no, do you hear! Particularly Phillip."

Margaret saw that Sabrina was becoming quite agitated, and fearing a relapse was imminent, nodded her agreement. "Very well, my love, if that is what you want."

She walked slowly to the door, aware that Sabrina was staring doggedly after her. She inched it open and slipped out into the corridor.

The Marquis of Arysdale towered over her, Charles at his elbow.

"Richard would like to speak with Sabrina, Margaret," her brother said.

She looked up into the marquis's darkly handsome face, dismissing the tug of feminine admiration his presence engendered. "I am sorry, your grace, but she refuses to see anyone."

"She will see me," Richard said sharply, and stepped forward.

Margaret put her hand upon his sleeve. "Your grace, I beg you will listen to me. She is distraught, surely you will understand that. So much has happened to her, and in so little time."

"Come, Richard," Charles said quietly. "Margaret is right. You must give her time."

The marquis looked undecided, his eyes still upon the closed bedroom door.

Margaret thought she heard him curse softly under his breath. He turned back to her, bending his dark eyes upon her upturned face. "You will tell Sabrina that I will return to speak with her this evening. She will not deny me entrance then." Before Margaret could form a protest, the marquis turned on his heel and strode back down the corridor.

Charles gazed after the retreating marquis, a worried expression on his face. "Clarendon will not be gainsaid,

Margaret. Sabrina will have some hours to consider her decision. Now, my dear, Mother is in the midst of most charmingly ridding us of our guests. You must come downstairs and make your good-byes."

"Does that include that cat, Teresa Elliott?"

"Yes, but she is most reluctant."

Margaret nodded briskly. "The sooner the better for that lady. My maid told me that she was wheedling about the servants for any tidbit of gossip. Phillip's appearance with Sabrina turned her green with jealousy."

Charles shrugged. "There is naught I can do, save see her on her way as quickly as possible."

"I shall be down in a moment. I must first tell Sabrina that Clarendon will not be refused."

"It was Phillip?" Sabrina asked when Margaret came back into the room.

Margaret shook her head. "No, 'twas the Marquis of Arysdale. He was most desirous of speaking with you, my love. Charles helped me to put him off, but only until this evening, I fear. You will have to talk with him, Bree, else he is likely to kick the door down."

"Very well," Sabrina said dully. She wondered perversely why it was not Phillip who demanded to see her. Indeed, she wondered how much longer he would remain at Moreland, but did not form her thought into a question for Margaret.

After Margaret left her, she let her mind wander to the carriage trip from Charles's hunting box to Moreland. Phillip had cradled her in his arms, unspeaking, his hazel eyes unfathomable. She had been thankful for his silence, for she felt so numb that she doubted she would have been able to respond to him.

She stared grimly at the closed bedroom door. Had Richard Clarendon been chosen to be the sacrificial husband? Somehow, she could not imagine the marquis doing anything that was not precisely to his liking. Although she did not have the experience of a season in London, she was not so naive as to believe that the marquis did not cut a wide swath through the female ranks. She sighed softly.

If Richard had decided to play the gallant, she would simply have to save him from himself.

Perhaps it was the flickering light of the candle touching her eyelids that awakened her. Sabrina opened her eyes, followed the candlelight to its source, and saw Phillip seated next to her bed, looking at her intently, his expression impassive.

As she had grown used to his presence at her bedside, his appearance in her bedchamber caused her to do nothing more than to blink several times.

"What time is it?" she asked, trying to clear her mind of sleep.

"After midnight. I rather hoped the candlelight would awaken you sooner or later."

Her thoughts wove themselves together at the sound of his voice. "What are you doing here, Phillip? We are no longer in Charles's hunting box, you know, and I would venture to say that your presence here is most improper. Not, of course, that it matters much," she added with ill-concealed bitterness, "seeing that I am already beyond the pale."

"You finally admit to the truth, do you, Bree?" he said, his voice as sharp as hers had been. He rose and sat down beside her, laying his hand across her brow. "You are feeling more the thing now?"

"Yes," she managed to say in a tolerably calm voice. "What are you doing here, Phillip?" she repeated.

"Richard informed me—he was in the vilest of moods incidently—that you would not marry him. He concluded that it was I whom you had decided upon. As I did not wish to cause wild speculation, I decided to pay you a visit after everyone had taken to his bed."

"Richard was mistaken in his perceptions, my lord," she said stiffly. "I told him that I did not intend to marry anyone." She closed her eyes a moment, picturing the marquis towering over her bed, his black brows flaring toward his temples, his expression incredulous. He had sounded rather like a frustrated little boy denied something he had expected would be his for the taking. "You refuse my offer, Sabrina?" he had demanded.

"Yes, Richard, though I am honored at your concern."

"We are not talking about concern! Dammit, I was to wed you in any case, 'twas all arranged."

"Not with me, your grace," she said flatly, plucking up her spirit.

"So you spend five days with Phillip Mercerault and you are ready to whistle me down the wind."

She looked away from him, somewhat angered at his blithe interpretation of the situation. "Richard," she said, hoping her voice sounded reasonable and calm, "you have made your gallant offer and are now freed of your obligation to me. My intention is to first of all visit my grandfather to assure myself that he is well cared for. Then I shall go to London, to my Aunt Barresford. You know, of course, that there is no place for me now at Monmouth Hall."

Sabrina opened her eyes at the sound of Phillip's voice.

"Well, whatever you told Clarendon, it is still his opinion that I am to be the lucky man."

She turned her gaze to Phillip, but said nothing.

"I would imagine, Bree, that you have considered your position and have probably decided upon some corkbrained solution. A solution, I am certain, that involves your aunt in London. Just what makes you think, my dear, that your aunt would joyously welcome an unexpected visit from her niece?"

"I have ten thousand pounds."

Phillip cocked a brow. "An heiress, in short. Excellent. Now everyone will believe that I have married you for your fortune, and your no doubt sizable dowry. Actually I much prefer being thought a fortune hunter rather than a noble, chivalrous fool."

"I shall not wed for the wealth I would bring a gentleman."

He nodded agreeably. "We shall put your fortune in your name or in trust for our children."

Sabrina opened and shut her mouth. He was building a wall of words, and she was throwing herself impotently against it. She thought she would prefer another interview with Richard Clarendon. At least with him, it had been she who had been the calm, rational one. "Phillip," she said, in an effort to focus his attention away from his logic, "it appears to me that you are taking your defeat at the wager in very good part. However, you may be sure that I shall not hold you to it. You may inform the other gentlemen, Richard included, that Sabrina Eversleigh can take care of herself without the assistance of you noble benefactors."

"What the devil are you babbling about?" he demanded, his impassive countenance suddenly alert. "What defeat at what wager?" Even as he uttered the words, he remembered Charles's lame jest about offering himself as the sacrificial husband. He dropped his gaze from her face.

"You cannot deny it, can you? You, Phillip, and your wretched marquis are the both of you eyeing each other like crowing bandy roosters, fighting to keep your ridiculous male honor as well as your freedom! Well, I tell you, I won't have it. I am not damaged goods and I refuse to shout to the world that I am, by leg-shackling myself to one of you. Now, I am very tired and have found you a bore. Good night, Phillip."

She flipped onto her side, away from him.

Phillip was silent for some moments. She felt the bed give way as he rose.

"The world is very seldom the way we wish it to be, Sabrina," he said finally.

"Then the world must change, and I shall force it to."

"I see that you must learn for yourself. The world will not change its rules for you, Sabrina. I presume that I will see you in London."

"Yes," she said. "But first, I shall visit my grandfather. If he needs me, I shall, of course, do what I must."

He drew a deep breath. "You have refused to attend me in any other matter, Sabrina. I beg you will listen to me now. Your grandfather is too ill even to recognize you. There is absolutely nothing you can do to help him."

"Don't you understand, Phillip? I must be certain that

he is being properly taken care of. You do not know Trevor. He has no love for any of us, least of all Grandfather. And only he stands between Trevor and the earldom . . . and all the Eversleigh wealth. I must go."

The viscount was silent, his gaze fastened on the dark shadows in the corner of the bedchamber. He looked down at her and said abruptly, "Will you trust me to see that the earl is properly cared for and that he is protected from your cousin?"

"But what can you do?"

"Will you trust me to see that all is taken care of, Sabrina?"

"But I cannot simply leave Yorkshire whilst he is ill!"

"I repeat, Bree, there is nothing you can do. Now, what is your answer?"

"I suppose," she said slowly, aware of her own helplessness, "that since I trusted you with my life, I can also trust you with his. Thank you, my lord."

"And will you not trust me with your future?"

"No, my lord."

She heard him sigh as he plunged the room into darkness. She smelled the smoking candle wick and pictured him standing beside her bed.

"Good-bye, Sabrina."

He did not want her to reply, she thought, for no sooner had he spoken than she heard his footsteps move away from her. She saw a dim shaft of light from the corridor before he closed the door behind him.

7

"I must congratulate you, Anisa! Your niece is a charming girl. Too slight perhaps, but still. You said she has been ill, at her home in Yorkshire?"

Lady Anisa Barresford drew her gaze from Sabrina, who was dancing a sober cotillion with a young hussar. "Yes, Lucilla, she was, evidently, quite ill, an inflammation of the lung, I'm told. Skinny as a hen's leg, but her pallor is all the crack, or so my daughter-in-law informs me."

"She has been with you but a week now?" Lady Lucilla Blanchard inquired.

Lady Barresford nodded absently, knowing quite well her friend's penchant for gossip. She thought that Madame Giselle had performed a wonder with Sabrina's blue velvet gown, in the Russian style. "You must add pounds, Sabrina," she had chided her but the day before. "The Russian style requires a full bosom to be truly elegant." Madame Giselle had cut the back of the gown a good inch lower, to draw attention to Sabrina's well-formed shoulders and back. She also applauded her decision not to push her niece to have her long hair clipped into a more modern style, for the glossy black mane looked breathtaking piled high on the girl's head, with two long tresses laid provocatively over her bare shoulder.

"You say the girl is an heiress, Anisa?" Lady Blanchard pursued, her eyes upon her younger son, Edward, who, she noticed disapprovingly, was making not the slightest push to be pleasant to Sabrina Eversleigh.

"She inherited her mother's money, of course. As to her portion . . ." Lady Barresford shrugged. She raised a plump, beringed finger and patted the crimped grayish curls at the side of her face.

"Good heavens!"

Lady Barresford looked sharply at Lady Blanchard and followed her sloe-eyed gaze to the drawing room door. Viscount Derencourt stood negligently beside the plump Blanchard butler, gazing indolently about the crowded room.

"What is Phillip Mercerault doing here, I wonder! Never have I known him to grace a small dancing party such as this. To be sure, I did send him an invitation, but still!" Lady Blanchard suddenly recalled her duties as hostess and rose quickly from her chair beside Lady Barresford, her full satin skirts rustling about her.

Lady Barresford watched her friend flutter toward the viscount, her face flushed with pleasure at the entrance of such a notable Corinthian. "Silly widgeon," she said under her breath, and turned her attention back to her niece. The cotillion drew to a close and she watched Sabrina curtsy prettily to the hussar and retrace her steps to her aunt's chair.

"You dance passably," she said, as Sabrina sat down beside her.

"Thank you, Aunt."

Lady Barresford frowned at her colorless tone of voice. She said sharply, " A little bit of animation on your part would hold you in good stead, Sabrina. To be sure, gentlemen have no admiration for a bluestocking, but still, they are put off by ladies who have nothing to say."

"I am sorry, Aunt, but I am a trifle fatigued." Actually, she felt not at all tired, but she knew that her precise, rather cold aunt would think her quite odd if she told her that it was her spirit and not her body that was fatigued. She forced a smile to her lips. Although it did not reach her eyes, Lady Barresford seemed to approve.

"This is your first appearance in London, child," her aunt continued, her voice less severe. "Not, of course, that I would ever wish you to be a flirt, but a little push to be pleasant would not be inappropriate." She paused a moment, remembering that she had spoken similar words to Sabrina's snirpish sister, Elisabeth. Not, of course, that it had done any good at all. An entire season she had squired Elisabeth about, and all for naught. "One long season," she said aloud. "Elisabeth simply did not catch, you know. You, I am persuaded, will not pose such a problem."

Sabrina raised her eyes to her aunt's face. "It matters not, Aunt," she said softly, "since Elisabeth is now married."

The sausage curls about Lady Barresford's face quivered as she tossed her head. "At last! Twenty-three years old and on the shelf, I thought. I did not meet your cousin, but at least he is part of the family." She added in a snide voice, "I would doubt not that your grandfather had a hand in the matter. The Eversleigh wealth and a bride. Yes, that was the bargain your cousin accepted."

"Sabrina, allow me to introduce the Viscount Derencourt. Phillip, you are acquainted with Lady Barresford. This is her niece, Sabrina."

Sabrina had known that she would see him in London, for he had told her so; but it was too soon. She had not had time to gain distance from her feeling for him, or to school herself in how to behave herself toward him. She slowly forced her eyes to his face.

"Lady Barresford . . . Miss Eversleigh. A pleasure to see you again, Sabrina." The gentleness of his voice nearly undid her. She nodded dumbly, unable to speak.

"I had no idea you were acquainted with my niece, my lord," Lady Barresford said, aware that Sabrina had suddenly become a tongue-tied stick of wood.

"Only briefly, my lady," Phillip said, pulling his gaze from Sabrina's lowered face. "A party at Moreland," he added at the confused expression on Lady Barresford's face.

"Ah, that is Charles Askbridge's country seat," she exclaimed, pleased with her memory. "And Charles's dear sister, Margaret, married Sir Hugh Drakemore. How does the child like marriage to one of London's erstwhile confirmed bachelors?"

Phillip thought of the glowing smile on Margaret's face when Hugh had arrived at Moreland but one day before Christmas. "I would say that she is tolerably happy, my lady." The small orchestra at the far end of the drawing room struck up a lively country dance.

"Would you care to join me in this set, Miss Eversleigh?"

"Yes, my lord," Sabrina said. Without looking directly up into his face, she placed her hand upon his proffered arm and rose. She looked a belated question toward her aunt.

"Yes, do enjoy yourself, child." As the viscount walked away with Sabrina on his arm, Lady Barresford felt a stab of apprehension. The viscount, although a charming, handsome man, and quite wealthy, was still a rake. Later, she must put a warning in Sabrina's ear. The girl was, after all, from the country, and it was doubtful that she had ever encountered in Yorkshire the likes of Phillip Mercerault. Except, of course, she amended to herself, that Sabrina had briefly met the viscount at Moreland. She resolved to keep her eyes on the both of them.

"It is a pity that you cannot as yet waltz," Phillip said softly into her left ear.

She gazed up at him warily and felt an almost physical pain at his nearness. "Why?"

"Because I wish to speak with you, of course."

The set formed and they were almost immediately separated. Sabrina pinned a smile on her lips and let her feet move her mechanically through the steps. She was out of breath at the end of the dance and turned away from Phillip to calm her breathing.

She felt his hand upon her arm. "You are feeling all right?"

"Yes, of course. I am simply not used to such exertion as yet."

"Would you care for a glass of punch?"

She nodded and allowed him to lead her from the drawing room across the corridor to the dining room, where the long table had been set with innumerable delicacies.

Phillip placed a filled glass in her hand and accepted for himself a goblet of champagne from a footman. "To London and your evident success."

She raised her chin. "To a world that does not need to be changed."

"To a world that does not as yet know."

"Yet, my lord? Do you intend to make an announcement?"

"It is hardly necessary. Your world right now is made of glass. It will require but one rock—but one vicious tongue—and it will shatter."

"I have done nothing to harm anyone. There would be no reason for such viciousness as you describe."

"You are a remarkable innocent, Bree. That, combined with your stubbornness, will be your undoing, I fear. Have you received my letter?"

A grateful smile lit her face. "Yes, Phillip, and I thank you."

"I believe you can calm your worrying, Sabrina, for as I said in my letter, your grandfather is improving steadily. He is a tough old eagle. Your rapacious cousin, Trevor, will chomp at the bit for many years before taking his turn. The earl is safe from Trevor, I assure you."

She frowned, her eyes upon his exquisitely tied cravat. "But how can you be so certain that he will be safe from Trevor?"

"Very simply, Bree. I, myself, spoke with the infamous Trevor."

"You did what?" She was glad at the moment that she had set down her glass, for she would most assuredly have dropped it.

"I do wish that you would listen to me, my dear, it would save much repetition. I visited Monmouth Hall and cornered both Trevor and your blushing bride of a sister. They deserve each other, you know."

She looked up at him rather helplessly.

"But why?"

"Why do they deserve each other, or why did I insist upon speaking to them?"

"Really, Phillip, you know very well which I mean! Given your self-proclaimed penchant for doing exactly as you please, I find it difficult to fathom why you yourself would go out of your way to beard the lion in his den!"

"Do you, Sabrina?"

"Your attempts at nobility do not fit with your character as you paint it, my lord. I have told you that I will not . . . take advantage of your guilty conscience, or your misguided sense of honor, or whatever it is that is making you act in this ridiculous manner!" She drew to an abrupt halt and added as an afterthought, "Not, of course, that I am not exceedingly grateful to you for protecting my grandfather."

"It was not such a terrifying experience, Bree. Whatever Trevor Eversleigh may lack, instincts for self-preservation are not among them. I told him quite succinctly that I would put a bullet through his heart if the old earl died. Of a certainty, your grandfather is now receiving the best of care."

"But Phillip, you know that if Grandfather died, you would have to meet Trevor on the dueling field. You would risk your life for him?"

"Not only for your grandfather, Bree."

"But I have freed you of any obligations whatsoever that Charles tried to foist upon you! Why, Phillip?"

"It is as you said, Sabrina. My guilty conscience," he replied in an amused voice.

"I would return to my aunt now, if you please," she said stiffly, and turned away from him. Suddenly, she whirled about, causing him to very nearly stumble into her. "Guilty conscience, my lord? I presume that there is nothing for you to feel guilty about! Even a hardened rake would not take his pleasure with an unconscious female!"

Phillip felt a moment of anger, then a burgeoning demon of mischief. He laughed softly and drawled in a sensuous lazy voice, "I was not aware that you had such intimate knowledge of hardened rakes. However, Sabrina,

I must point out to you that you were not precisely unconscious during those early days. You were in a fevered, almost frenzied state. Do you not recall how I warmed you
when you were so frigidly cold?"

Hazy memory stirred and she felt herself go white. He
had warmed her with his body, had pressed her closely
against him. She trembled, recalling his hands moving up
and down her back, cradling her against his chest. He
could easily have done anything he wished with her. All she
could remember was the dizzying warmth of him. She
backed away from him, splaying her hands in front of her
in a gesture of denial.

"I do not believe you!" she gasped. "You are mocking
me and I will not have it, do you hear!" She whipped
about, picked up her skirts, and fled down the corridor
back to the drawing room, to the safety of her aunt. She
ignored the several pairs of startled, curious eyes that
watched her flight.

He stared after her, wondering why the devil he had
said such an outrageous thing. Even though she had angered him with her ridiculous charge about assaulting her
virginity, he should have held his tongue. He shook his
head, surprised at himself. Every time he spoke with her,
he seemed to put up her back and push her further away
from him. He was behaving as perversely as she was.

He said polite good nights to his hostess and took his
leave. Some hours later, after having consumed a half
bottle of brandy at White's, he had his hackney draw up
at Martine's apartment on Fitton Place.

It was some minutes before Dorcus, Martine's maid,
butler, and chef, cracked the front door open a few inches
at his insistent knocking, demanding irritably who was
trying to raise the dead.

When she saw him, she drew back with a startled, "My
lord, 'tis after two in the morning!"

"And a fine morning it is, my girl," Phillip agreed, and
chuckled at his own drunken wit. He tossed Dorcus his
greatcoat and hat. "No need to announce me, I'll surprise
your mistress."

He trotted up the stairs, clutching at the bannister

several times to keep his balance, and burst unceremoniously into Martine's bedchamber.

A long candle suddenly burst into wavering light.

"Mon chou! Quelle entrée turbulente!"

She propped herself up on her elbows and parted her lips into a slow, lazy smile.

"Good evening, madam," he said grandly, and swept her a drunken bow.

She sat up and allowed the covers to drop to her waist, revealing her creamy rose and white breasts.

He groaned and shucked off his clothes, leaving them where they lay in the middle of the floor.

"Quelle sottise," Martine chided him softly. She pulled back the covers and drew him down into her arms. *"Mon dieu,* but you reek of brandy."

"I am neither a cabbage nor foolish, but I do reek." He grinned, and buried his face in her full breasts. "And speak English, my wits are too addled for any more translations."

She gave a husky laugh and stroked his curly chestnut hair. "I hope you have not drunk too much, my Phillip, to give us both pleasure."

"I could give every damned woman in London pleasure," he growled, "including that stubborn little chit." He cupped her breast in his hand and covered the rosy nipple with his mouth.

Martine let herself be drawn into the exquisite sensation he was creating with his tongue. She made a slight moue with her full lips when he suddenly released her.

Phillip raised unfocused eyes to her face, his hands, out of habit, still stroking her. "The little fool! I've compromised her and still she won't have me. One minute she accuses me of being noble, rants about my misdirected honor! The next she lashes out at me for taking advantage of her during her illness. She even had the gall to accuse me of losing some hair-brained wager, in short, of having to be the sacrificial husband!"

Martine blinked her creamy brown eyes at his incoherent speech. "You compromised a lady, my Phillip?"

"Of course I didn't! What do you take me for, Martine, a rutting bounder?"

Martine lifted a languid hand and brushed her fingers through his tousled hair. "But my dear Phillip, did you not just say that——"

"She would have died if I hadn't taken care of her," he muttered by way of explanation. He laid his head on her bosom again for a moment and tapped his fingertips on her shoulder in muddled frustration.

She shifted her weight beneath him. "I am your drum, *mon chou?*" she asked presently, covering his tapping fingers with her hand.

"Even Clarendon wanted her," Phillip said aloud. "Why the devil can't she see that social ruin is nipping close at her heels?"

"But if you were not a rutting bounder and did not compromise her, why is this disgrace biting her feet?"

Phillip groaned at this travesty of a translation and flipped over on his back. The weaving light from the single candle at the bedside sent spiraling fingers of light toward the ceiling, and he could make out a patch of plaster that was cracked and in imminent danger of falling on the bed. "Call the damned carpenter, Martine! I have no taste to have my head cracked open whilst we are in the midst of lovemaking!"

"But my Phillip, how can the carpenter prevent your cracking your head? Surely you do not wish this person to watch us."

"The ceiling, dammit!"

"Ah," she said, nodding her head in seeming understanding. "I cannot understand why this girl refused Clarendon. A most romantic figure, that one!"

"He's a rake and unworthy of her."

"But are you not also an unworthy rake?"

"Stop twisting my words, Martine! Of course I am, but not in the same degree. Clarendon would have really compromised her, taken gross advantage of her innocence, had it been he who had found her."

Martine pondered this anomaly for some minutes without success, then harked back to two words that quite struck her fancy. "Clarendon, he also wanted to be the sacrificial husband to this girl that nobody compromised?"

"It was Charles Askbridge—the idiot—who said that. Your romantic Clarendon would have shied away had he thought of himself as a sacrifice."

Martine sighed at this digression and lazily ran the tips of her fingers in light stroking circles over his chest, downward to his muscular belly. "How hard you are, *mon chou*," she marveled, splaying her fingers outward.

"You know I spar at Gentleman Jackson's boxing salon," he said absently, his attention returning to the cracked plaster overhead.

Martine gave a low, gurgling laugh. "I don't think your Gentleman Jackson has anything to do with this hardness."

"Indeed not!" He grinned crookedly and pulled her on top of him. Her sleepy brown eyes widened perceptibly as he kneaded her buttocks. He felt her soft mouth close over his and her tongue touch his lips. More out of habit than from any burning desire, he lifted her hips and eased himself inside her. She brought up her legs and straddled him. A tiny frown appeared on her forehead. "I do not understand, Phillip. You tell me many times that you do not want a wife—that you do not want to be foot-bound."

"Leg-shackled."

"Ah yes," she said softly, moving herself slowly over him. "But you act to me like the man with the guilty conscience. Yet you have done nothing to harm this girl?"

"For God's sake, Martine, she spent nearly a week with me—alone. And that wretched pair, Elisabeth and Trevor, were spreading tales about her wantonness. At least when I saw them, I made it clear—in no uncertain terms, mind you—that they were to keep their mouths closed. But no doubt the damage has already been done."

Martine let herself give in to the demanding ache that was building in her body. She gasped when he closed his hands over her breasts and whispered softly, "This girl whom you did not seduce, would she like this?"

Phillip thought of the small, slight Sabrina pressed hard against the length of his body during her raging fever. He saw her violet eyes widening in shock when he had intimated that he might have taken her during her fevered state. He could feel again her consummate embarrassment at his intimate care of her. Although his wits were muddled with too much drink and a rapidly building desire, he quickly brought himself to heel. A gentleman did not discuss a lady of quality in such explicit terms, much less with his mistress. He realized dimly that it was not Martine who was being impertinent, but he himself.

"Enough said about the lady," he muttered thickly. Before Martine could question him further, he wrapped his fingers in her short fair curls and pulled her mouth down to his.

It was a clucking, disapproving Dambler who admitted his exhausted master into his bedchamber near to dawn the next morning.

"Don't preach at me, you old Methodist," Phillip growled, as his valet removed his hopelessly rumpled clothing.

"The nighttime, my lord, is for sleeping and not for carrying on and—so forth," Dambler said severely as he eased his master between the sheets.

"Particularly so forth. Turn the clock back to midnight if it pleases you. Curse you for a meddler anyway!"

"What would her ladyship say?" Dambler persevered, twitching his nose as he blew out the candles.

Phillip grinned despite his aching head. "You did yourself in there, old man. My mother was quite a high flier in her day."

He heard a disgruntled *hurrumph* from his valet and could picture the wispy-haired Dambler standing in the darkened room, shaking his head at his master's filial disrespect.

"Go back to bed, man, and keep the servants out of this room until after noon, if you please."

"Yes, my lord," Dambler said stiffly and bowed toward the bed, out of habit. He turned at the door. "Does your lordship have any activities planned for the evening?"

"I have just finished the evening, thank you."

"The *next* evening, my lord."

"No." Phillip rubbed his aching head, an action that brought both relief and memory. "Hellfire . . . yes, Dambler. I had clean forgot. It's off to that sacred boring shrine, Almack's, to play St. George again."

"A noble gentleman, St. George, my lord."

"If he was anything like me, then he was a bloody fool!"

Miss Teresa Elliott, her arm placed gracefully upon her brother Wilfred's sleeve, glided toward the patronnesses across the large main hall at Almack's.

"What a bunch of old dragons," Wilfred whispered toward his sister's ear, as his myopic gaze took in the three ladies seated close together in their stiff-backed gilded chairs. "If you hadn't worn Mama out with all your soirees, balls, and whatever else it is you do——"

"Do be quiet, Wilfred! It will not hurt you to be away from your wretched books for one evening, and I must have an escort, you know that."

"Find yourself a husband, Teresa. Maybe you will snag some poor wretch who will be willing to let you diddle him about."

She replied with a self-satisfied smile that made her brother want to pinch the slender white arm reposing on his sleeve.

"Don't be so sure of yourself, miss!"

"You're a stuffy old stick, Will, and I won't have you prosing at me! And for your information, brother, I have decided upon one of the most eligible bachelors in London."

"And who might the poor devil be?" Wilfred asked, gazing down at her classic profile with no enthusiasm.

She pouted and tossed her head. "It's unlikely that he will attend this evening, for he finds Almack's a bore. However," she added complacently, "I expect he will come about—once we are married."

"Who is this weak-willed ass?"

"Mind your tongue, Will, else I'll tell Mama."

"Just try it, Miss Conceit, and I'll smack you on the head with my thick volume of Homer."

Miss Elliott could not respond to this provocation, for the Duchess of Wigan and her meek spouse were bending welcoming smiles upon her.

"All sticky smiles, ain't you, sister, when it's someone you want to impress. Damn, but that ridiculous feather the duchess is wearing made me want to sneeze. Now, Teresa, who is this paragon you've set your sights on?"

"It's doubtful you would even know him, for he moves in most elevated circles. He is a Corinthian, not a worthless scholar."

Wilfred snorted disdainfully. "A Corinthian? Nothing more worthless than that, m'dear."

"I'll have you know that it is the Viscount Derencourt."

"Phillip Mercerault—Beau Mercerault?"

"Yes," she said, ignoring the incredulity in his voice. "If you ever bothered to pull your nose from your infernal studies, you would know that I have ridden in the park with him and, indeed, was at Moreland with him before Christmas." She frowned slightly, remembering that the visit had not at all met her expectations. "If it hadn't been for that stupid girl who interfered, I am certain that he would have—"

Wilfred interrupted her suddenly. "I thought you said Phillip Mercerault never attended Almack's."

"He doesn't," she began, then followed Wilfred's pointed gaze. "Good heavens! He must have found out that I would be here this evening. How clever and romantic of him to surprise me!" She tugged at her brother's sleeve. "I beg you to be polite, Will!"

Wilfred stifled a yawn and nodded absently.

"We must first greet Lady Jersey and the Countess Lieven, and that cold Mrs. Drummond Burrell."

"Snotty, all of 'em. Bet all they read is that fool Byron."

Delicate color suffused Teresa's cheeks in her excitement as she greeted the patronesses most charmingly. Wilfred, thank the lord, muttered at least intelligible how-do-you-does and tugged at his cravat only once.

"Pretty little chit," Countess Lieven said behind her fan to Sally Jersey. "Nice manners."

Sally Jersey only nodded, her rather protuberant brown eyes searching through the growing throng of dancers in the middle of the floor. "Perhaps," she said after a moment, "Miss Elliott's manners will grow less charming when she meets the newest addition to this year's debutantes. Indeed," she added thoughtfully, "it would appear that Miss Eversleigh has already made a notable conquest. Phillip Mercerault asked my permission to lead her in a waltz."

Mrs. Drummond Burrell, who had given no impression of even having attended to the ladies' conversation, turned her haughty gaze to Lady Jersey and said placidly, "It would appear to me that the viscount will shortly find himself caught between two ladies. The man has great charm. It will prove interesting to see him extricate himself from the encounter."

Teresa bore Wilfred toward the viscount, pausing to give only cursory greeting to a young gentleman who seemed most willing to take Wilfred's place at her side.

She was within five feet of her goal when the viscount turned away to speak to a small, dark-haired girl who was standing next to Lady Barresford. In the next moment, he was leading the chit to the dance floor. Teresa stopped dead in her tracks. "How dare he!" she hissed.

Wilfred, who had expected to be thoroughly bored parading about after his nonpareil sister, quickly altered his opinion. He drawled, "Looks to me like that little beauty has cut you out with your viscount. Maybe you boasted victory a bit prematurely, sister."

"Oh do be quiet," she snapped, biting her lower lip. "Undoubtedly he was simply being polite. Come, Will, I must say hello to Lady Barresford."

Teresa was once again frustrated in her wishes, as Lady Barresford lowered her turbaned head in close conversation with Lady Blanchard.

"Drat," she muttered in vexation. She looked toward Phillip and the girl he was waltzing with, and saw him throw back his head and laugh at something the chit said. Without warning, she grabbed Wilfred's arm.

"You will dance with me. And mind you, Will, don't step on my toes!"

"Quoth the green dragon of jealousy . . . the lady's eyes are slits," Wilfred recited.

"I will thank you, Will, to keep your ridiculous poetry to yourself!"

Phillip whirled Sabrina in a wide circle toward the periphery of the dance floor. "So what do you think of Almack's?" he asked, smiling down at her.

"It is most pleasurable, particularly the dancing. And you, my lord, do you often come here?"

"Rarely. I find it rather a bore, if you must know."

"I hope that you have not put yourself out on my account."

"I have told you, Sabrina, that I never put myself out on anyone's account. I hope you will learn that I normally do exactly as I wish." Except where you are concerned, Sabrina, he finished silently to himself. She appeared to have forgotten their rather turbulent encounter of the evening before, and he wondered wryly if she was coming to her senses.

"You must try for a little conversation, my dear," he said gently, calling her attention back to him. "You do not wish to bore me, I am certain."

Her violet eyes widened and flashed at him.

"Ah yes, a little vivacity enlivens your countenance, Sabrina. Richard spoke of your being as vivid as life itself. I would not quibble if you had a mind to impress me in the same way."

Before she could respond, he tightened his hand about her waist and whirled her about the perimeter of the dancing floor, in wide, dipping circles. She was panting breathlessly and laughing as he drew her to a slow, sedate pace.

"Please do not stop, it is so very pleasurable!" He grinned at her and she rushed into flurried speech to hide her discomfiture. "How wrong you are, Phillip. Almack's is not at all a bore. And everyone is being so kind."

He whirled her about again in the large circles she so much loved. "I must agree, Bree, this is a delightful evening. You dance rather well, I might add, for a merchant's offspring."

"And you, my lord, are simply begging for me to tread upon your toes."

"The Italian crepe you are wearing is most becoming," he said in an amused voice, disregarding her threat. "I applaud your aunt's choice of the dark amber."

"Then you may compliment my taste, sir. Not everyone tries to give me orders, you know." A small frown puckered her forehead. "How do you know that it is Italian crepe? You are the first gentleman I have known versed in female attire."

He gave her a flashing smile. "A rake, my dear Sabrina, is perforce a master of many things. If you like, I shall escort you to a small milliner's shop, just off Bond Street. I can think of several charming hats that should set off your coloring to perfection."

"If you are so knowledgeable, my lord," she snapped, "then your perceptions should tell you that I do not care at all to hear such nonsense."

He felt her fingertips tapping on his shoulder and thought, a slight smile on his lips, of his previous night with Martine. "Suffer with me, my dear, the waltz is nearly ended."

The fingertips ceased their tapping. "If you would but stop being outrageous and trying to put me to the blush, I assure you that I would not suffer at all in your company."

"I am honored by your accolade, Sabrina, and am delighted to hear that you do not find me altogether insufferable." He lowered his chin to the curls atop her head and said in a pensive voice, "I am quite determined to be the second St. George. As a damsel in distress, I do think it unwise of you to scorn my services."

"Your services, my lord, are quite unnecessary."

"Which services do you refer to, Sabrina? I have, after all, performed such varied ones for you."

"Now you are being insufferable, Phillip!"

"Quite right you are. Do forgive me." She gazed up at him through her lashes, her expression suspicious. Whilst she was thus occupied in examining his smug apology, the orchestra struck up another waltz and he whirled her toward the middle of the dance floor.

"Another waltz! How kind of you, my lord, I do enjoy it so very much."

He saw the speculation in the eyes of those about them, and sternly repressed a twinge of conscience. He had been right to think that Sabrina, in her ignorance of London society, was sublimely unaware that two dances, particularly waltzes, pronounced to the world that there was more than simple acquaintance between them.

After some moments, he said, "I must leave London for several days, to go to my home in Essex. I shall be back no later than Monday. Would you like to ride in the park with me when I return?"

"They allow Cits in Hyde Park, my lord?" she inquired demurely.

"Since you will be in my company, there is no need for you to worry."

She tilted her head back. "I swear to you that one day, Phillip Mercerault, I shall have the last word!"

"Since I am ten years your senior and will doubtless reach my dotage before you, it is a vague possibility."

Sabrina quelled the desire to rip up at him for this latest presumption, and changed the topic. "I know your home is in Essex. However, I know little else about it."

He laughed down at her, his white teeth flashing, amused at her earnest tone of voice. The lady had finally found a safe topic, one that would keep her at her ease and him at his distance. He slowed their pace and relaxed his hand about her waist. "Have you ever traveled in Essex, Sabrina?"

She shook her head, relieved that she had guided him, at least for the moment, to an unexceptional subject.

"As you know, my family home is called Mercerault Ashby, the Ashby part dating back to the late sixteenth century to an heiress who greatly helped to mend the Mercerault fortune at the time. The house and lands are in the parish of Great Waltham and came into Mercerault hands in the early seventeenth century, following the demise of the last Langley, Sir Anthony, by name. That illustrious gentleman, I might add, although a brave naval officer, was also a wastrel of a landlord. In fact, he sold off the manor and lands to my ancestor, the newly created viscount, Lord James, to rig up his own private fleet of ships to attack the Spanish. Poor fellow got a sword through his gullet on the coast of Spain for his troubles. In any case, with the Ashby money, Lord James set about to turn himself into a true English landowner. I think you will approve my home, Sabrina. Although it doesn't have the faded romance and crumbling grandeur of Monmouth Hall, it does give one a sense of permanence."

"But what does Mercerault Ashby look like, Phillip?" she prodded.

"It is weathered red brick, some soaring gables, and a lot of ivy crawling to the roof. There is a large nursery in the east wing."

At his addition of this quite unnecessary detail, her interest vanished and she turned stiff in his arms.

He cocked an eyebrow and continued smoothly, "In addition to the nursery, there is also an exquisitely ornate library and drawing room. The ballroom at the back of the house is fairly dripping with carved cherubs and winged ladies from the ceiling—really quite disconcerting, particularly when one is dancing."

The music came to a halt, and Phillip seemed prepared to keep her with him for yet another waltz. Sabrina said suddenly, "Look, Phillip, my aunt is beckoning to me. I do believe that she is frowning! I could not have done anything objectionable, since I have danced with you, and quite passably, at least according to you."

"I shall return you to her. It is likely she wishes you to meet other gentlemen." He hoped that Lady Barresford would not give Sabrina too stern a raking down for dancing two waltzes with him.

"I suppose you are right," she said on a small sigh. "Will you waltz with me again after I've done my duty with the other gentlemen?"

He smiled at her ingenuousness and, regretfully, shook his head. "Not tonight at any rate, my dear. I have an engagement and must take my leave."

He returned Sabrina to her aunt, noting well the speculative light in that lady's eyes. "My lady. Sabrina, I shall see you on Monday." Sabrina nodded and felt a stab of disappointment as she watched him make his way to the patronesses to bid them good night.

"It would appear," Mrs. Drummond Burrell said toward the viscount's retreating figure, "that his lordship managed to escape with his skin intact."

"I must say that Miss Elliott looks none too pleased," Lady Jersey added, a wry smile on her plump face.

"At least the girl has the good sense not to dash after him," Countess Lieven said, not to be left out.

"Oh dear," Lady Jersey said behind her fan. "I do believe that Miss Elliott has decided to meet her rival."

"Dear Lady Barresford! How delightful to see you again. My mama sends her best regards."

Sabrina turned about at Miss Elliott's words. What an incredibly lovely girl, she thought. She dismissed Phillip from her mind for the moment, promising herself that when she saw him again, on Monday, she would give him a scathing set-down for the trick he had played on her. However had he managed to keep a straight face when she, ninny that she was, had asked him for a third waltz?

She waited patiently for her aunt to introduce her. Her eyes fell upon a slender young man with narrow shoulders and reddish hair that seemed to stick up about his head at odd angles. She heard the girl saying, "And this is Wilfred, my brother."

Wilfred sketched a bow, all the while uneasily eyeing his sister who was staring with glittering eyes at the dark-haired girl at Lady Barresford's side.

Lady Barresford nodded pleasantly toward the uneasy Wilfred. "Sabrina, my dear, this is Teresa, and her brother, Wilfred."

Sabrina made her curtsy and said pleasant how-do-y'do's.

Teresa said gaily, "Do let me take Sabrina from you

for a few minutes. I vow I should like to become better acquainted."

Sabrina wondered silently what would happen to poor Wilfred.

"Do you not have the next dance with Miss Ainsley, Will?" Teresa said firmly to her brother.

Sabrina smiled to herself at the perfectly blank expression on Wilfred's face.

"Miss Ainsley," Teresa repeated slowly, stressing the young lady's name.

"Ah, yes, of a certainty I do," Wilfred said, and backed away.

"Do not keep my niece too long, Teresa, for there are many others I would have her meet."

"Of course not, Lady Barresford," Teresa said pleasantly, and promptly bore Sabrina off.

"You are new to London, I gather," she said, seating herself on a small sofa and patting the place next to her.

"Yes, I have been here with my aunt but a week."

Teresa continued sweetly, "I saw the viscount dancing with you, Miss . . . Barresford?"

"Eversleigh," Sabrina corrected.

"Ah yes, Miss Eversleigh. Was dear Phillip giving you lessons? I vow your experience cannot be so lacking as to demand two successive waltzes."

Sabrina, who had been openly admiring this lovely girl, blinked in confusion at the sweet voice and the undeniably acid words. "I much enjoy the waltz, Miss Elliott," she said carefully.

Teresa's eyes widened as memory suddenly fell into place. "Eversleigh, did you say? How very interesting. Would it be, Miss Eversleigh, that you have just arrived from Yorkshire?"

"Yes. My home is in Yorkshire, near to Leeds."

Miss Eilliott's nostrils flared and she gave a high, sharp laugh. "Then you are, of course, well acquainted with Phillip Mercerault."

Sabrina sensed danger. She tried to tell herself that Miss Elliott was most likely being a cat because she had a tendre for Phillip and was simply jealous. But she took in the lady's narrowed, gleaming eyes and her tight lips, and quickly rose. "If you will excuse me, I must return to my aunt. I am really rather fatigued."

"Fatigued, Miss Eversleigh? I should imagine so, given your penchant for unusual and tiring activities. Undoubtedly it was you who was giving lessons to the viscount and not the other way around."

"I think, Miss Elliott, that you must explain your most unusual words," Sabrina said coldly, drawing herself up to her full height. "I find your innuendoes quite tasteless."

"Innuendoes, Miss Eversleigh? You needn't play the innocent with me, I assure you. How many lies did you tell your aunt so that she would introduce you into society?"

"I think I hear a jealous lady speaking," Sabrina said softly. At an audible gasp from Teresa, she continued in what she hoped was an indifferent voice, "There is really no need for you to behave in such an ill-bred manner, Miss Elliott. The viscount is merely a friend, and you are most welcome to him."

"Why you vulgar little slut!" Teresa gasped. "If Phillip is but a friend, then what would you term your cousin, Trevor Eversleigh?"

Sabrina did not question how Miss Elliott knew of Trevor. She wondered with a sickening knot in her stomach if her new-found life of one week was crumbling about her feet. Had Phillip been right?

Teresa saw the color drain from Sabrina's face. "I was a guest at Moreland. Ah yes, I see that you cannot deny it. The gentlemen were in quite a fix, I assure you, trying to figure out what was to be done with you. Did you enjoy your five days with Phillip? I have heard it said that he is most kind to his . . . discarded mistresses."

Sabrina thought wildly that Miss Elliott was but one person. Surely all of society could not be so malicious. She heard Miss Elliott continuing to speak, as if from a great distance. "Do you intend to continue your sluttish behavior in London? Everyone at Moreland was appalled that a girl of good family would seduce her own cousin, and her sister's husband at that."

Sabrina remembered her words to Phillip about making the world change. As she gazed into Miss Elliott's gloating face, she realized she had been wrong. Society would not change its rules for her; she was nothing better than an outcast. She threw back her head and said in a tightly controlled voice, "It is ridiculous that I should try to defend myself to the likes of you, Miss Elliott. I pity you, for you have a cold, venomous nature."

"I need no pity from a harlot."

Sabrina turned on her heel and made her way slowly back to her aunt. Perhaps you should have tried to reason with Miss Elliott, explained everything to her, she told herself, but the idea of so demeaning herself made her cold with anger. If she did not have her pride, she would have nothing. She wondered, almost dispassionately, what would happen to her now.

8

Sabrina stood quietly beside a window of the small drawing room of her suite at the Cavendish Hotel, gazing over the tops of red and gray brick buildings toward Bond Street. Although the window was tightly closed against the winter wind, she fancied she could hear the people on the street below speaking to each other as they passed by her window, carrying on civil conversations about whatever it was people discussed when they were not alone. She turned away from the window. She heard Hickles, her newly-acquired maid, moving about in the next room. At least she was not completely alone, although it was difficult to count Hickles as anything remotely resembling a confidant. Sabrina grimaced as she pictured her maid, an obese older spinster who contrived to look somehow disapproving even when she smiled, a rare event during the past three days. You cannot afford to be choosy, my girl, she told herself stoutly.

Her thumbnail found its way to her mouth. At least she was not destitute. To be sure, she had been treated with marked suspicion when she had paid the necessary visit to Hoare's Bank to secure her funds in her own name. There had been nothing her Aunt Barresford could do to prevent her from using her own money, although Sabrina was quite certain she would have had she been able.

She sat wearily down in a stiff-backed brocade chair and stared blankly at the wall opposite her. She smiled bitterly, remembering how she had still felt some hope after her disastrous confrontation with Teresa Elliott just five days before. Although her aunt had looked at her rather oddly when she had pleaded a headache, she had accompanied her home without questioning her.

How glib she had been, telling Phillip that she would change the world. The very next day she had learned what it was like to receive haughty stares from beak-nosed ladies and be cut dead by several acquaintances supposedly friends of her Aunt Barresford. One gentleman she had met that disastrous evening at Almack's ogled her openly on the street.

Sabrina's confrontation with her aunt came about that very afternoon. She had intended to tell her aunt the whole of it but was forestalled by Lady Blanchard, who was waiting for them upon their return, her face bloated with eagerness. Sabrina went to her room, reasoning that she was, after all, the granddaughter of an earl and not some poor relation. Perhaps Aunt Barresford would understand and be able to smooth the matter over with society. She had not long to wait for her aunt's summons to the library.

"Sit down, Sabrina."

Sabrina looked searchingly at her aunt. Her cheeks were a mottled red and her eyes were bright and hard. "Lady Blanchard has spoken to you?" she asked, careful to keep her voice neutral. She glanced about the library, half expecting to see that lady still in attendance.

"Can you doubt it?" Lady Barresford asked, her voice tight with suppressed anger.

"Aunt, I beg of you not to be angry with me," Sabrina said earnestly, easing herself into a chair. "I wanted to tell you what had happened in Yorkshire but——"

"But you could not bring yourself to confess to such wanton behavior!" Lady Barresford interrupted coldly. "Lord, first Elisabeth and now you. At least your sister did not come to my home with her reputation in shreds, hoping to pull the wool over my eyes!"

"Aunt, you must listen to me. I do not know what Lady Blanchard told you, but you must believe that it is all lies, started by that wretched girl Teresa Elliott."

"Ah, so you deny running away from Monmouth Hall?"

"No, of course not. I had to, you see, because Trevor tried to . . . rape me. I could not stay!"

"He tried to rape you? A likely story that, my girl! A man who has been married to your sister for but one month? Now I suppose you'll tell me that you did not spend five days—alone—with Phillip Mercerault."

"I was ill. He saved my life. There was nothing more than that, Aunt, you must believe me! 'Twas Charles Askbridge who made Phillip believe that he had compromised me, but I would have none of it. I did nothing wrong!"

Lady Barresford ceased her furious perambulations in front of her niece and stared down at her in disbelief. "Are you telling me that the viscount agreed that he had compromised you? He made you an offer of marriage?"

Sabrina said quietly, "Yes, but I refused him."

"That is a lie!" Lady Barresford fairly shrieked at her. "No girl would be such a fool as to turn down Viscount Derencourt, much less one who has spent five days alone with him! What you really mean to tell me, isn't it, my girl, that he offered you a carte blanche?"

Sabrina shook her head stupidly. "I do not understand you, Aunt."

"You became his mistress and he offered to let you continue in that role. Now do you understand, Miss Innocence?"

"Phillip could never be like that, Aunt, I assure you!"

Lady Barresford shook her head in disgust. "I wish you would stop play-acting, Sabrina. Now do keep quiet so I may decide what is to be done with you."

Yet another person to decide what to do with Sabrina Eversleigh, she thought bitterly, staring down at her toes.

"You will go home to Yorkshire," Lady Barresford said with sudden decision. "You will contrive, I trust, to be conciliating with Elisabeth and Trevor, for there is the earl to think of. You would not wish to make him more ill than he is now."

Sabrina raised her eyes to her aunt's face. "I cannot go

back, Aunt," she said quietly. "Though you do not wish to believe me, Trevor did try to rape me and I do not doubt that he would behave in the same despicable manner were I to return. As to Elizabeth, I can no longer live in the same house with her."

Lady Barresford said sharply, "Then, my innocent niece, what do you intend to do? You must know that after all that has happened, I cannot allow you to remain here."

Sabrina rose abruptly to her feet and said with what calm she could muster, "You are wrong, Aunt, about all of it. You will not even consider that I am telling you the truth. I will be out of your house as soon as I can pack."

"And just where do you think you are going, miss?"

"I will not be on the streets, Aunt, if that is what worries you. You forget that the money you have freely been lavishing on the both of us belongs to me. I bid you good-bye, Aunt."

"Miss Sabrina."

Sabrina drew her gaze from the wall to her maid's heavily jowled face. "Yes, Hickles?"

"It is tea time. Would you like me to order it up?"

"Yes, thank you, Hickles," Sabrina said quietly, choosing to ignore the ill-disguised impatience in her tone. How odd it is, she thought, staring after the woman, that servants can always sense when all is not as it should be. Of course, someone of Hickles's strident character knew quite well that she was the only one to provide Sabrina, an eighteen-year-old girl, with any air of respectability.

Sabrina watched the clock on the mantelpiece move its arms slowly into evening. She had no desire to leave the Cavendish Hotel for fear that she would meet someone she knew. She thought of the gentleman who had openly ogled her, and shuddered.

She realized with something of a start that it was Tuesday morning, when the clock finished chiming its twelve strokes. She was to have ridden in the park with Phillip on Monday. She wondered if he had been delayed in Essex and was unaware of her plight.

Phillip had known what would happen, had warned her

again and again, and she had spurned his protection. She
looked at herself in the narrow mirror over the mantelpiece. Her face was set and there were dark smudges
making half circles below her eyes.

"You are a fool," she said to the pale image, "a stupid,
witless fool." She tried to imagine the future, the days
stretching out endlessly into months and years. She felt
sudden fury at the injustice of it all and smashed her
fisted hand into the mirror. The glass shattered and she
looked stupidly at the blood that was beginning to trickle
down her fingers.

Toward dawn an idea came to her. The world had not
changed, but she had. She had allowed herself to wallow
in self-pity, to act the broken, helpless female. She had
foolishly nurtured romantic ideas about a future that
could no longer be hers. It would require resolution to
carry out what she had in mind, but she would find it
before the day was out, she told herself, and finally fell
into a deep sleep.

In one fact, Sabrina was wrong. The viscount had returned from Essex to London on Saturday, earlier than
expected. He sat in the library of his townhouse on Tuesday, staring thoughtfully into space, his fingers wrapped
about a folded piece of stationery.

It had required a good deal of resolve on his part not
to go to Sabrina as soon as he had become aware of the
full extent of her disgrace, but he had guessed that his
arrival at the Cavendish Hotel on Saturday would only
have made her more obdurate. He could easily imagine
her raging anger and bitterness, her sense of injustice at
what had happened.

He unfolded the note and read it swiftly through once
again. A smile lifted the corners of his mouth. She had a
business matter to discuss with him, did she. At least she
hadn't lost her pluck. It seemed to him now that he had
done the right thing by not going to her immediately. She
had finally come to her senses.

At half past four in the afternoon, Viscount Derencourt
presented himself at the Cavendish Hotel. A heavy

woman of indeterminate age and equally forgettable countenance admitted him, her manner one of open curiosity.

"I am the Viscount Derencourt. You may announce me to your mistress." He spoke in his haughtiest manner, guessing that Sabrina had had to endure sniffing disapproval from her battle-ax of a maid.

"Yes, my lord," Hickles muttered crossly.

"After you have announced me, you may take yourself off," Phillip added in his most uncompromising voice. He saw the woman's nostrils quiver briefly in disappointment before she turned and led him into a depressingly small drawing room.

"Miss Sabrina, the Viscount Derencourt is here to see you."

Although Sabrina had dressed herself with care, Phillip was appalled at her appearance. Her face was pale and drawn and she stared at him with painful uncertainty.

"My lord, I am delighted that you could come," Sabrina said with forced lightness. "Hickles," she continued, turning to her maid, "you may go now. Do dress warmly, for it is quite chilly outside."

Hickles allowed herself a disapproving sniff before removing herself from the drawing room. A young girl receiving a gentleman—and alone! She supposed it was to be expected, given the peculiar behavior of her mistress the past three days.

Phillip shrugged out of his greatcoat and gloves. As Sabrina relieved him of them, he said sharply, "What did you do to your hand?"

"Nothing of importance, my lord," she said, and whipped her clumsily bandaged hand behind her back. "I thank you for coming. Will you please take a seat?"

He nodded, and eased his large frame into the proffered chair.

"Tea, my lord?"

Again he nodded. He saw that her hands were shaking as she poured the tea. A few drops spilled onto her hand and she winced. He was on the point of pulling out his handkerchief to help her when he stopped himself. She was behaving quite well. If he showed her his concern, she would likely think that he was pitying her.

He accepted the cup, took one sip, and set it down, for it was wretchedly weak. He thought to make some unexceptionable conversation, but she was looking at him with such apparent dread that he decided not to mince matters. Better to get it over with, and quickly.

"I received your note, my dear. You have a business matter to discuss with me?"

"Yes," she said finally, her eyes darting from his face to a point just beyond his left shoulder. "I suppose you know why I am here."

"Yes," he said calmly. "I have been back in London since Saturday."

She momentarily forgot her steady, rehearsed lines, and turned on him. "Then why did you not——" She broke off abruptly and bit her lower lip.

"It is a long story, Sabrina, and one I will not bore you with at the moment," he said gently. "Your business matter?"

She drew herself up ramrod stiff in her chair and recited her speech. "You were right, my lord, about everything. I find that I am disgraced, all because of one lady, Miss Teresa Elliott, who, I believe, is much enamored of you. As you said, my lord, 'twould take but one vicious tongue and the damage would be done. My aunt, unfortunately, was not at all inclined to take my part in the matter; indeed, she was most desirous that I remove myself from her house as quickly as possible." She paused a moment, thinking she heard a snort from Phillip, but when she met his eyes, his glance was impassive. He nodded for her to continue.

"In any case, my lord, I have given the matter much thought. I have never been without friends nor so much alone in my life, and I do not care to continue in this way."

So even marriage to me is preferable, Phillip thought wryly. He stilled his feelings of wounded consequence, realizing that it had cost her a great deal to admit her feelings to him.

"So what is it that you wish to do, Sabrina?"

"I wish to make you an honorable offer, my lord. I would that you would marry me. In return, you shall have my remaining nine thousand pounds and my dowry, which, I believe, is quite sizable." She added by way of explanation, "My Aunt Barresford dipped quite liberally into my funds, but still, it is nine thousand pounds."

"As great an heiress as the Ashby lady, in short. A most tempting business offer, Sabrina. Now, let me understand you. If I marry you, you will turn all your fortune over to me?"

She nodded, eagerly. "In addition to my money, my lord," she continued, "I offer you your . . . freedom." There, she thought, it is I who have offered the marriage of convenience, so that he will not have to.

Phillip said harshly, "I have my freedom, madam. Is there naught else I can expect from you?"

She looked away, unwilling to let him see the pain his words brought her. "I offer you all that I can, my lord." She added silently to herself, 'Tis no more than you can offer me, Phillip.

"And in return for filling my coffers and offering me my . . . freedom, I am to save you from disgrace, give you the protection of my name?"

She nodded, tight-lipped at his cold appraisal.

"Very well, Sabrina, I will accept your business offer," he said in a measured voice. She gave an almost audible sigh of relief. He gazed at her pensively for a long moment. "I seem to recall that you would not marry where there is no love."

She whipped back her head and snapped, "You cannot be so dull-witted as not to see that everything has changed!"

He said nothing, merely sat back in his chair and stretched his long legs out in front of him, lacing his fingers behind his head.

Sabrina's nerves grew taut with the lengthening silence. "Would you care for more tea, my lord?"

Phillip sat forward suddenly and tapped his fingertips

together. "Tell me, Sabrina, when I have mended your tattered reputation, what then will be your intention?"

She set the poised tea pot back down and blinked at him, totally at sea. "Intention, my lord?"

"Married ladies of fashion often amuse themselves with lovers. You have offered me my freedom. Is it your intention to dally in like manner?"

She turned as white as her collar. "After all that has happened to me . . . how could you ever think such a thing, much less speak of it so brazenly! I would not want any of *that!*"

"Marriage involves many things, Sabrina. Most wives, I venture, would expect much more from their husbands than the simple token giving of their names."

For one interminable moment, Sabrina felt Trevor's mouth grinding against hers, his fingers probing at her, painfully squeezing her breasts. She felt dazed and confused. "I will, of course, do my duty, my lord," she whispered finally, her eyes lowered to her lap.

Phillip drew back and gazed at her bent head, appalled at himself. He had acted the bastard, causing her needless pain. He had even pressed her about lovemaking when any half-witted fool would realize she would be terrified at the thought. It came to him with sudden insight why he had so crassly pushed her. She had offered him everything she had to give—her money. But nothing of herself. Why should he expect anything from her that he himself was not prepared to give?

He rose and placed his hand on her shoulder. She stiffened at his touch.

"Sabrina," he said gently, "please forgive me. Believe me, my dear, I am most delighted to accept your offer of marriage."

She looked up at him, her expression grave. "Will my shame bring you disgrace also, Phillip?"

"No," he said honestly. "Most will believe that I have done the right thing by you. As for the others . . ." he shrugged. "Trust me to see that no one will ever hurt you again."

"My—my money is sufficient for you to make the . . . sacrifice?"

He said lightly, "If I ever find myself at *point non plus*, I shall simply strangle you and find myself another heiress."

His jest brought a wan smile to her lips. "In that case, my lord, I shall practice the most stringent economies."

He pulled her to her feet and lightly kissed her brow. "Perhaps we can begin by my teaching you how to make viscount's bread."

She nodded, nestling her cheek against his shoulder. She said in a muffled voice, "I shall try to make you a . . . comfortable wife, Phillip."

He gave a low, deep laugh. "My God, Sabrina, spare me such an appalling future!"

9

Phillip shifted his position by the mantelpiece in the library of his townhouse, and looked first at Charles Askbridge and then at Lord Alvaney.

"I believe, Ned," he said, addressing Lord Alvaney, "that you have heard the whole of it. Can you think of anything to add, Charles?"

"No, only that I am relieved that Sabrina has finally come to her senses."

Lord Alvaney's long thin nose quivered as he harked back to Trevor. "Shocking bad *ton*, Phillip, and from the future Earl of Monmouth! To think that a well-bred girl could be treated in such a fashion. It's positively medieval."

Phillip nodded, his hazel eyes narrowing.

Charles said, "At least Phillip has ensured that Trevor and Elisabeth will do no more tale bearing."

"I only wish that something else could be done to the bounder," Lord Alvaney pursued.

Phillip said wryly, "I can't very well put a bullet through my wife's brother-in-law, Ned."

"I suppose not," Lord Alvaney said, much disappointed.

"More sherry, gentlemen?"

Phillip refilled their proffered glasses and returned to his place by the fireplace. "Now that I've told you this touching story, Ned, you must know that I will need your assistance."

"Methinks my persuasiveness is the most apt term, Derencourt!"

"In a word, yes," Phillip agreed. "Well, gentlemen, can it be done?"

"If we are, shall we say, a bit ruthless," Lord Alvaney said, fingering his snowy cravat. "There is but one problem that I foresee, and that is Miss Eversleigh's aunt, Lady Barresford. If she can be brought around to see reason, then I daresay we shouldn't have much difficulty with the rest of the people involved."

There was a distinct gleam in Phillip's eyes. "My dear Ned, do allow me to handle the lady. Not only will she reinstate Sabrina in her good graces for all society to see, she will also hold the private wedding at her home. The wedding festivities will, of course, be held here."

"How much time do we have, Phillip?" Charles asked.

"The wedding will be on Saturday—in short, gentlemen, we have four days."

"It's miracles, you want, my dear fellow."

"Yes indeed, Ned. If I did not, I would not have enlisted your aid." Phillip raised his sherry glass in a toast. "To my imminent demise as a bachelor."

"The ultimate sacrifice," Charles said ruefully, and downed the remainder of his sherry.

Lord Alvaney pursed his thin lips together, already deeply involved in his strategies. A sudden smile lit up his foxlike features, and he slapped his knee. "A challenge to wile away the winter hours." He rose. "If you gentlemen will excuse me, I'm off to White's."

"Thank you, Ned," Phillip said quietly, as he shook his friend's hand.

Lord Alvaney raised a haughty brow. "I say, old boy, can you really imagine anyone surviving in London society if I were to cut him dead?"

After Greybar, the viscount's butler, had shown Lord Alvaney from the library, Charles turned troubled eyes to Phillip.

"What do you intend to do about Teresa Elliott? It is she, you know, who brought the whole thing about in the first place."

Phillip shrugged. "If it had not been Teresa, I daresay it would have been someone else. I suppose I shall pattern my actions after Ned's. In short, I shall cut the lady."

"It's Sabrina I'm worried about," Charles said seriously. "What if Teresa treats her badly?"

Phillip grinned. "I would wager, Charles, that after we get this damned wedding over with and Sabrina has a chance to settle down, Teresa Elliott will discover quickly that she is no match for the Viscountess Derencourt."

The following morning, after fortifying himself with two strong cups of Spanish coffee and a rare haunch of sirloin, the viscount drove his curricle to the Barresford townhouse. Although the day was overcast, he was in good spirits; indeed, he was looking forward to his meeting with Lady Barresford. He jumped lightly from his curricle, tossed the reins to his tiger, Lanscombe, and walked up the wide front steps.

"I shall announce myself," he said firmly to the butler who stood wide-eyed at the front door. He heard the man groan as he made his way to the Barresford drawing room on the second floor. Damn, but servants were awake on every suit!

"I bid you good morning, ma'am," he said cheerfully, as he walked into the drawing room.

Lady Barresford pressed her hand against her bosom and gave a sharp gasp. "My lord!"

"As you see, my lady." He quickly took in the lady's glittering eyes as well as the pen and stationery spread in front of her on a small writing table.

"You will forgive me, I trust, for paying you a visit at such an early hour. However, I see that you are already busy with your . . . correspondence. Now I can provide you with good news to write."

"I have nothing to say to you, my lord!" She rose to her feet and waved an imperious finger toward the door.

"Surely, ma'am, you will find something to say to your future nephew-in-law."

Lady Barresford lowered her finger and stared at him open-mouthed. "You have offered for her?"

"I have offered for Sabrina on many occasions, ma'am. I daresay it was your exceptionable treatment of her that finally made her accept my suit."

"You dare to call my behavior into question!"

"What I would say, my lady, is that Sabrina does not appear to be blessed with family members who, as a matter of course, take her side and trust her word. However, at present, I am more concerned with society's behavior. I think that we can, together, contrive to shut the gleefully gossiping mouths."

"She is a disgrace to the Eversleighs, my lord, and to the Barresfords! Lies she told me, all lies. Bold as brass she is——"

"Sabrina told you no lies, ma'am," Phillip interrupted quietly. "It is immaterial to me whether or not you believe her or me. What is important, however, is her acceptance into society, as my wife."

"No one with any decency will ever again admit her. As for you, my lord, were I you, I should seriously wonder how many men she has dallied with before you so obligingly offered for her!"

Phillip forced himself to keep his voice level. "I have had enough of your tiresome venom, ma'am. You are speaking of your niece and my betrothed. You will now oblige me by sitting down and listening to what I have to say."

Lady Barresford appeared undecided for a moment, then sat down on the edge of a chair.

"Sabrina and I will be married here in a small ceremony on Saturday. I will return her to you tomorrow and you will treat her with the respect she deserves."

"You young jackanapes! After all that the little wretch has done to me, to my reputation!"

Although Phillip would have preferred to give the lady his comprehensive opinion of her character, he realized that he could bring her about more simply. "In short, ma'am, we have a scandal that threatens to boil shortly over the pot. As you said, your reputation will be sadly in question. Would it not be preferable to scotch all gossip now? Can you think of a better solution than to have Sa-

brina safely wed to me? I assure you that my friends are
at this moment putting a stop to most of the gossip-mon-
gering. You will not have to fear for your position in society, ma'am, if you give in now."

She rose and took several stalking steps about the
room. "But my friends," she wailed, turning. "They are
already aware of my feelings in the matter!"

"I suggest you inform your friends, ma'am, that new
facts have come to light and your niece is quite innocent.
Indeed, she has been much maligned, and you, because you
are her aunt, wish to be the first to right all the wrongs
done to her."

Lady Barresford cried, "But a wedding on Saturday,
'tis impossible!"

"With your abilities and energy, ma'am, I would never
despair of the outcome. I will, of course, pay for all the
expenses, including an appropriate gown for you."

He thought he heard her utter a very unladylike oath
under her breath. "Very well," she said slowly, "but if she
is not accepted, you have no one to blame but yourself."

Phillip proffered her a respectful bow. "Would you
wish to have my secretary's services?"

She shook her head absently, and Phillip knew that she
was already planning the necessary arrangements. "I will
bring Sabrina to you tomorrow morning." At the darkening frown on her forehead, he added sternly, "I expect
her three days with you to be pleasant, my lady."

As he turned to take his leave, Lady Barresford said,
"I hope you will not regret your chivalrous action, my
lord." As he merely smiled at her, she added in a curious
tone, "What makes you so certain that the girl is telling
the truth about her cousin, Trevor?"

"Ma'am, I know Sabrina. And, I might add, I also
know Trevor Eversleigh. I would that you not forget that
Sabrina is now in my care. I bid you good day, my lady."

10

"No one would ever take you for a bride, my girl, were it not for that expensive gown the viscount provided you."

Sabrina turned away from the gaunt female image in the mirror. "Phillip did not buy the gown, Aunt, I did."

" 'Tis all one and the same," Lady Barresford snapped, fingering her own exquisitely fashioned silk gown. "You have no money now. As your grandfather is too ill to be approached in the matter, I, of course, had my solicitors draw up the marriage contract. All you have now is a husband, and one, I might add, who has many pleasant demands on his time."

Sabrina was thinking about the shakily-written letter a footman had delivered the previous evening from her grandfather. He had assured her that he would be well enough to greet her and her new husband in but a short time. He had not mentioned any of the less pleasant circumstances surrounding her sudden marriage and she wondered how much of it he knew. Her pleasure at his letter had carried her through until now. She turned at her aunt's words. "What do you mean, Aunt, by pleasant demands?"

Lady Barresford snorted. "You don't have to play off your tricks with me, girl! I know you are well aware of the pleasures men take with women, though it appears that you've pulled the wool over the viscount's eyes."

Sabrina tugged at the itchy Brussels lace at her throat and chose to ignore her aunt's insult. "Please, Aunt, what do you mean?"

"Very well, act the innocent. You're not such a fool as to believe that the viscount has led a celibate life. Nor can you expect him to change his comfortable habits just because he is wedding you."

Sabrina gulped down the knot of anger in her throat. Her aunt was perfectly correct—theirs was, after all, a marriage of convenience.

"Is it time to go downstairs, ma'am?"

"Yes, it is time. For God's sake, girl, pinch your cheeks! You're colorless as a specter." Lady Barresford turned on her heel and walked toward the door, her manner as stately as her gown.

Sabrina closed her thumb and forefinger about her cheek and pinched herself. Her maid, Hickles, emerged suddenly from the corner of the bedchamber where she had been conveniently unobtrusive. "Will you need anything else, my lady?" she asked, her voice trembling with suppressed excitement.

"Yes," Sabrina said softly, turning. "It would please me greatly, Hickles, never to see your face again." She swept up the train of her gown and walked from the room, without a backward glance at her maid.

"Well, I for one think Sabrina was a lovely bride. Perhaps a trifle pale, but hardly a wooden doll." Margaret Drakemore turned away from Madelaine Bingly, her small hand fisted at her side.

Lady Bingly raised a pained eyebrow. "Such loyalty, my dear Margaret! Do finish with that stupid flounce, girl," she snapped to the maid who was kneeling before her mending a torn ruffle in her gown.

Lady Dorchester drawled from her seat before a mirror, "Now, Madelaine, it is surely time for Christian charity." Particularly, she thought with a small grimace, since her spouse, Lord Dorchester, was a good friend to Viscount Derencourt. She, for one, would not cut the new viscountess.

Lady Bingly did a small pirouette. "There, no one could tell that that oafish Colonel Sandavar put his foot through the flounce." She waved away the maid and turned to the still fuming Margaret. "I believe I hear a waltz striking up, my dear. Let us go back to the ball-room before our husbands think we have run away from them. Such an exciting adventure for Miss Eversleigh . . . or rather, the viscountess."

Margaret, who had never cared for the squint-eyed Lady Bingly, rose to her full height. "I have told you the facts of the entire matter, Madelaine. It is really quite small of you to continue in this vein."

Lady Dorchester rose from her seat and gave a final pat to her auburn hair. "Margaret is correct, Madelaine," she said in her affected drawl, "what's done is done." As she swept from the dressing room, she said over her bare shoulder, "At least the viscount will not have a shrinking bride on his hands tonight. How perfectly quaint that the wedding should follow the wedding night."

Lady Bingly tittered and moved to follow Lady Dorchester. "Or was it a wedding week, my dear Lady Dorchester? With the viscount's winning manners, it must have been a most interesting experience."

"Wretched cats," Margaret muttered under her breath.

"I wonder if the viscountess is perhaps breeding. An excellent reason for so hastily placing a gold band on Miss Eversleigh's finger."

Margaret heard the carrying words, as, she suspected, she was meant to. At least, she thought, her spirits rising a bit, most of the guests were behaving as they should, with no slighting comments about Sabrina. The small wedding held in the drawing room of Lady Barresford's townhouse had gone off without a hitch, her brother, Charles, having acted in the stead of Sabrina's family. She wished that the wedding dinner and ball had been kept similarly small, but Phillip had insisted. "I have no wish to add coals to the smoldering fire," he had said. "Sabrina will dance her wedding waltz with me before as many of the *beau monde* as we are able to accommodate. This will be no fly-by-night wedding."

Perhaps, Margaret thought, Phillip had been right. But it did not help matters that Sabrina looked so white and drawn. Margaret dismissed the maids and walked slowly back down the oak staircase to the ballroom.

Sabrina shrank back into the shadows until Margaret disappeared from her view down the winding stairs. She had not been meant, of course, to hear the cutting words, but she had. She quelled her indignation and drew a long sigh. She forgot the thick tresses of hair that had worked themselves loose from their pins and made her way quickly back downstairs.

"Hold still, Bree, and I'll fix your hair."

"Phillip!" Color rushed to Sabrina's cheeks. He stood two steps below her, a slight smile playing about his mouth. She realized with a start that she had been so closed into herself for the entire day and evening that she had scarce even been aware of him. She looked at him now, devastatingly handsome in his severe black evening clothes. There can be no more beautiful a man, she thought.

"You have eyelashes like a girl," she said foolishly.

The smile became a wide grin. "I trust that is all I have that is like a girl's. Come here, Sabrina, before your hair falls into your face."

She obeyed, her steps slow and careful for she feared tripping on the hem of her wedding gown. She felt his long fingers move deftly to draw her hair back into place.

"There, you are once again presentable, viscountess."

But I do not feel like a viscountess, she wanted to tell him. He placed his thumb under her chin and forced her to look up at him.

"It is almost over," he said gently, his thumb stroking the line of her jaw. He felt her tremble and wondered with a sudden frown what she was thinking, for she had said very little during the day. Like Margaret, he thought she looked pale and ill. "There is but one more waltz that you must dance with me. Then, little one, you may retire."

Lady Dorchester's words flashed through her mind. "But I don't wish to retire," she said in feverish haste. She saw that he was frowning at her and added in a strained voice, "Whatever you wish, my lord."

He wanted to tell her that she had nothing to fear from him, that he would not force himself upon her, but the strains of a waltz floated to his ears and he abruptly drew her hand through the crook of his arm.

"Our waltz, Sabrina," he said only. "For God's sake, raise your chin. This is, after all, supposed to be a most happy and memorable night."

She flinched at what she thought to be irony in his voice, but quickly squared her shoulders and thrust her chin in the air.

The colorfully attired group of ladies and gentlemen obligingly parted their ranks as Phillip led Sabrina onto the dance floor. She looked up fleetingly into his face and saw a set smile on his lips. He is smiling for the benefit of our guests, she thought miserably, pretending that our marriage is to his liking.

She saw Lady Dorchester from the corner of her eye and missed a step. She felt Phillip's arm tighten about her waist.

"Smile, Sabrina, else everyone will think that you are not happy with your choice of husbands."

Her lips parted into a travesty of a smile.

"That is not much better. Now you look like you're off to the Tower of London and the chopping block."

Her eyes were drawn back to Lady Dorchester and she saw the lady whispering to Lady Bingly behind her fan.

"Only men have choices," she said in a bitter voice.

"You are quite wrong, my dear. I have had no choice since the morning I found you in Eppingham Forest. Surely I am not such a bad bargain."

"That is not true, Phillip," she said in a low voice. "I offered you a business . . . arrangement. It was your choice to accept it or reject it."

He realized that she was becoming overwrought and hastened to choose a topic that would soothe her. "Are you convinced now that your grandfather is on the mend?"

A genuine smile lit up her face. "Yes. Although," she added, her smile dimming a bit, "his handwriting is not as it used to be."

"He will recover fully, you will see."

The waltz drew to a close and Phillip drew her into his arms and planted a light kiss on her lips. "There, viscountess, it is over," he whispered into her hair, amid applause and laughter from the ladies and gentlemen.

He drew her forward to stand at his side to receive their guests' parting greetings. Sabrina felt her color rise at some of the more spicy suggestions from the gentlemen. She firmly planted a smile on her lips and counted the minutes until they would all be gone.

One of the last guests to leave was Lady Barresford. She paused at Sabrina's side. "You have carried this off quite well, niece. You are fortunate that the viscount is an honorable man."

"Thank you, Aunt," Sabrina replied, her voice colorless.

Lady Barresford nodded toward the viscount. "I bid you good evening, my lord. I leave you to your blushing bride."

Phillip took Sabrina's hand and squeezed it. "Sabrina is far too exhausted to blush, ma'am, even though I am certain that she would be inclined to do so at the few tasteless comments she has been forced to endure this evening."

"That's as may be," Lady Barresford said obscurely, drawing herself up.

Sabrina saw with relief that Greybar was hovering beside Lady Barresford, her ermine wrap on his arm. "Thank you, Greybar. Her ladyship is on the point of leaving."

Lady Barresford grunted audibly and allowed Greybar to assist her into her wrap. "Well, niece, you have made your bed, and now you may lie in it."

To Sabrina's surprise and discomfiture, Phillip threw back his head and laughed. "A most excellent suggestion, ma'am."

Lady Barresford sniffed and sailed majestically from the room.

Phillip turned to Sabrina. "Now, little one, it is time for you to lie in your bed."

She gazed up at him uncertainly.

He nodded at her and led her unresisting to the staircase. "I will send Doris to you, my dear." He patted her hand and turned away.

" 'Tis like an angel you look, my lady," Doris said to the pale figure standing in front of the long mirror, swathed from neck to toe in a white silk nightgown. Sabrina nodded abstractedly, and Doris smiled to herself. Lord, but the viscount was a fine figure of a man. The new viscountess was lucky to be wedded to such as he. She finished brushing the long black hair that hung in deep waves to Sabrina's waist and stepped back. "Is there anything else I can do, my lady?"

"No, thank you, Doris."

Doris curtsied and softly closed the door behind her.

Sabrina turned slowly from the mirror and let her eyes rove again over the large bedchamber. It was severe and masculine, all straight lines and sharp angles, not at all unlike its master, she thought. She flinched slightly as she gazed at the huge bed, a carved oak affair set on a dais in the middle of the bedchamber, with no hangings to soften its stark presence. She picked up a branch of candles, carried it to the bed, and set it on the bedside table. Phillip had told her that carpenters would be at her disposal to redo another bedchamber for her down the corridor. Perversely, she wondered why he did not wish her to share his room.

Sabrina slipped in between the sheets and drew the covers up to her chin. She stared up at the dark oak beams that criss-crossed the length of the ceiling. She strained to hear Phillip's footsteps. She felt her own nakedness under the covers and drew her knees up to her chest in an instinctive protective gesture. You're being a fool, she chided herself. Phillip is kind and gentle and will not hurt me. Yet how different her wedding night was to be from what she had expected. She had fancied, as she supposed every girl did, that her wedding night would be an exciting, very romantic adventure, not a prospect to be dreaded. But she did dread it, for there was no romance,

no pretense of love. Indeed, she scarce knew the man she
had bound herself to.

In the next few minutes, she found herself shaking her
head, as she thought back to the five days she had spent
with Phillip. Their time together had certainly been
unique, she thought ruefully, remembering her bath. She
supposed, upon further reflection, that she did perhaps
know him better than most girls knew their husbands on
their wedding day. At the very least, she did not have to
concern herself about excessive virginal modesty, since
Phillip had taken so intimate care of her.

Sabrina glanced at the clock on the bedside table. It occurred to her, as she watched the minutes tick by, that he
should have come to her by now. When the candles gut-
tered in their sockets, she reached over and snuffed them
out. She lay in the darkness, the covers bunched up about
her chin. He is not going to come, she realized finally,
staring up at the darkened ceiling. It came to her suddenly that she wanted to become his wife, to have him
make love to her. She shook her head at herself. She had
offered him a marriage of convenience and he had accepted it. Evidently, there was nothing more he wanted
from her. She sighed softly, wishing that she too wanted
nothing more from him. Her physical exhaustion finally
stilled her thoughts, and she fell into a light, restless sleep.

"If I may say so, my lord, a most joyous occasion and
splendidly carried out."

The viscount raised his eyes from his brandy and
looked at his butler, Greybar, a man as stolid and comforting as the huge columns that held up the house. He
smiled, knowing how Greybar dearly loved to plan occasions.

"You have done excellently, Greybar. My thanks to all
the staff."

"If you will allow me, my lord," Greybar continued, "I
and the entire staff wish you and the viscountess much hap-
piness." Greybar hoped his felicitations were appropriate,
for he as well as the lowest scullery maid was well
aware of the facts surrounding the viscount's hurried

wedding. "Poor little mite," Mrs. Hawley, the housekeeper, had pronounced, shaking her crimped gray curls. "At least after the wedding, we shall keep her safe and sound with us." It was on the tip of Greybar's tongue to rearrange this thought a bit for his master's benefit, when the viscount rose from his leather chair before the fireplace and stretched his large frame. "I thank you, Greybar." He looked away for a moment into the dying embers. "I do not doubt that you are aware that your mistress has come through a rather trying time."

"Yes, my lord," Greybar said without hesitation, pleased to receive his master's confidence.

Phillip turned and bestowed a genuine smile upon his butler, one that had secured him the unending affection of his staff. "She is young, Greybar, and untried in London ways. I have decided against taking her to Essex, at least for the time being. She must learn her way here, in London, and I trust that you will assist her. A dinner party, say next week, will be just the thing to start her off."

An answering smile indented the butler's thin cheeks. "'Twill be a great pleasure to assist her ladyship, my lord."

Phillip tossed down the remainder of his brandy. "Off to bed with you now. It's been a memorable day, but a long one."

After Greybar bowed himself out of the library, Phillip turned back to the fireplace and negligently kicked the smoldering embers with the toe of his boot. He supposed that Sabrina was by now sound asleep. He looked for a moment taken aback, wondering just where the devil he was going to sleep. Yet another sacrifice to make for you, Sabrina, he thought ruefully.

All in all, his thinking continued as he walked up the stairs, he and his friends had pulled the whole matter off quite nicely. Now, in great measure, it was up to Sabrina to recover her spirit and make her own mark in society.

Before he fell asleep in a too-short bed in a guest bedchamber, he congratulated himself as the Viscount Derencourt on securing such a wife as Sabrina. She was of impeccable breeding, and would be quite lovely once she put some meat on her bones. Although he looked forward to making love to her, he could afford to give her all the time she needed to forget her experience with Trevor.

He was aware of feeling quite pleased with himself as he drifted off into sleep.

11

Late the next morning, the viscount faced his wife over the breakfast table. "You slept well, Bree?"

"Very well, Phillip, once I was able to go to sleep." Although she looked at him hopefully, he did not appear to notice anything beyond the words themselves.

"Excellent," he said, and began to carve himself a generous portion of rare sirloin.

"You know," she continued, still hopeful, "I don't feel at all married. Indeed, I don't feel at all different than I did last night."

Thinking that she was in need of assurance that all would be well now, he said gently, "You have but to look at your third finger, Bree. There is nothing more for you to fear, I promise you."

Sabrina gave up and concentrated on her scrambled eggs. She became suddenly aware that he was speaking to her. "Forgive me, my lord, what did you say?"

"I said that I will have Peter Stradling draw up the necessary papers so that your funds will return to your name."

She gazed at him stupidly. "You will what?"

"Sabrina, it is most discouraging that you find your breakfast of more interest than your husband. I said that your money is your own again, to do with just as you please."

Sabrina lowered her fork and stared at her husband, stupified. "But why?"

"Sabrina, I neither want nor need your money. For heaven's sake, you might at least thank me. You're quite independent now."

She tried to control her temper. "Is it, my lord, that

149

you believe me a simple female, with such niceties as bargains and honor beyond my ken? It is not *my* money, Phillip," she said with as much calm as she could muster. "We made a bargain, a business agreement, do you not remember?"

"Our bargain," he said slowly, "was at your insistence." He shrugged. "It allowed you to save face and the both of us to do what had to be done."

"You arrogant, smug bastard!" she cried, flinging down her napkin. "How dare you treat me like some simpering foolish female whose only motive was to lure your high and mighty lordship into marriage! Save face, indeed! What I offered you in return for your precious Mercerault name was all that I could, my lord. It was an honorable offer and I had thought that your acceptance was to be taken in the same light."

He drew back at her torrent of words. "I fail to understand how you can so twist what has happened, Sabrina. Nor do I understand your need for unladylike invectives."

"My invectives have nothing to do with the point! Why do you seek to destroy my honor and treat me like some buffle-headed child with no sense? Surely, that is within your comprehension!"

"Very well," he said coldly, glaring down the long expanse of table at her, "I shall keep your funds. Further, madam, if you wish it, we can hold a reckoning at the end of each quarter. I will expect you not to exceed your allowance. Is that what you want, Sabrina, to dance to my tune?"

She rose slowly and placed her hands, palms down, upon the table. "Anything, Phillip, is preferable to being in your debt. As for your continuous self-touted honor in my regard, I would that you would choke on it!"

"It was my wish that you would regain your spirit after you were safely wedded, ma'am. However, if that means that you're going to be an irrational, stubborn mule——"

" 'Tis better than being an arrogant, conceited ass!"

"I will thank you not to interrupt me again, Sabrina!"

"I shall do precisely as I please, my lord. I have, after all, paid you quite handsomely for that right."

"You have much to learn, viscountess," he said, now quite as angry as she was. "As for rights, you shall do what I tell you. An earl's granddaughter you may be, but more to the point is that you are now my wife. Why do you not take yourself off to your room until you've learned some manners?"

"I think not, my lord," she flung back at him. "Perhaps Charles Askbridge would like to take me for a ride in the park. He, at least, is not an overbearing tyrant."

"Don't push me, Sabrina, else I shall remove you to Essex and let you cool your termagant's tongue in peaceful solitude."

She flung back her head and regarded him with thoughtfully pursed lips. "Such words, my lord, do not fit quite right with your so chivalrous view of yourself. Does my honorable, sacrificial husband wish his disgraced wife to fling herself in undying gratitude at his feet?"

"Such an act would undoubtedly improve your character!"

There came a discreet knock at the dining room door. "Damnation," Phillip growled.

"Enter," he called, shooting a warning frown toward his wife.

"Your carriage is ready, my lord," Greybar announced, his eyes fastened on his master's snowy cravat.

"I have no further wish for the carriage, Greybar. You may tell Lanscombe to bring around my curricle."

"Yes, my lord," Greybar said, trying to hide his discomfiture.

When he had closed the dining room door behind him, Phillip turned again to his wife and proffered her a slight bow. "Since it is obvious that you have no wish for my company, I shall take myself off. It is one of your duties to plan the menus with Mrs. Hawley. You will tell her that I shall be eating at my club this evening and will not be here for dinner."

Sabrina inclined her head and nodded. "Such economies you already allow me to practice, my lord. If you will but continue in this vein, I doubt that I will ever have to give you a dutch reckoning. I wish you a good day."

She turned on her heel and walked swiftly past her husband from the dining room.

In an excess of ire, Phillip took himself off to Gentleman Jackson's boxing saloon, there to wear himself to a sweating frazzle with one of Gentleman Jackson's instructors.

"I would have thought, Derencourt, that you had found more pleasant ways to relieve yourself of such energy."

Phillip lowered the towel he was using to mop his face. The Earl of March, not long married himself, was regarding him with an amused gleam in his gray eyes.

"Good afternoon, St. Clair," Phillip said between heaving breaths.

"Allow both Kate and me to wish you happy on your marriage. We only just returned from St. Clair, else I would have been there to waltz with your bride."

"My bride," Phillip growled, unable to keep his ill humor to himself, "is at this moment amusing herself with Charles Askbridge. She informs me that Charles is not an overbearing tyrant."

"And you, I take it, are."

"Yes, the silly chit, and after all I have done for her."

The earl gazed with some interest at this outburst from a normally quite contained and polished gentleman. "I suppose it is a stupid question, Phillip, but what have you done for the lady?"

"Why I. . . ." He looked at the earl pointedly.

The earl continued dispassionately, "It would appear to me that you have secured the hand of a lovely girl, who, in the normal course of events, would have been beseiged by any number of hopeful gentlemen vying to lead her to the altar."

"Damn you, Julien," Phillip growled, flinging aside his towel. "I'll thank you to keep your valued opinions to yourself. She is my wife and she'll do as I tell her."

"Alvaney, confirmed bachelor that he is, would likely agree with you. I, on the other hand, will offer you but one more opinion. Don't try to break her to bridle, Derencourt. With that, my friend, I bid you good day."

Phillip rose slowly and flexed his tired muscles. He stared balefully after the earl's retreating figure.

Sabrina handed her sable-lined cloak to Greybar and stood quietly as a footman divested Charles of his greatcoat and gloves.

"Would you, my lady, and Lord Charles care for tea?"

"Yes, Greybar, in the drawing room, if you please."

"Lord, but it's cold today," Greybar heard Lord Charles say to the viscountess as he followed her into the drawing room.

Sabrina removed her bonnet while Charles moved to the fireplace to warm his hands over the bright blaze. After some moments, he turned to watch Sabrina fidget about the room, unable, it seemed to him, to contain her restless energy. Although he thought it deuced odd to be asked by a newly-wedded lady to escort her to the park, he had complied, even managing throughout the afternoon to keep his questions to himself. Sabrina had chattered away so persistently throughout their ride, about the most trivial of topics, that Charles now found himself thankful for her silence. He had known Sabrina all of her life, and her show of insouciance today did not at all deceive him.

He began carefully. "Where is Phillip? I expected to see him upon our return."

She ceased her perambulations and her shoulders slumped forward. "I really have no idea, Charlie."

"Do you expect him shortly?"

"It is his house. I suppose he will return when it pleases him to do so."

At her waspish tone of voice, he drew back. "Listen, Bree, for this entire afternoon I've listened to you carry on like a magpie. Now I ask you a simple question as to the whereabouts of your husband, and you turn into an ill-tempered shrew. For God's sake, Sabrina, you've only been married for two days!"

"I might have known that you would side with him!"

"Side with him. Dammit, I don't even know where he

is! Come, Bree," he said, softening his voice, "tell me what is amiss between the two of you."

Greybar entered bearing the heavy silver tea tray. While Sabrina was fussing with the cups, Charles was left to contemplate just what the devil had occurred.

When Greybar bowed himself out of the drawing room, Charles asked, "Now, tell me what happened to make Phillip escape from his own house." His direct approach proved successful. Sabrina thwacked her teacup into its saucer and snapped, "You see, Charlie, you are siding with him. Why does it not occur to you that it might not be my fault?"

"Because I've known you all your life. I am used to your freaks of temper, whereas poor Phillip——"

"Poor Phillip, is it! I'll have you know that he was abominably condescending and overbearing!"

"Enlighten me, Sabrina."

Sabrina drew an audible breath. "It's my wretched dowry and inheritance. Phillip informed me this morning that he was having the money returned to my name . . . so that I would be independent."

"A hanging offense indeed!"

"Are you telling me, Charlie, that Phillip did not tell you of our business agreement?"

"Business agreement? Please make some sense, Bree."

She looked down at her hands and began to pull relentlessly at her thumbnail. "After that terrible night at Almack's, he stayed away from me. It was I who approached him about marriage. It was an honorable bargain we struck, Charlie. He gave me the impression that he needed my money, that we had come to an agreement that benefited us both."

Charles gazed at her, thunderstruck. "You truly believed Phillip to be in need of funds?"

"I did, then. I am, after all, an heiress of sorts."

"Well, now you realize that Phillip never wanted nor needed your money. Lord, he would have followed the same course even if you hadn't a sou. It sounds to me as if you forced him to subterfuge so that he could do the right thing by you."

"Then the bargain he struck with me was a sham . . . a lie."

"Recall that you turned him down several times. He felt responsible for you, even though it was you who plunged him helter-skelter into this entire mess."

"But I did not want him to offer for me because of that. I did not want a sacrificial husband. Don't you understand, Charlie?" she pleaded. "I wanted to bring him something, anything, besides my sullied reputation."

"If you will cease worrying about your own honor. . . ."

Sabrina felt tears stinging the back of her eyelids and angrily choked them back. "He doesn't love me," she cried, the words rushing out. "He would never even have known me, much less married me, if it hadn't been for the most wretched of circumstances."

Charles walked swiftly to the settee, sat down beside her, and gently patted her shoulder. She turned and buried her face in the intricate folds of his cravat. "I think he must believe me guilty of being a . . . wanton," she choked, "for he has not touched me."

Charles felt as though deep waters were closing over his head. "Nonsense," he said in a heartening voice. He pulled her away from his fast-wilting cravat and gave her shoulders a slight shake. Although he could not understand why Phillip, a renowned rake of the first order, would not make love to his own wife, he sought to reassure her. "He merely wants to give you time, Bree. You were quite ill, you know. And so much happened to you that would, perhaps, give you a fright of . . . that sort of thing."

She said slowly, pulling herself together, "Do you really think so, Charlie? Then . . . I suppose it is up to me to show him that I am not at all exhausted . . . or frightened."

Charles had difficulty repressing an unholy grin of amusement. The Viscount Derencourt was to be seduced by an eighteen-year-old girl, who was his wife.

"Perhaps then," Sabrina continued, weaving her thoughts aloud, "Phillip will change his mind about this being a marriage of convenience."

Charles smiled at her and squeezed her hand. "And you will try to keep your sharp tongue leashed? I would imagine that Phillip is in as much of a muddle about all this as you are. He is quite new to marriage, you know."

"As am I, Charlie. As to my sharp tongue, I vow that you have never heard Phillip unleash his!"

As this was indeed the case, Charles merely shook his head and rose. "I must go now. Perhaps Phillip will return soon. And as for you, Bree, why don't you treat yourself to a mammoth dinner—you must add pounds you know. No man wants a wife who's a skinny little twit."

"Out with you, wretch!"

"Phillip! *Mon Dieu!*" For a moment, Martine was startled out of her normally languid composure. She pulled a lovely Norwich shawl more closely about her shoulders, and rose.

"Good evening, Martine. Why the surprise? Am I not welcome here?" He strolled over to his staring mistress and planted a light kiss on her lips.

"Bien sûr, mon chou."

"English, if you please, my dear."

"Of course you are welcome, my lord." She searched his face, drawn as she suspected most women were to his beautiful eyes.

"This is but your second day of marriage, *mon chou,*" she chided him gently.

"Indeed, an irrefutable fact."

"You have wed the girl whom you did not compromise."

"As well you know. Whatever else she may be, at least she is now safe."

"The disgrace, it is no longer biting her feet?"

"No, even her feet are safe." Phillip turned to the sideboard and poured himself a glass of port. Martine watched him silently as he quickly downed the port and filled his glass again.

"Did the carpenter come and fix the damned ceiling?"

"Oh yes. A most saucy man, that one! You need have no more fear about the concussion."

"Excellent." He set down his glass and gave her a mocking bow, waving his hand toward the door. "Will you join me upstairs, madam?"

"It will be fatiguing, my lord, but I shall contrive."

As she was lazily removing her gown upstairs in her elegant, very feminine bedchamber, she turned to the viscount, who was standing next to the fireplace staring at nothing in particular. "Phillip," she said softly.

He grunted, still not turning to her.

"The little one—she is alone?"

Phillip's head snapped up at her words and he turned on her with a thunderous look. "Why the devil do you call her that?"

Martine drew off the straps of her chemise and allowed the soft material to float to her waist. His eyes did not move from her face. He is behaving most strangely, she thought. "I called her that because I have seen her."

"Where?"

"In the park today. She was riding in Charles Askbridge's phaeton."

She saw his hazel eyes darken, and was not fooled by his negligent shrug. She wriggled lazily out of the rest of her clothes, stood naked before him for a moment, and walked slowly to the bed.

She stretched her arms toward him and said in a silky voice, "Do you not wish to see for yourself that you will not get the concussion?"

"How did she look?" he asked stiffly, making no move toward her.

"She looked," Martine said quietly, "as if she was trying to forget something, an unhappy episode, perhaps."

"I'll thank you not to pry, Martine."

She arched a sleek eyebrow. "But I do not pry, my Phillip. It was you, after all, who did the asking."

"Sometimes your English is quite remarkable," he said acidly, as he pulled off his clothes.

He seemed for a time to be unaware of her presence. She watched him silently, enjoying the beauty of his muscular body in the firelight.

"The little one—her eyes are most unusual. What is the word, my Phillip? Not purple, I think."

"Violet."

"Ah yes. Violet. Most vivid, her eyes."

She saw the powerful muscles in his arms tighten and his hands clench. She felt a shiver of desire and forgot about his wife. "Come here, my lord," she whispered, holding out her arms to him.

He said in an almost angry voice, "Dammit, I shall always have my freedom."

Martine gazed at him thoughtfully, but had not time to respond to him, for in the next instant he was upon her, his hands caressing her fiercely.

He did not take time to bring her to pleasure.

She winced as he thrust into her, wondering if he was trying to hurt her, himself, or perhaps his viscountess.

He took his pleasure quickly and fell on top of her, his breathing harsh. She stroked his curling hair and ran her hands down his back.

"It is I who have the concussion, Phillip—and not on my head."

Phillip raised his head and smiled perfunctorily as he looked into her languid brown eyes. "It seems," he said more to himself than to her, "that I must needs cause hurt. I shall do better next time, I promise you."

He kissed her lightly, passionlessly, on the mouth and rose from the bed.

"I will see you again, my lord?" she asked, turning on her side toward him.

"Of course," he replied shortly.

"Ah, yes, I forgot. It is all a matter of your freedom, is it not?"

He stared at her hard for a long moment, his gaze unreadable. "Perhaps," he said finally, his voice level.

She watched him dress himself and rose from her bed only when he needed her assistance to shrug into his coat.

"It is late. I must go."

"Take care, my lord," she said softly. She returned to her bed, listening to his footsteps on the stairs. She heard the front door open, then close. She gazed about her elegant bedchamber, her expression thoughtful, and blew out the candle beside her bed.

The small ormolu clock on the mantel rang out two long strokes. Sabrina lay wide-eyed in the darkness, waiting to hear Phillip's footsteps on the stairs. She wasn't at all certain how one went about seducing one's husband, but she had sufficient confidence in herself not to despair of the outcome.

She stiffened suddenly at the sound of footsteps outside the bedchamber door. She heard him pause and then his footsteps sounded down the corridor until they were lost to her hearing. Very well, my husband, she said to herself, you have given me sufficient time to recover from my fright with Trevor and you from your ridiculous nobility. She forced herself to lie quietly for some minutes longer to give him time to remove his clothing and settle into his bed.

She rose finally and walked to her dressing table to light a candle and gaze at herself in the mirror. Her eyes were sparkling with excitement. She quickly brushed her hair and, clad only in a white silk nightgown, slipped out into the corridor and walked to his temporary bedchamber.

She inched the door open and paused, nonplussed at the sound of stentorian snoring. She grinned in the darkness and walked stealthily to the bed, only to gaze down at her husband in consternation, for he was lying on his back, still attired in his evening clothes, his arms flung away from his sides. Not quite the romantic scene I imagined, Phillip, she thought, as she bent over to touch him.

She stiffened suddenly and whipped her hand back. She sniffed again and a cloying rose scent assailed her nostrils. It was a woman's fragrance. He had been with another woman, and on the second night of their marriage. He was nothing but a rake, a womanizer. He had played her false without even giving her a chance.

She crept silently from the room, trembling with humiliation, the sound of his blissful snoring in her ears. It was all she could do to prevent herself from flinging something at him.

She raged at him in her own bed, calling upon every invective she knew to ease her pain. She felt tears swimming in her eyes and angrily choked them away. He had gone to another woman without giving her a second thought; he cared not one whit about her. She only wished that she could be as indifferent to him as he was to her.

" 'Tis near to noon, my lord, and a lovely day it is, I might add. The day will fair be gone if your lordship does not rise soon." Dambler whipped back the heavy pale yellow velvet curtains, bringing bright sunlight into the room.

Phillip cocked open an eye and gazed at his valet with loathing. "You old preacher," he mumbled, running a hand through his tumbled hair. "No one would believe me if I told them my valet gave me my marching orders."

A hint of a smile appeared in Dambler's rheumy eyes, but he continued severely, "And still in your evening clothes, my lord! You should have rung for me, no matter how late the hour. It's much too old you're getting for such nonsense, my lord."

"I don't know why I bother to tolerate you," Phillip growled as he swung his long legs over the side of the bed. "You're worse than a Methodist. At least those prosing fellows would not invade my bedchamber."

"I will have Elkins bring your bath, my lord," Dambler continued imperturbably.

Phillip grunted in agreement. At least, Dambler chose to think it agreement.

"Is her ladyship up and about, Dambler?"

"I believe her ladyship is with Mr. Stradling, my lord, planning the menu for the dinner party."

"Lord, I had clean forgot the wretched affair. It is Thursday night, is it not, Dambler?"

"Yes, my lord. If you don't mind my saying so, her ladyship is one who knows just as things should be done. Mr. Stradling has already sent out the invitations."

Phillip dropped his last article of clothing into Dambler's outstretched arms. "It seems that I am to become a useless fribble in my own house."

"If your lordship would deign to remain at home at

least one night out of seven, I venture to think this would not be the case," Dambler said with gentle severity.

"I'll shave myself, thank you, Dambler. With the mood you're in, you would just as likely as not nick my throat with the razor."

Dambler chose to ignore this bit of ill humor. "Her ladyship has set the decorators and the carpenters to work on her suite, my lord. She told me in that sweet way of hers that it wasn't fair for your lordship to have his feet hanging over the end of a guest bed."

"So her ladyship has a sweet way about her, does she? Are you certain that we are talking about the same ladyship?"

"My lord!" Dambler expostulated, a pained expression on his face. " 'Tis but three days you are wed!"

"Yes, and two months ago I would have been sleeping in my own bed!" Phillip drew himself up sharply. He was being altogether surly, and although Dambler had known him since he had been in short coats, he should not be filling his valet's ears with such comments. "Never fear, old man, I shall be the model husband when I go downstairs."

He found Sabrina in a small room downstairs. His secretary, Peter Stradling, sat near her, a tablet on his lap and a pen in his hand.

"Good morning, Sabrina, Peter," he said easily as he strolled into the room. "You are planning the orgy we are to have Thursday night?" Although Sabrina was gowned charmingly in a pale jonquil yellow morning dress, her face was pale and there were dark smudges under her violet eyes. He felt a stab of concern for her. He managed to quell this feeling when she said sharply, "Good morning, my lord. Peter and I are planning a dinner party. I fear it will be up to you to plan your own orgies."

Phillip gazed at Peter Stradling, whose pleasant, sensitive face was undergoing a series of uncomfortable expressions. "Would you care, my dear, to discuss it over luncheon?"

"There is really much to be done, my lord," she protested.

"Then we will speak of it over luncheon," he repeated, his tone brooking no denial.

"I have many other matters to attend to, my lady," Peter said hastily, one blue eye on his master. When he rose from his chair, the tablet slid from his lap and thumped to the floor. Phillip thought he heard an oath from his normally staid and mild-tempered secretary, and grinned despite himself.

"My dear?" He offered his arm to Sabrina.

Sabrina inclined her head in good grace and placed her fingers lightly on her husband's sleeve.

He looked down at her, sudden amusement crinkling the corners of his eyes.

"I do not see what you find so diverting, my lord," she said stiffly, looking straight ahead of her.

"Still angry with me for my ill-timed gallantry with regard to your money, Bree?"

She looked at Phillip blankly for an instant, a look that was not lost on him. "There is something else you wish to rip up at me about other than your erstwhile fortune?" He felt her fingers tighten on his arm.

"Of course not, my lord," she said in a tight voice, refusing to meet his gaze.

"I simply wanted to be certain, Bree," he said in the same bland voice. "In our short acquaintance, you have managed to point out so many flaws in my character."

"It would appear, my lord, that the list grows each day. I trust you enjoyed yourself yesterday for the entire afternoon and the evening."

"Indeed, my dear. But then I always do when I find myself in pleasant company. But let us not quibble. How are the arrangements going for your first dinner party?"

She did not answer until he had seated her at the dining table. "My dinner party, my lord?" she queried, serving herself a slice of ham. "You do not intend to grace us with your presence?"

"I trust you will eat more than that," he said, eyeing the small serving she had dished onto her plate.

"I am not hungry."

"You are supposed to be flourishing now that you are married to me, Sabrina, not going into a decline."

"Flourishing, my lord?"

"I was hoping that your shrew's tongue would become slower when you put flesh on your bones." He grinned at her and wolfed down a large bite of ham.

"I am pleased that you find your wit so very amusing, my lord," she snapped, and tossed her napkin beside her plate. "If you will excuse me, there is much that needs my attention—my dinner party, you know."

"Sit down, my lady. It is most rude for you to leave the table before your husband has finished. Besides," he added at the mutinous expression on her face, "I would like to know what you have planned—so that I may either approve or disapprove your schemes."

"You are being most provoking," she said, and slipped back into her chair. She realized that she was still hungry and served herself another helping of ham.

As Phillip was delighted to see her eat, he forbore to comment on her show of perversity. "Well?" he asked presently.

"Well what?"

"The dinner party, my dear. What delights have you planned?"

She thought of the kind of delights that he obviously preferred and grew so angry that she bit her cheek.

"Perhaps, Sabrina, I could give you instruction on how not to injure yourself whilst eating. I seem to recall that by the time I had achieved my eighteenth birthday, I had quite mastered the art of chewing my food."

"As I am certain you had mastered many arts, my lord!" She lowered her hand from rubbing her cheek and glared at him.

"Why thank you, wife. It has been far too long a time since you paid me a compliment. Yes, I suppose I am accomplished in many areas," he added modestly. "I do hope that you will not forget my excellent doctoring of you."

Although he was being insufferable, Sabrina was willing to give the devil his due in this particular instance.

"I cannot forget that, my lord," she said in a low voice.

"Nor your memorable bath. Lord, what a mop of hair you have!"

"Had I not been so weak, I could have managed quite well by myself."

"Ah, the lady finally admits that she had need of my humble services." He polished off the remainder of his ham, wiped his mouth, and sat back in his chair.

"I have no more need of your services, Phillip, humble or otherwise!"

"You will always have need of me, Sabrina." He lowered his voice and she felt gooseflesh rise on her arms at his caressing tone. It took her a moment to remember that he was a lecherous devil and that she wanted nothing to do with him. She tossed her head. "Enough of your nonsense, my lord. Do you or do you not wish to hear about the soiree Thursday evening?"

Phillip rather regretfully motioned for her to proceed, for, though he was loathe to admit it, he enjoyed sparring with her. At the end of her recital of the dinner menu, he found that he was nodding in approval.

"Impressive, Bree. Perhaps it is not at all a bad thing to have one's wife bred in the wilds of Yorkshire. Allow me to select the wines, and I vow we will have to drag our guests from the dinner table."

Sabrina found that she turned quite pink with his praise and minded not one whit that he changed the wines she had chosen. She continued, "I had Peter commission the Huxley group for the dancing. I do so love to waltz, and Greybar told me that they have quite a fine way with the music."

Phillip cocked an eyebrow. "Dancing? I thought this was to be only a dinner party."

"I know that hiring an orchestra is quite dear, but I shall pay for it myself," she said defensively.

Phillip could not resist teasing her. "You do work miracles, my dear. I had thought that all of your vast wealth was now in my hands. Just how do you intend to pay for the orchestra?"

She wanted to kick herself, for he had rolled her up,

foot and guns. "I will deduct the cost from my quarterly allowance. I trust you will not prove niggardly in that regard."

"Of course not, my dear. Never would I want it said that Viscount Derencourt dangled his wife on a skinny string. If you are willing to forgo new gowns and the like, I do not think you will have to borrow from me to pay for your orchestra."

"You are insufferable," she choked, and pushed back her chair with such energy that it nearly tipped over.

He was at her side in an instant, steadying her teetering chair. He placed a hand on either arm and said softly, "You cannot dance if you break your leg, Bree. Or is it that you wish for me to care for you again?"

She stared into his hazel eyes and knew that she would much enjoy his doing anything he wished. She reached out her hand to cover his, but drew it back quickly. He was a faithless bounder and she would not let him add her to his string of conquests. She sat stiffly in her chair, waiting for him to remove himself.

Phillip straightened and frowned down at her. He had seen the desire in her violet eyes and her tentative gesture with her hand. Damn Trevor anyway for giving her such a fear of men. There can be no greater irony, he thought as he turned away from her rigid figure, than that Beau Mercerault is married, and his wife is still a virgin.

"What gown do you intend to wear?" he asked evenly.

"Rose satin," she managed. "It has not yet arrived from the dressmaker."

He nodded absently, not really heeding her words.

"Is there anything else you wish to discuss, my lord?" he heard her ask in a polite, formal voice.

"No, Sabrina, there is nothing else," he said, his voice sounding unnaturally harsh, even to his own ears. He turned away from her and walked to the curtained bow windows.

Sabrina withdrew from the dining room, feeling quite miserable. The arrival of her rose satin gown later in the day from the dressmakers did not even bring a smile to her lips.

12

Doris lovingly coaxed a final dusky curl into place atop Sabrina's head and stood back, eyeing her mistress expectantly.

" 'Tis lovely you look, my lady," she said finally to gain the viscountess's attention.

"Oh, forgive me, Doris. You have worked marvels." Sabrina rose and regarded herself from all angles in the large mirror. The rose satin gown with its layers of Valenciennes lace edging the bodice and long sleeves made her appear most elegant, she thought, and not at all thin. Her hand was reaching for a single strand of pearls when there came a soft knock on the door. She nodded absently to Doris and began to finger the clasp on the necklace.

"My lord!"

Sabrina swung around at her maid's exclamation and inadvertently drew in her breath. Phillip stood in the doorway, dressed in severe black velvet. His cravat was so snowy white, she thought fancifully, that it looked to be cold to the touch. It required all her resolution not to tell him how handsome he looked.

She felt her husband's eyes upon her, his hazel eyes taking in every detail, like those of a man judging a piece of horseflesh, she thought, pursing her lips.

"But one more item, my dear, and you will have all the gentlemen languishing at your feet."

"Good evening, my lord. What is this item?"

Phillip smiled at her and extended his left hand. A long, narrow jewelry box lay on his palm. "I trust it will be the perfect complement to your beauty."

She hunched her shoulders at this display of gallantry, but nonetheless took the box. Nestled in the velvet interior was a delicately wrought diamond necklace.

She gasped. "Phillip, it's exquisite! I've never had a diamond anything before," she said naively.

She fumbled a moment with the clasp. Strong fingers closed over hers. "Do allow me, Sabrina. I don't want to have to send the thing to Rundle and Bridge so soon for repairs."

She felt the coldness of the diamonds flat against her throat, then the warmth of his fingers touching the back of her neck. She thought he must feel her trembling and sent him a fleeting glance over her shoulder. He was fastening the necklace and did not appear to notice.

"There. Look in the mirror, Sabrina."

As she was slow in gathering her scattered wits back together, he placed his hands on her arms and gently turned her toward the mirror. Her eyes were drawn to his face standing behind her rather than to the diamond necklace. He grinned.

"What is this, my dear? You distrust me so much that you fear what I will do if you take your eyes off me?"

"Of course not," she said, her voice a trifle breathless. She gazed at herself and drew a wondering breath. "I don't look at all like myself."

Phillip merely laughed and turned away to gaze about her bedchamber. "Are you all settled in now, Bree?"

"Yes. The paint still smells a bit, but as you can see, the decorators have done magnificently."

Phillip ran his hand over the top of a pale blue velvet chair, done in the French style. She mistook his action, and said sharply, "Of a certainty, the style and fabric did cost dearly, but I shall, of course, pay for it out of my allowance."

He slewed his head about to look at her, cloaking the startled look in his eyes in but an instant. He saw that her bristles were up and said only, "Allow me to congratulate you on your economic abilities."

She blanched, for the price of her rose satin gown amounted in her mind to an exorbitant figure.

"You may, of course, consider the necklace as a wedding present," he added in a teasing voice.

"You are all kindness and generosity, my lord!"

"So I have been told many times, my dear," he replied.

"I had thought that roses were your favorite gift," she snapped, without weighing her words.

"Roses? Really, Bree, it is most difficult to secure such blossoms this time of year."

She bit her lip and turned away from him. She had no intention of letting her wayward tongue betray to him that she knew of an attachment of his who reeked of a cloying rose fragrance.

He gazed thoughtfully at her a moment, then proffered her his arm. "It is time to greet your guests, Sabrina. I have one surprise for you, a gentleman who was not on your original invitation list."

"Who might that be, my lord?"

"If I told, it would not be a surprise. Patience, viscountess."

The twenty guests who sat down at the long dining table amid laughter and rustling gowns included not one unknown face. As the viscount was seated at the other end of the table, she had to curb her impatience. It was probably a miserable jest, she thought, frowning slightly down the expanse of table toward her laughing husband. She gave over her attention to Lord Alvaney, who appeared most willing to keep her amused.

As the meal progressed to the baked pheasant, Sabrina glanced down to where her Aunt Barresford was seated and was relieved to see a smile on her relative's glacial features. No one had refused her invitation, and Sabrina wondered with some cynicism if the guests had come merely to see if she would embarrass herself.

She was forced to marvel at her husband's adept handling of their guests. Both gentlemen and ladies alike appeared to bask in his attention, tossed with cavalier charm first to one, then to another. To her prejudiced eye, there was but one other gentleman to rival him. The Earl of March, seated near the middle of the long table, his beautiful countess at his side, appeared to be in his element, just as was the viscount. As for the Countess of March, that young lady had been most kind to her. "My dear," she had whispered in a conspiring voice before dinner in the drawing room, "we must discuss how best to strip this woefully masculine domain of its bachelor pretensions. You must visit me in Grosvenor Square and we will settle upon a strategy."

By ten o'clock, the ballroom boasted enough dancing couples to delight any aspiring hostess. "Your husband has done quite well by you, Sabrina," her Aunt Barresford remarked, surveying the assembled company with grudging approval. "I vow that Teresa Elliott must be having a fit not to have been invited."

"You mistake the matter, Aunt," Sabrina said softly. "I made certain that she received an invitation. If she chooses not to come, it is her affair."

"What a strange girl you are!" Lady Barresford exclaimed.

"I want no enemies, ma'am. But look, Miss Elliott has arrived, and with her brother. Poor man, he looks like a goose being served up for the dinner table."

If Wilfred Elliott did not precisely feel like the dinner goose, he was experiencing some discomfort. His sister's dark eyes were glittering dangerously. He said in a low, controlled voice, "You have ranted and carried on for the past week, sister, and now you will make a push to be pleasant."

"Just look at her," she whispered fiercely, "lording it all over everyone, just like she belonged."

"She does belong. I have told you countless times that if you value your social position, you had best wipe that scowl off your face. I do not think that Viscount Derencourt is a man to tolerate such nonsense."

Teresa was forced to hold her peace as she and Wilfred came to the viscount and viscountess in the receiving line.

"How delightful that you could come," Sabrina said, nodding pleasantly to both Miss Elliott and her brother.

Teresa inclined her head, her eyes on the viscount's profile.

"My lord," Sabrina said, tugging slightly at Phillip's sleeve, "Miss Elliott and her brother, Wilfred."

Phillip turned from a brief conversation with Lord William Ramsey. His hazel eyes instantly lost their compelling warmth.

"So naughty of you, my lord, to wed yourself so quickly to Miss Eversleigh," Teresa chided in a silken voice. "I vow that I as well as the rest of London had scarce time to really get to know her."

Phillip gave Sabrina a quick glance promising full retribution, for she had not told him that she had invited Miss Elliott this evening. "I would rather say, Teresa," he said in the blandest of voices, "that if I had not convinced her to wed me so quickly, I might have lost the most beautiful lady in London to another gentleman." Before she could draw her breath, Phillip turned to her brother. "Will, I trust that your Homeric efforts at scholarship are not proving too rigorous."

"Not at all, my lord." Wilfred bowed, a pronounced twinkle in his eyes. "Homeric," he added as a bemused afterthought. "Very witty, my lord."

Phillip bowed as the Elliotts made their way into the ballroom.

"Such a whisker, Phillip," Sabrina whispered. "The most beautiful lady in London indeed!"

"Do you question my taste, Sabrina? Or, for that matter, my word?"

Another couple claimed her attention and it was some ten more minutes before Phillip turned again to Sabrina. "Dance with me, Bree. I think we have finally greeted every guest."

"And not one of them your 'surprise,' Phillip."

"Perhaps he did not wish to come," he said as he took her arm.

He could not swing her in the large circles she so much enjoyed for all the crush of dancers. "I believe, my dear, it is safe to say that tonight is a success."

Sabrina was smiling, her eyes alight with pleasure. "You see, my lord, not everyone is unkind in London."

He groaned. "I might be wed to the most beautiful lady

in London, but with utterances like that, I am inclined to believe that she is also the most naive."

As his speech contained a delightful compliment, Sabrina chose to ignore the remainder. "The Countess of March, Kate St. Clair, has been most kind to me, I must admit." Sabrina arched a black brow into a pert expression. "She said that she would help me rid your house of all its masculine pretensions."

Phillip remembered the earl's words to him several days before at Gentleman Jackson's. He said more to himself than to her, "Julien certainly follows his own advice. Never have I seen a young lady less broken to bridle."

"What is all this about breaking ladies to bridle?" Sabrina demanded, bristling.

A space cleared on the dance floor and Phillip suddenly whirled her around in smooth, wide circles. When he drew her back into a more sedate pace, she was panting and laughing at the same time. "How well you dance, my lord!"

"Did I not tell you that a rake must perforce be accomplished?"

Yes, she thought, gazing straight ahead into his cravat, accomplished and profligate. He felt her draw away from him and frowned over the top of her head. How touchy she was, and he was but jesting.

"I believe," he said as the music came to an end, "that our surprise guest has arrived. If I am not mistaken, he wishes to dance with you."

Sabrina, attuned to the particular nuances in Phillip's voice, in this instance heard a certain coldness. She turned sharply and found herself facing Richard Clarendon.

"Richard!" she exclaimed, and swept him a curtsy.

Richard Clarendon gazed down at the slender, vibrant girl before him and for a moment forgot all his gallant banter. "You are well, Sabrina?" he asked stiffly.

"Most well, your grace."

"I am delighted that you could come, Richard," Phillip said softly. "My wife dearly loves to waltz. Indeed, she

has worn me to a frazzle. Perhaps we could have a chang-
ing of the guard, so to speak."

"Mayhap Richard does not care to dance," Sabrina
temporized, confused by her husband's unusual request.

Richard Clarendon merely nodded to Phillip and took
Sabrina's arm. She smiled up at him shyly, craning her
neck, for he was some inches taller even than the viscount. He whirled her away into the throng.

"Good God, Phillip! What the devil are you doing?"

Phillip turned to see Charles Askbridge standing at his
elbow, a frown of disbelief puckering his forehead.

Phillip gazed down a moment at his well-manicured fingernails. "Clarendon just arrived in town, and he is a
friend, Charles. Would you that I barred him from my
home?"

"By the look on Clarendon's face, I would say that he
still wants her. Are you not placing Sabrina in a rather
awkward position?"

"I prefer it when you are more circuitous in your questioning, my friend," the viscount drawled. "If you will excuse me, I must play the attentive host." He turned on his
heel, leaving Charles Askbridge staring after him.

Sabrina felt the silence growing uncomfortable. "Your
mother and son are well, Richard?"

"Yes," he said only. Sabrina wondered at the with-
drawn tone of his voice.

"Have I offended you in some way, Richard?"

His dark eyes flashed a moment. "Of course not," he
said softly. "It is I who have offended myself."

"I do not understand you, your grace."

"I do not many times understand myself, Sabrina," he
said, shaking his head. The girl in his arms was now the
Viscountess Derencourt and there was nothing on earth
that could change that fact. "I read of your marriage."

She said in an even voice, "It has been nearly a week
now."

He wondered, looking down at her, what would have
happened had he not removed himself to one of his
northern estates after her refusal of him at Moreland, had
he, like Phillip, been in London to be with her after Ter-

esa Elliott had done her damage. He did not fault Phillip for the course of action he had followed; he only wished that it had been he who had been her rescuer. He saw that she was looking at him questioningly and quickly changed the topic.

"I visited Monmouth Hall before coming to London. Your grandfather does much better. That weasel cousin of yours assured me a dozen times if he assured me once that the earl would recover."

"I had a letter from Grandfather the day before the wedding. He sounded in good spirits. Did you visit with him, Richard?"

"Yes, but only briefly. He still tires easily."

"And Elisabeth?"

Richard restrained himself. "She appears to enjoy being mistress of the manor." Actually, he thought, it was quite likely that it was her only pleasure. It was becoming quite common knowledge that Trevor had tossed up the skirts of every comely maid at Monmouth Hall, all under the nose of his wife. He thought that Sabrina had read his mind when she asked, "Does Trevor treat Elisabeth kindly?"

"In public, I daresay," he replied honestly. "I am glad that you are out of that household."

"Poor Elisabeth," she said sadly. "Trevor is such a cruel, selfish creature. She would not listen to me."

"I cannot recall Elisabeth ever listening to anyone." He said suddenly, "You are too thin, Sabrina."

She glanced up at him, startled. "You and Phillip!" she laughed. "If the two of you have your way, I shall be fat as a flawn by spring."

She felt his hand tighten about her waist and blinked at him. His dark eyes glittered intensely and she wondered what he was thinking.

Richard wished now that he had not come, for the tug of attraction he felt for her was still too strong for his own peace of mind. Although he thought dalliance with married ladies a most satisfactory pastime, the idea of a flirtation with Sabrina was distasteful to him. I must be becoming a moralist, he thought ruefully to himself.

"Your ball is a grand success," he said, pleased with the hint of indifference in his voice.

"Yes. Phillip has really done quite well by me." No sooner were the words out of her mouth than she regretted them. Even to her own ears, she sounded bitter. If she thought the marquis would ignore her lapse, she was mistaken.

"You are not happy?" he demanded sharply. His grip tightened about her fingers and she thought that the fine bones would bruise with the pressure.

"What an absurd question!" She laughed, her voice a trifle high. "I am no longer that naive girl from Yorkshire, your grace. One learns to pay the piper in this fair and just land."

The waltz drew to a close. Richard drew her hand through his arm, his fingers warm and caressing over hers. "Come, Sabrina, let us try some of your punch."

She nodded, looking for her husband from the corner of her eye. She saw him in laughing conversation with a striking auburn-haired girl whose name she could not remember. "I should like that," she said in a low voice, and turned her gaze away from the viscount.

"Oh dear," she exclaimed suddenly at the sound of tearing material. She stopped dead in her tracks and looked down, annoyed with her own carelessness. "I've caught my gown," she said, examining the torn flounce. "Do forgive me, your grace, but I must leave you and pin it up else I shall be tripping all over myself the next time I dance."

"Do allow me to assist you, Sabrina," Richard said with a wolfish grin. "I am really quite accomplished at such tasks, you know."

"Somehow you do not fit my image of a proper lady's maid, Richard."

"Lord, I hope not! I think that you will find me very deft, nonetheless."

Sabrina shook her head, laughing. "You and Phillip are like two peas from the same pod. The both of you must always have the last word. Very well, your grace, there is a small room just down the corridor that should provide you, me, and my flounce sufficient privacy."

Phillip observed Sabrina and the marquis stroll from the ballroom, Richard holding her arm rather too possessively, he thought.

"If you will excuse me, Miss Patteson," he said to the auburn beauty at his side, flashing his most beguiling smile, "I have just recollected a small errand I must do."

He made good his escape from the ballroom just in time to see Sabrina laugh up at Richard and walk away with him down the corridor toward the back of the house. Although he didn't wish to, his feet carried him after them. He saw Sabrina open the door to the small room she had been using for her own private parlor and close it after her.

His fists clenched at his sides and he felt cold fury wash over him. He admitted to himself that his invitation of the marquis had been far more than a simple gesture to a friend. He had wanted to be certain that Sabrina cared nothing for Richard Clarendon. As he gazed toward the closed door, he thought Sabrina's behavior was inexcusable. He turned on his heel and strode back to the ballroom.

"Some assistant you are, your grace," Sabrina chided Richard lightly, as he sat with loose-limbed grace on a small settee, watching her stick pins in strategic places in the flounce.

"Consider me your inspiration."

"Muses are useful for such things as poetry and the like, not for such mundane tasks such as this." She laughed as she spoke and carelessly jabbed her finger with a pin. "Ouch!" She put the injured finger in her mouth.

"Now I can be of assistance, Sabrina." Richard rose and knelt down in front of her, taking the throbbing finger and inspecting it. A small drop of blood rose to the surface and Richard, without thought, licked it away, then gently kissed the finger.

Sabrina sat very quietly, gazing down in perturbation at his bent head of black curling hair. "Richard . . ." she began, not really knowing what she should say.

He groaned and rose quickly, flinging her hand away from him. He ran his hand distractedly through his hair.

"God, I'm sorry, Sabrina. I did not intend. . . ."

Sabrina rose and placed her hand on his sleeve. "You need say no more, Richard. 'Tis forgotten. As a friend, you must——"

"Dammit, I don't want to be your friend! You know that I would have married you, despite what happened between you and Phillip."

She stiffened and drew herself up very straight. She felt every bit as bleak as her voice sounded. "Nothing happened between Phillip and me. And I confess that nothing is ever likely to happen."

An arrested expression appeared on the marquis's swarthy face. Good God, he thought, thunderstruck, she's in love with him. The impropriety of the situation struck him forcibly. In her innocence, she had thought nothing of accompanying him to this room, alone. All she needed at this point was more vicious gossiping. He smiled at her very gently, slowly lifted her hand, and lightly kissed her fingers. "I meant no insult, my dear. It is my wretched tongue and, unfortunately, rather too many experiences with women totally unlike yourself. Everything will right itself, Sabrina, you will see. Now, I must take my leave. You must return to the ballroom and your guests before you are missed. *Au revoir,* Sabrina.

He turned on his heel and left the room, leaving her to stare after him.

At two o'clock in the morning Sabrina was so weary that she could barely restrain her yawns as her maid brushed out her hair. Her bedchamber door opened suddenly and Phillip's reflection appeared in her mirror.

"You may leave now," he said to the maid, and stood at the doorway until Doris had passed out of the room. He kicked the door closed with the heel of his boot.

Sabrina swiveled about in her chair and regarded him with some surprise, for the tone of his voice was curt. "You have sent home the final hangers-on?"

"Yes." He sprawled into a chair opposite her and began to tap his fingertips together.

"We did not waltz again, Phillip," she said, for want of anything better. "Indeed, you were so taken up with the ladies that I feared they would never leave."

His hand waved away all of her words. "You, at least, had the good sense to return to the ballroom before the gossips took notice."

"I tore the flounce on my gown and had to pin it up."

"How quick you are to come up with a plausible explanation. Unfortunately for you, my dear, I saw you go with Richard Clarendon to that very private room of yours."

Sabrina grew very still. "What are you saying, my lord?"

"I am saying, Sabrina, that I gave you the opportunity to prove your indifference to Clarendon but you behaved with the greatest impropriety."

Sabrina flew from her chair, her face suffused with angry color. "By God, my lord, this passes all bounds! You have the audacity to burst into my bedchamber and tell me that you invited Richard here to give me some sort of test?"

"No, of course not. I can well control my own wife without recourse to subterfuge. However, Sabrina, I must now question your feelings toward Clarendon."

"You are a lecherous hypocrite! Get out, Phillip, I have no more patience for this nonsense!"

He rose like a graceful beast readying to spring. "Remember, madam, that this is *my* house and I shall do precisely as I please." He strode to her and grasped her shoulders in a firm grip. "I will not tolerate Richard Clarendon as your lover, or any other man for that matter."

"Take care, my lord," she said flatly. "You begin to sound like the jealous husband. Where there is no love, the ground must be too arid to cultivate such an emotion."

"I will not be cuckolded, Sabrina. You had your flirtation with Clarendon this evening, but there it will end. I would that you contrive to show some gratitude after all I have done for you."

She was speechless with fury. She drew back her hand to slap him, but he caught her wrist and bore her arm back down to her side.

"You conceited, self-righteous beast," she spit, trying to wriggle free of his hold. "Just because your character is despicable, you must cast me into the same mold. As to your ridiculous gratitude, my lord, I begin to believe that spending my days in that miserable hotel, shunned by society, was preferable to living in the same house with you!"

"Don't push me, Sabrina," he growled at her.

"Push you! I have done nothing to you, if you but had the intelligence to realize it!" His grip loosened at her spate of words, and she jerked free of him. She took several steps back from him, rubbing her throbbing wrist.

"Sabrina," he began uncertainly, reaching out his hand toward her.

She flinched at his gesture and moved even farther away from him. "You tell me, my lord, in no uncertain terms that this is your house, that I am nothing more than society's cast-off, dependent upon your generosity and good graces for my keep. Tell me, Phillip," she continued, her voice deadly calm, "what price would you affix to my bedchamber? I would gladly pay you for it, since being a grateful pensioner is hardly to my liking."

"I was mistaken," he said slowly, his eyes searching her face. "This room is yours. I bid you good night, Sabrina." He turned and walked quickly away from her to the door.

Her voice rang out clear and taunting. "Do you not wish to hear all about your wanton wife and her seduction of the Marquis of Arysdale? I vow you would not be bored with the telling!"

Phillip's hand tightened about the doorknob, but he did not turn. He heard the hysterical pitch in her voice and kept his mouth shut. He closed the door quietly behind him, leaving her standing in the middle of the room, her eyes bright and glittering with unshed tears.

13

During the next several days, Sabrina treated her husband
with a calm, detached submissiveness. Her behavior
baffled Phillip and he found more often than not that he
avoided her presence, for he simply could not make her
respond to him.

After breakfast one morning, he found himself gazing
at her with growing concern. She sat very quietly, her
hands folded in her lap and her eyes downcast. She appeared to him like a wax doll, the immense vitality of her
extinguished. He thought hopefully of the mare he was
buying for her from Tattersall's. Anything, he thought, to
bring the sparkle back into her eyes.

"Would you care to attend Almack's this evening?" he
asked, remembering that she dearly loved to waltz.

She glanced listlessly out of the window at the gray,
overcast winter day. "If it would please you, my lord."

"I am asking you what you would prefer, Sabrina," he
said evenly.

She lowered her head. "I thought you found Almack's
a bore, my lord. It looks as if it might snow today," she
added vaguely.

"I enjoy waltzing with you," he said calmly, controlling
his growing impatience. "It matters not if it snows."

"I see," she said and rose from her chair, drawing her
blue silk shawl more closely about her slender shoulders.
"I will, of course, do your bidding."

"Sit down, Sabrina," he said sharply.

Without a word, she sat down.

He saw that her fingers were nervously knotting the fringe on her shawl. "I have asked you for your desire in this matter. It is not a question of your doing my bidding."

"But my desire must perforce be to do your bidding, my lord," she said flatly.

"Very well. My bidding is for you to cease acting like a spiritless old horse." He thought he saw a spark of anger in her eyes and found that he wanted nothing more than to have her cut up at him. But she remained infuriatingly silent. "Perhaps Richard Clarendon will be present. I realize that he is naught but a friend. Perhaps you would care to see him." He felt a pang of guilt even as he essayed what he hoped she would perceive as an apology for his behavior the night of their ball.

"In that case, my lord, I should much desire to go."

Her calm, unexpected reply made him blink. "You what?" he asked sharply.

She gazed at him unflinchingly. "I said," she repeated softly, "that I should like to go. As you said, my lord, it matters not if it snows."

He wasn't at all certain now how she had perceived his apology about Clarendon, if indeed, she had thought it an apology at all. He eyed her with growing frustration.

"Perhaps, my lord," she continued with great humility, "I could borrow the diamonds for the evening? I know they are very dear to you, but I promise to be most careful."

"The bloody diamonds are yours!"

She rose and dropped him a deep curtsy. "I am most grateful to you, my lord, for your generosity. Will you be here for luncheon?"

"I will throttle you if you do not cease this ridiculous game, Sabrina!"

"Game, my lord?" She gazed at him blankly. "I but endeavor to be the kind of wife you wish."

"Then let me inform you, madam, that you are not succeeding!"

She looked away from him. Yes, she thought bleakly to herself, what you wish, Phillip, is that you had never met me in the first place. "Perhaps, my lord," she said quietly, "you could be more specific as to your requirements."

He threw up his hands. "I will not be home for luncheon," he growled, turned on his heel, and slammed out of the dining room.

Sabrina walked slowly to the wide bay windows and pressed her cheeks against the chill glass. She supposed that she had wanted to push him to anger, but, she realized, it had solved naught.

She wandered into the library and for want of anything else to do, selected a novel from one of the lower shelves and curled up in a curtained window seat.

She opened the small vellum tome of *Manon Lescaut* and forced herself to concentrate on the French story. Her attention soon wandered to the light flakes of snow that pattered gently against the windowpane, dissolved into small drops of water, and streaked in slender rivulets down the glass. She traced the brief existence of each splashing snowflake with the tip of her finger.

She must have dozed, for her head snapped up at the sound of voices in the library.

"I merely wanted to ask you, my lord," she heard Peter Stradling say to Phillip, "for it indeed is a strange bill to receive from a tradesman."

She shook off the vagueness of her sleep. Phillip's voice held her motionless in her seat.

"Ah yes, the carpenter. Martine informed me that he was a saucy one." The viscount sounded mildly amused. "For your information, Peter, I had thought I would be killed during the night by a piece of falling plaster in the bedroom. Do pay the man."

Sabrina's fingers tightened about the thin book until they showed white. Martine. They were talking about Phillip's mistress! She had been taught that one never learns well of oneself by eavesdropping, but she could not bring herself to make her presence known. She could picture the grin on Peter's face. Even her husband's secretary was well aware that he kept a mistress!

"There is another bill that concerns Mademoiselle

Beauharnais, my lord. It is a gown from Madame Giselle. The total, I think, is a trifle excessive."

Sabrina heard the brief rustling of paper as, she supposed, the bill changed hands.

"It is a bit exorbitant," she heard Phillip agree, without much interest. "As I am off to see the lady, I shall ask her about it. Anything else pressing, Peter?"

"Well, actually yes, my lord," Peter said in a rush. "I have prepared a speech on the Corn Laws for you to consider presenting in the House of Lords."

"My dear Peter," Phillip said on a gentle sigh, "you must needs continue to try to thrust me into the political arena. I am well aware of the Corn Laws, my dear fellow. But you know I have no particular liking for imposing my opinions on that stodgy group of gentlemen who seem to spend all their waking hours fussing about one thing or another."

"But my lord, the Corn Laws are terribly controversial, let me assure you! Why, just the other day, Lord Melberry. . . ."

Sabrina stopped listening. She felt such humiliation and anger that she could barely keep her place. To hear Phillip speak so cavalierly of his mistress to Peter Stradling, and with such masculine insouciance, made her forget all her vows of submissiveness.

She heard Phillip say jovially to his secretary, "As I am about to depart, Peter, why don't you likewise take yourself off to the political dens, for, say, a bit more research on these confounded Corn Laws."

She heard receding footsteps and Peter's fervent voice. "Thank you, my lord, I do need a few more facts. Then, perhaps, my lord, you would consider becoming more involved. . . ."

The library door closed upon the rest of Peter's words. Sabrina bounded from her hiding place and shook her fist at the closed door. She had married the greatest hypocrite imaginable. She was to remain chaste, untouched by even her husband, whilst he blithely continued his profligate pleasures.

Phillip had told her to cease being a spiritless old horse. Very well, she would certainly grant him his wish!

She drew up suddenly, realizing that she had not the faintest idea where Phillip's mistress lived. She rushed to the large mahogany desk and spotted the infamous carpenter's bill on top of a neat stack of papers. Written on the paper was an address on Fitton Place. She quickly memorized the address, straightened the bill on its pile, and quietly let herself out of the library. She saw Greybar standing near the front door looking toward her, a curious expression on his face.

"His lordship has left, Greybar?"

"Yes, just this moment, my lady."

"Call me a hackney. I wish to leave in ten minutes. No longer, mind!"

"Yes, my lady."

Thirty minutes later, Sabrina found herself staring at a two-story brick townhouse, sandwiched between other houses in a very quiet, unpretentious area of London. She pulled her ermine-lined cloak more closely about her and stepped quickly from the hackney. From the corner of her eye, Sabrina saw Lanscombe, Phillip's tiger, climb into the box and prepare to drive the curricle around the corner. How like Phillip, she thought, to ensure that his horses received the proper exercise while he dallied about inside. She wondered how long poor Lanscombe was to tool the curricle about before fetching his master. Sabrina saw Lanscombe's jaw drop open when he spotted her. He gazed at her dumbly, shaking his head.

Sabrina turned her back on him, walked up the front steps, raised her gloved hand, and pounded upon the door.

After some moments the door slid cautiously open and a frowning maid's face appeared.

"What be it that you want?" Dorcus demanded suspiciously, eyeing the strange lady.

"I want my husband," Sabrina said coldly, and before the look of consternation had fully formed on the maid's face, she shoved the door open, pushing her aside. She was standing in a square entranceway. On one side she could see into a small drawing room. Straight ahead of her was a slightly winding staircase that led to the upper floor. She heard a light, tinkling laugh from above, and without further thought, grasped her skirts and rushed to the stairs.

"Wait!" Dorcus squawked. "You can't go up there!"

Sabrina ignored the maid and quickened her steps. She followed the sound of a woman's heavily French-accented voice to a door that stood some inches open. She stood for an instant, indecisive. At the sound of Phillip's low laugh, she pushed the door open and rushed inside. She drew up short, panting.

She stood inside a large bedchamber, dominated by a huge bed. Upon the bed a woman lay upon her back, clothed in nothing but alabaster skin. In an instant, Sabrina took in every detail of her exquisite body. But it was Phillip who quickly captured her attention. He was standing next to the bed, quite as naked as his mistress. She had never before seen a naked man and stood gawking at him in astonishment. His body was beautiful, far more exquisite than a woman's. He was long, hard, and muscular, all angles and sharp lines. Inevitably, her eyes fell to his swollen manhood, and bright color stained her cheeks.

The brief frozen tableau suddenly turned into furious life.

Phillip, who had been reaching to touch Martine, turned to see his wife burst into the bedchamber.

He whipped his hand back. "What the devil are you doing here?" he yelled at her. Although Sabrina was staring at him, it did not occur to him to cover himself.

"Mon dieu," Martine whispered softly, her sleepy eyes widening with great interest.

Sabrina dragged her eyes away from his body, looked again at his naked mistress, and yelled back at him, "I think I should ask you the same question, my lord! You miserable bounder! You are my husband."

Phillip had never felt more foolish in his life. Damnation, this couldn't be happening. He took several furious steps toward her.

"And you are my wife, madam! Why the devil aren't you at home, where you belong!"

"It is *your* home, do you not remember, my lord? I don't belong there, I merely reside there."

"Dammit, Sabrina, I will not tolerate such outlandish behavior! Go home immediately, I shall deal with you later!"

"You call my behavior outlandish, my lord! How dare you serve me such a turn! Do I mean so little to you that you do not hesitate to humiliate me? Does our marriage mean so little to you?"

"Our marriage, madam, was meant to provide you a home and the protection of my name. 'Twas you who wished that, do you not remember?"

"You bastard," she yelled, trembling with fury. "You have the audacity to rant at me about taking Richard Clarendon for a lover, when all the while you are . . . dallying whenever it pleases you!"

"You will take no lover, madam!"

She stared at him, unable to believe the perversity of his thinking.

"If you will but recall, Sabrina, it was you who offered me my freedom. It was you who insisted upon our business arrangement."

"Ah, so it suits you, my lord, to insist upon your freedom whilst I am to play the role of the docile virgin wife, who blithely disregards your rakehell activities?"

"Docile and virgin are your words, Sabrina, not mine! Now, I will have no more of this. Take yourself home, you are ranting like the lowest trollop in Soho."

"You filthy hypocrite!" she screamed at him. "I catch you with your mistress and you have the nerve to call *me* a trollop!" She flailed at his chest with her fists.

"Mon dieu," Martine said again, raising herself up on her elbows.

Phillip clamped his arms about Sabrina, and dragged her to the small dressing room adjoining the bedchamber. He kicked the door closed with his bare foot. "Stop it, Sabrina," he said fiercely, shaking her.

She became rigid in his arms and he released her. She took a stumbling step backward. She opened her mouth, but he interrupted her.

"Your behavior is inexcusable. I will not have you questioning my actions. Now you will take yourself quietly away from here, else I will seriously consider sending you to Mercerault Ashby to learn your place."

"My place! Damn you to hell, Phillip, I have no place! Now you have humiliated me, stripped me of even any pretense of honor! God, I hate you!"

"That's enough," he shouted and grabbed her shoulders.

Sabrina drove her knee with all her strength into his groin. He dropped his hands, stared at her in amazement, and then doubled over in pain.

Sabrina whirled away from him, steeling herself against the pain she had brought him. She pulled the door open and, without another look at his mistress, fled from the bedchamber.

For several minutes, Phillip thought death would be preferable to the exquisite waves of pain that bowed him to his knees. As the bouts of nausea slowly receded, it was Sabrina's death that he contemplated. He pulled himself shakily to his feet and walked slowly back into the bedchamber. Without a word, he swiftly began to dress himself.

"My lord," Martine whispered, seeing the slight grimace of pain furrowing his brow as he shrugged into his clothes, "what happened?"

"She kicked me in the groin."

"Ah. She was very angry, that one. Most enterprising."

"She will regret it," he growled, his head snapping up.

"What is it you intend to do, my lord?"

"Murder might be a fine start!" He sat down and tugged on his hessians.

Martine held her tongue, for she realized that he was far too angry to listen to reason. She felt a stab of alarm for the viscountess and shook her head. Did not Phillip see that the little one was in love with him? Such fire from a lady born!

Phillip pulled on his coat, nearly splitting the stitching at his shoulders.

Martine heard him mumble something about his freedom. He turned at the door. "I will be back later, Martine."

She said nothing, and leaned back against the pillow, listening to his galloping footsteps on the stairs.

Lanscombe said not a word as his master jumped into the curricle and grabbed the reins. The furious working of the viscount's jaw did not bode well for the viscountess, he thought. Like a frightened little animal, she had flown down the steps, running full speed toward a hackney.

Twenty minutes later, the viscount pulled his stallions to a steaming halt.

"Stable 'em," he said shortly, and jumped down from the curricle.

"Aye, my lord," Lanscombe said to the viscount's retreating figure.

"Is the viscountess here?" Phillip demanded of Greybar.

"Yes, my lord, she arrived home but a few moments ago. She went to her room, I believe."

Phillip took the stairs two at a time. He strode down the corridor, his greatcoat swirling about his ankles. He stopped at Sabrina's room and pulled at the doorknob. It was locked.

"Open the door this minute, Sabrina!"

Her voice came back to him, loud and quite clear. "Go to the devil, my lord! I have no wish to talk to you, much less be forced to endure your loathsome presence!"

Angry cords stood out on his neck. He took a step backward, raised his booted leg, and crashed his foot against the door. He heard splintering wood. He aimed one more kick nearer to the lock and the door flew open, straining at its hinges.

Sabrina stood with her back against the windows. "How dare you come bursting into my room! Get out of here!"

He advanced toward her, his hazel eyes narrowed and blazing.

Sabrina whipped her hand up from the folds of her skirt. She was clutching a riding crop tightly in her fingers. "Stay away from me, my lord!"

"The only thing I will stay away from is your knee!"

"I mean it, Phillip!" She raised the riding crop.

"Try your best, you little witch."

She swung it at him, but he took a swift sideways step, and gripped her arm just above the elbow. As he bore her arm down, she tried again to kick him. He turned to his side, letting her strike his thigh.

He twisted the riding crop from her hand, threw her over his shoulder, and strode from the room.

"Let me down, you bastard!" she cried, flailing with all her strength at his back.

He ignored her fists and a terrified, open-mouthed maid in the corridor, and dumped her to her feet inside his bedchamber. He turned and swiftly turned the key in the lock.

"Now, madam, it is time for you to learn who is master here!"

She stumbled away from him, scurrying to the far corner of the room, but he grabbed her about the waist in one powerful arm and hauled her toward a chair.

"Let me go," she shrieked, clawing at his arm.

He pulled her down on her stomach over his legs and jerked up her gown. She struggled wildly as he ripped at her underclothes.

"So you wished to take your riding crop to me, did you, Sabrina!" He brought the leather thongs down against her naked buttocks.

She cried out in shock and pain and struggled more fiercely against his hold.

He became aware that she ceased struggling against him. He shook himself free of his fury and stared down at her. Her buttocks and thighs were a mass of red welts, some of them trickling blood. He flung the riding crop away from him, appalled at what he had done. She lay limply over his legs, only her shoulders quivering slightly.

He grasped her under her arms and hauled her upright. She was staring at him mutely, her violet eyes dark pools of pain.

He sternly repressed the desire to beg her forgiveness and without a word, he strode to the door, pulled the key from his pocket, and locked it behind him.

Sabrina gazed stupidly at the locked door. Very slowly, she walked to the bed and eased herself face down upon the covers.

Phillip walked back downstairs and came face to face with a white-faced butler. "No one is to disturb her ladyship. Is that clear, Greybar?"

The man nodded dumbly. Although he did not know precisely what had happened above stairs, he had never before seen the viscount show so little control. He looked up to see Dambler walking slowly toward him, his face set and drawn. "I've talked to Lanscombe," Dambler said softly. " 'Tis a fine mess we're in now."

Phillip hailed a hackney and returned to Martine's apartment. He found her just as he had left her. There was no welcoming smile upon her face.

"I told you I would return," he said sharply, shrugging out of his coat.

Martine regarded him somberly. "You have hurt the little one?"

"I do not wish to discuss the matter."

"Did you hurt her?" she repeated stubbornly.

"She tried to take a riding crop to me. I whipped her with it, that is all."

"The little one is half your size, my lord. Hardly a fair contest, I should say."

He ignored her and continued to peel off his clothes. There was a spot of blood on his finger that he had not noticed. He stared down at it, remembering how her body quivered each time he brought down the riding crop. He turned to stare blindly into the glowing embers in the fireplace. Damn, what was wrong with him? What the devil had he become?

"You are quite blind, my Phillip," he heard Martine say softly.

He turned to face her and Martine was taken aback at the haggard expression on his face.

" 'Tis not a wife of convenience that you've got, my lord."

"No, you are right. Now I've a wife who hates the very sight of me."

"Being blind has also made you a fool," she said gently. "The little one loves you."

"She doesn't love me," he said in a hard voice, turning again to the fireplace. "She never would have married me had it not been impossible for her to do otherwise."

"The little one also has great pride," she said, marveling at his stupidity. "After all, *mon chou*, an excess of indifference would not have brought her here."

"The devil! She won't even let me touch her."

Martine shrugged elaborately. "How sorry I am for you, my lord," she mocked softly. "An accomplished rake who has not the wherewithall to seduce his own wife."

"This entire conversation is damned ridiculous! I'll thank you to keep your thoughts to yourself in the future, Martine." But he began to pull on his discarded clothes.

Martine merely smiled at him, saying nothing further.

Once dressed, Phillip turned and said briefly, "I am going to my club. There, at least, I will not have to be bothered with women."

"As you will, my lord," she said to his retreating back.

The viscount hailed a hackney and told the man to take him to White's. No sooner had he leaned back against the worn leather squabs than he let out a loud oath. He leaned out the window and reversed the hackney's direction.

When he entered his home, he found both Dambler and Greybar regarding him with profound disapproval. "Just what is the meaning of your sour looks?" he asked coldly.

"Greybar and I were discussing her ladyship, my lord," Dambler said carefully. "It appears that she has locked herself in your bedchamber."

"You are the both of you a couple of meddlesome old crows. I locked her ladyship in my bedchamber, as you both know very well. Now, if I may be excused before you have both rung a peal over me, I will see to her."

He turned on his heel and walked stiffly up the stairs.

Phillip quietly unlocked the door and stepped inside. In the dull gray afternoon light, he saw Sabrina on his bed, lying perfectly motionless on her stomach, her face turned away from him. Her yellow gown exposed only the soles of her bare feet. Her black hair fell down her back onto her face in a tumbled mess, nearly obscuring her averted profile.

"Sabrina," he said softly, sitting down beside her.

She did not reply and he gently pulled her hair away from her face.

"What is it you want, Phillip?" she asked dully, her voice slightly muffled by the pillow.

"To see that you are all right."

"I would be quite all right if you would but leave."

He gazed at her hips and saw faint streaks of blood showing through the yellow muslin. "I will do as you wish, after I have taken care of you."

"I will take care of myself!" She reared up on her elbows and glared at him.

"Even one as remarkably talented as you are, Bree, cannot effectively minister to your own bottom."

Sabrina drew a deep, resolute breath and rolled herself away from him to the other side of the bed. Slowly, she forced herself to rise. "May I return to my own room now, my lord?"

He walked around the end of the bed to face her. "No, my dear. Come, lie back down. I do not wish you to hurt yourself more than I have already done."

She felt stinging pain in her thighs and buttocks that brought tears of humiliation to her eyes. "Let me go," she choked out and tried to walk past him.

"Please obey me in this, Sabrina. There is no one else but I to take care of you. I cannot believe that you would prefer your maid." As she made no further move away from him, he eased her with great care into his arms and placed her face down onto the bed.

As she held herself stiffly, Phillip continued persuasively, "It is not the first time I have taken care of you, Bree. At least in this, you may trust me."

She nodded, reluctantly. He slid his hand under her stomach and lifted her slightly to pull up her gown. He gazed down, furious with himself at the sight of her white shift streaked with blood. When he tried to ease it up, she quivered with pain, for the material had stuck against her buttocks and thighs.

"Do not move, Bree, I will be right back." Some ten minutes later, Phillip returned, laden with warm water, salve, bandages, and laudanum.

She was lying as he had left her, save that her arms were crossed above her head, forming a pillow for her forehead.

"I will try to soak the material free. But first, Bree, I want you to take some laudanum."

He measured several drops into a glass of water and eased her up to allow her to drink it without choking. She downed it without hesitation, hoping that it would dull the pain sufficiently so that she wouldn't disgrace herself.

Phillip began carefully to soak the shift with warm water. After some minutes he tried again to pull the material free.

Although the laudanum was making her groggy, Sabrina could not help the whimper of pain that escaped her lips.

"I am sorry, Sabrina, but I must do it." In one firm movement, he pulled her shift free of the clotted blood. She cried out, half rearing up. "There, it is done now." Gently, he pressed her back down on her stomach. "The rest won't hurt nearly as much, Bree, I promise you."

He cursed himself long and fluently as he stared down at the mass of welts. After he had bathed her, he realized with no little relief that most of the cuts were not so deep as he had first suspected, only a few of them drawing blood. He dried her and began to rub in the salve. As his fingers touched the white softness of her thighs, he realized that his hands were shaking.

He was recalled to his senses at the sound of a choking

sob. Sabrina tried to stop her trembling. Perhaps Trevor was right, she thought, stuffing her fist in her mouth, pain and pleasure were inexorably bound together. She felt his fingers abruptly leave her and only the stinging, insistent pain remained. She heard Phillip speaking to her, but the laudanum had so dulled her mind that she could make no sense of his words.

Only vaguely did she realize that he was raising her and unfastening her gown. She felt the cold air touch her bare skin as his hands eased her breasts free of her clothing. She felt a light cover being tucked in about her and she fell into a deep, dreamless sleep.

14

Sabrina carefully perched on the edge of her desk chair as she wrote her letter to Phillip. She looked up after several minutes to gaze through her bedchamber windows. Heavy-bellied clouds, laden with snow, hung low in the early morning sky. She glanced at the clock on the mantelpiece, quickly added several more lines to her letter, and turned away to finish packing her portmanteau.

She fastened the straps, dragged the portmanteau to the door, and turned to look one last time about her room. It was a lovely room, the light blue and cream colors exactly to her taste. She saw her letter on the writing desk, and returned to read it one last time.

"Dear Phillip," she read. "I have returned home, to Yorkshire and my grandfather. I am truly sorry if my abrupt departure causes you embarrassment. I am also sorry for many other things, Phillip, least among them my outrageous behavior of yesterday. You were perfectly right. I had no right to act the wounded wife and take you to task for having a mistress.

"You will perhaps believe me the perfect hypocrite now, but I find that I simply cannot continue as we have. I find that I cannot hold to our agreement. I know that your freedom is important to you. But I know too that I am unable to be but one of the women to share your life.

"It is time for me to return where I belong. I have no real fear of Trevor, for as you have said, he values his own survival above all things.

"I know, Phillip, that you have great pride. I ask that

194

in your pride you will not feel yourself honor-bound to come after me. I have made my decision and it is what I want.

"Again, my lord, I am truly sorry for all the unpleasantness I have brought you. Adieu."

Sabrina glanced one last time about her bedchamber, pulled her cloak closely about her, and made her way downstairs.

She bestowed a bright smile upon the dubious Greybar. "Doris informed you that I wished a hired carriage. Is it here?"

"Yes, my lady," he said unhappily. "Would you not prefer to wait until his lordship returns? He informed me that he would not be gone for long."

"No, Greybar. I do not wish to await his lordship's return. Now I must take my leave of you."

"My lady," he began.

"Good-bye, Greybar," Sabrina said. She walked quickly from the house into the cold morning. She stepped into the carriage and waved her gloved hand to the butler, who stood shivering and uncertain on the front steps.

The horses started forward and she was tossed back onto the squabs. The sharp stinging in her bottom made her turn quickly onto her side. She drew a carriage blanket over her legs and pillowed her face in her hands.

The weary horses pulled to a steaming halt in front of Monmouth Hall early the following evening. Sabrina gazed at the great weathered stone ediface, its jagged surfaces worn smooth through the centuries. Smoke billowed from the massive fireplaces that towered twenty feet above the slate roof and sharp points of candlelight dotted the latticed windows.

She paused a moment before the great oak doors, her stomach knotting in fear at the prospect of seeing Trevor again. She pulled herself upright and applied her strength to the iron, griffin-headed knocker.

"Lady Sabrina!" Ribble exclaimed upon seeing the small disheveled girl standing on the doorstep.

"Good evening, Ribble. How good it is to be home

again! Grandfather is all right, is he not? I have not received a letter from him in almost a week."

Ribble had grown quite used to Sabrina's rapid, tumbled speech during the eighteen years he had known her. He merely smiled at her reassuringly. "Of a certainty, the earl improves by the day." He strained his eyes beyond her. "His lordship?"

"He is not with me," Sabrina said simply, and walked into the large flagstoned entrance hall.

"Sabrina!"

She turned toward Elisabeth's high, breathless voice to see her sister clutching the railing at the bottom of the staircase.

"Would you please see to my coachman and my portmanteau, Ribble?" Sabrina asked before turning to her sister. She listened with half an ear to Ribble issuing orders to two footmen who had but moments before stood gawking with undisguised curiosity at the Returned Prodigal.

"You are looking lovely," Sabrina said warmly as she walked toward her sister, her arms outstretched. She wished that she had not made the gesture, for Elisabeth seemed to have to force herself to suffer Sabrina's quick embrace. In truth, Sabrina thought, Elisabeth looked positively haggard. Although her gown was new and stylishly cut, it seemed to hang off her thin shoulders, its color accentuating the sallowness of her skin. Wisps of fair hair had escaped the bun she habitually wore at the nape of her neck, giving her an almost bedraggled appearance. But it was her sister's eyes that gave Sabrina pause. They held no joy; they were dull and lifeless.

"What are you doing here?" Elisabeth asked in a low voice.

"I have come to stay with you for a while. Elisabeth, are you all right?"

Elisabeth said coldly, disregarding Sabrina's inquiry, "Now that you are arrived, I suppose I cannot send you away. Where is the viscount?"

"He is, for the moment, still in London. I wanted to

see you and Grandfather, Elisabeth. I have felt so helpless not being here with him."

"Doubtless he will wish to see you. You nearly caused his death, sister. I trust this time you will conduct yourself properly."

"Elisabeth, you know I was guilty of no misconduct. I beg you will not distort the truth, at least to yourself." Sabrina gazed steadily into her sister's eyes, and it was Elisabeth who looked away first.

Elisabeth gave a grating, shrill laugh. "If you were guilty of nothing, sister, how is it that you are so very brave now? With your husband still in London, you have no protection from Trevor—if it is protection you need."

"It is very simple, Elisabeth. You know that Phillip would kill Trevor if he dared to lay a hand on me."

Under Sabrina's calm gaze, Elisabeth's fair features seemed to crumble.

"Well, well, what have we here! My little sister!"

Sabrina saw Elisabeth go rigid at the mocking voice of her husband. Sabrina turned slightly and watched as he languidly made his way down the stairs, his eyes never leaving her face.

"As you see, Trevor," Sabrina said evenly.

He stopped at the bottom of the stairs, making no move toward her. "And where is your marvelously fierce husband?"

Elisabeth answered quickly. "The viscount is in London. Sabrina has come to visit Grandfather."

"Such an honor for the old gentleman. You will find him sadly changed, little sister, but quite alive."

Sabrina saw that Ribble was listening intently to their conversation and hastened to say, "If you would not mind, Elisabeth, I should like to visit Grandfather now. I shall be quite content with a tray, if it would not be too much trouble for Cook."

"Undoubtedly, Cook has already heard that her precious Sabrina has returned, and is preparing a feast."

Sabrina flinched at the cold sarcasm in her sister's voice. "It matters not," she said quietly. She moved away toward the stairs, keeping as much distance as she could between herself and Trevor. "I gather that Grandfather is in his room?"

"Certainly," Trevor drawled, splaying his white hands. "The old gentleman rarely allows either Elisabeth or me into his exalted company."

He strolled to his wife and drew her hand through his arm. "Of course, your sister and I have little need for anyone else's presence. Is that not true, my love?"

Elisabeth's eyes were on the toes of her blue kid slippers, and she nodded dumbly.

"I believe I asked you a question, Elisabeth."

Sabrina felt the blood pound at her temples as she watched Trevor slide his fingers to the soft skin on the inside of Elisabeth's arm and pinch her cruelly. Sabrina could not help herself. "Leave her alone, you beast!"

"Shut up, Sabrina!" Elisabeth turned her pale face to her husband. "As you say, Trevor, it is quite true." She lowered her voice, glancing at Ribble from the corner of her eye. "Go now to see Grandfather, Sabrina. I am rather tired this evening and will see you in the morning."

"You do not think that our little sister would care to have tea with us—before you retire, my love?"

"I think not, Trevor," Sabrina said, wishing for a moment that she had Phillip's strength. "Until tomorrow, Elisabeth." She turned and walked up the stairs.

Jesperson, the earl's valet, opened the door to the vast bedchamber and sitting room. "Welcome home, my lady," he said softly, his impenetrable dark eyes brightening ever so slightly at the sight of her. "His lordship knows you have arrived and is anxious to see you."

"Thank you, Jesperson. I thank you for caring for him and . . . protecting him."

A flash of deep emotion crossed the man's face before it resumed its impassive facade. "This way, my lady."

Childhood memories stirred as Sabrina followed Jesperson through the sitting room to the long, rectangular bedchamber beyond. The small treasures she had collected in her young days were still displayed atop a huge mahogany desk: colored rocks from the streambed, polished by the rushing water to a smooth, silken surface; a string of amber beads left her by her mother; a tattered kite whose long cloth tail lay wrapped limply about it.

Her grandfather's bedchamber had not changed since before she was born. It was dominated by dark blue damask hangings. Thick Aubusson carpets covered the planked floor, swallowing the sound of her heeled slippers. The earl sat in his chair before the roaring fireplace, wrapped in his favorite velvet burgundy dressing gown, his twisted fingers clutching the arms.

"Grandfather!" she cried, and ran to him, hurling herself into his arms.

She felt his gnarled fingers stroke her hair, and she slipped down to her knees, her head upon his legs.

He was long silent, and Sabrina felt sudden fear that he had believed Trevor and Elisabeth's stories about her. In her letters to him, she had not written of what had happened, fearing to hurl him into a tragic confrontation. She raised her head slowly and gazed into his fierce blue eyes.

"How much like her you are," the earl said softly. He let the tips of his fingers gently trace the contours of her face. "It is such a pity that you never knew your grandmother." He seemed to recall himself, shaking off bittersweet memories. "You are a beautiful, vibrant woman, Sabrina. I suppose I must give due credit to that viscount of yours."

Jesperson said from beside the earl's chair, "Would you care for tea, my lord?"

"Aye, and some of Cook's delicious macaroons. My granddaughter must be hungry after her journey."

"Yes, please, Jesperson, I am quite famished." When the valet left the room, Sabrina eased herself up and drew forward a small footstool.

"You are looking well, Grandfather," she said lovingly, stroking his hand.

"I am but an old eagle chained to his nest, Bree. Even my spirit grows weary."

"You are an old poet who loves the simile and I refuse to allow you sole claim to weary spirits."

He smiled, the criss-crossed lines about his eyes

deepening even more. "What does a chit like you know about spirits and such?" A frown crossed his forehead. "You have seen your sister?"

"Yes, and Trevor also." She tried to keep her voice neutral, but the earl would not allow it.

"She has become even more of a whining termagant married to that scoundrel ne'er-do-well."

"Perhaps, Grandfather, she is not happy."

The earl snorted, looking away from her face for a moment. "Your sister, more's the pity, will never be happy either with or without her husband, for she has naught but dislike for herself. She always wanted to be the great lady, lording it over those about her, but it has brought her nothing."

Sabrina nestled her cheek against the warm softness of the earl's dressing gown, and felt the skin of his leg stretch against the bone.

"She never visits me anymore," the earl continued. " 'Tis her guilty conscience, perhaps. Don't look so surprised, Bree," he added as Sabrina brought her head up to gaze at him. "Never did I believe the filth she and Trevor told me. Lord, what a mistake I made, bringing that honey-voiced fop here to Monmouth Hall. Still, he is Elisabeth's husband. That fact alone must still my hand against him."

"You simply did your duty by your heir, Grandfather, and to Elisabeth. As to what happened. . . ." She shrugged. "But enough of this! We are together again and I want naught but that you get well again."

"You came home because you have no place else to go."

Her head whipped up at his softly spoken statement and she forced a smile to her lips. She had forgotten his uncanny ability to guess her thoughts. She wondered fleetingly if he had done the same with her grandmother. She thought too of her few letters to him. Had she failed to cloak her unhappiness? She had no chance to frame a suitable response, for Jesperson entered, bearing a tea tray in his hands.

"Cook thought you would be wanting more than just

macaroons, my lady," Jesperson said. Sabrina gazed greedily at piles of ham, chicken, and warm bread.

"It appears that I can have no private thoughts," she said lightly, avoiding her grandfather's eyes. "Thank Cook, please, Jesperson. It looks delicious."

The earl sipped his tea, not speaking until Sabrina had eaten her fill. She sat back on the footstool with a contented sigh, licking her fingers.

"Now tell me, Sabrina, why have you come here without the viscount? I have not met him, of course, but Richard Clarendon had nothing but praise for him. That was a surprise, I might add, seeing that Richard wanted you for himself."

She stared down at the faded pattern in the carpet. "Phillip is generous, Grandfather, and ever so gentle." A crooked smile crossed her lips as she thought about her still tender bottom. "I would have died had he not found me."

The earl nodded for her to continue.

"He is a good man, a man with a very strong character and a temper that only I seem to be able to call forth."

"You paint the picture of an estimable man, Sabrina."

She nodded and turned her face into the shadows.

"Then why did you leave him?"

"Why, Grandfather, how could you think such a thing! Why I——"

"Sabrina, I felt the shape of you whilst you were still in your mother's womb. I watched you howl with fury when you emerged into the world, all red and wrinkled, so angry at leaving her warm belly. Even as a small infant, your violet eyes were bright with wonder and honesty. You have not changed. Dissimulation is not part of your nature. It is time for you to tell me the truth."

Sabrina gazed down a moment at her short, blunt fingernails, and drew a deep breath. "He does not love me, Grandfather. If you must know, he wed me only because he felt his honor impelled him to do so. He laughed about his being St. George and I, the damsel in distress. We agreed to a marriage of convenience, indeed, I offered him his freedom. He did not even try to come to me. Oh,

Grandfather, I did the most terrible thing to him, and yet, I know that I would do it again."

"Something outrageously honest and worthy of an Eversleigh, I trust."

A ghost of a smile flitted over her mouth. "I found out that he kept a mistress. I went to her apartment and found them together."

The picture of such a confrontation brought a smile of amusement to the earl's lips. "And what happened, Bree?" he managed, with scarce a tremor.

"I kicked him in the groin. He was quite naked, and I suppose that I hurt him badly."

"Oh lord," the earl groaned, unable to say more lest he burst into laughter.

"He was most angry."

"Understandable."

"He followed me home and whipped me with a riding crop. I am still a bit sore." She rubbed her bottom in an unconscious gesture.

"You left him then?"

"No, he soon returned and cared for me. I did not wish him to, but as I have said, he has a strong character. Yesterday morning, he left the house for a while. I hired a carriage and came here."

The earl gazed thoughtfully into her violet eyes, Camilla's eyes. He thought it likely upon brief reflection that his spirited wife would have done the same to him had he been inclined to take a mistress.

"He does not love me," she said harshly, breaking the silence. "And he desires his freedom above all things."

The earl leaned forward in his chair and took one of her hands into his. "Tell me, Sabrina, do you love him?"

Her fingers clenched in the palm of his hand, and she spoke finally as though the words were wrenched out of her. "I am sick with love for him."

"Certainly a wifely kick in the groin should have convinced him of your feeling," the earl said, without thinking. He saw the stricken look on her face and hastened to draw her forward into his arms. He wished that he had met the viscount so that he could truthfully reassure her.

He stroked the masses of raven hair. "We shall simply wait and see what happens, Sabrina." He looked into the orange flames in the fireplace and saw another face, so like Sabrina's, from a past that had long since turned to ashes and memories. "You are Camilla's granddaughter. Believe me, Bree, no man who knew her would have ever willingly let her go."

Ribble pulled open the front doors and gazed for an instant in blank surprise before his leathery features split into a wide smile.

"My lord! Her ladyship will be so pleased. She didn't tell us precisely when to expect you."

"I daresay her ladyship will be quite surprised to see me," Phillip said as Ribble divested him of his greatcoat and gloves. He looked up at the sound of rustling silk.

"So you have come, my lord."

He proffered a slight bow. "As you see, Elisabeth. I trust you have taken good care of my wife." He wondered silently what Sabrina had told her sister.

"She arrived only yesterday evening, my lord. Indeed, I have scarce seen her. She has spent most of her time with Grandfather."

"The earl continues to improve?"

Elisabeth shrugged. "Sometimes I wonder if he will not live to see the next century. Undoubtedly the arrival of his granddaughter has enlivened his spirits."

"I have found that Sabrina's presence enlivens the spirits of most around her. Where is she, Elisabeth?"

Elisabeth waved her hand in an indifferent gesture. "With the earl, I should imagine. I have not seen her today."

She turned and said in an imperious voice to Ribble, "Escort his lordship to the earl's suite."

"Perhaps I shall see you later," Phillip said as he turned to follow the butler up the staircase.

Phillip dismissed the butler with a pleasant smile and knocked on the earl's door.

"My lord!"

"Good day to you, Jesperson. The earl is here?"

"Of course, my lord. He will be delighted to finally meet your lordship."

As they walked through the sitting room to the bed-chamber beyond, Phillip asked quietly, "You have had no . . . interference in your care of the earl?"

"No, my lord, not since you and the marquis came to visit."

"Excellent. Is my wife with the earl?"

"No, my lord. He sent her away about an hour ago. Wanted her to get some color in her cheeks, he said."

"She is riding?" the viscount asked, his voice incredulous.

Jesperson shook his head. "No, my lord. She said something about not feeling like a gallop today."

"I daresay she wouldn't."

Jesperson opened the adjoining door to the earl's bed-chamber and allowed the viscount to pass in front of him into the room. Phillip drew to a halt and looked at the old man who sat hunched forward in a chair by the fireplace, a tartan blanket wrapped about his legs. The earl turned his head slowly and the viscount found himself staring into a pair of lively blue eyes, sunk beneath a craggy brow. A smile touched his lips.

"You, I presume, are Sabrina's husband," the earl said in a resonant voice.

Phillip walked forward and took the earl's twisted fingers in his hand. "Yes, sir, I am Sabrina's husband. Phillip Mercerault, by name."

"Sit down, my lord."

Phillip did as he was bid, easing his large frame onto a faded brocade settee opposite the earl.

"Forgive my travel dirt, sir. I did not wish to take the time to change."

The earl waved an indifferent hand. "Sabrina will be surprised to see you, lad, though I must admit that I am not."

"It is likely that she will be, sir. As you can imagine, I am here to fetch her home."

The earl shifted his gaze from the viscount's handsome

face to his hands. Always, he thought, a man's character is evident in his hands. He approved of what he saw. He said slowly, his eyes going back to the viscount's face, "Therein lies the problem, I believe. She might choose not to go with you. This is her home, you know, and I won't force her to return with you."

Phillip, who had been well aware of the earl's scrutiny, sat forward, his eyes narrowing. "Forgive me for being blunt, sir, but Sabrina is my wife, and will do as I bid her. And that, sir, is an end to it."

The earl's blue eyes twinkled. "It surprises me, lad, that my granddaughter hasn't taken a whip to you for such high-handedness."

Phillip smiled. "Actually, sir, she has."

The earl found this admission to his liking. He tried to square his shoulders, but the movement was painful. He said quickly, seeing the look of concern on the viscount's face, "Keep your seat, lad. I find age and infirmity rather a bore, but it is naught but what awaits all of us. What is of the most importance now is my granddaughter. She spoke of you as being kind, my lord, kind and noble."

"She has tried to strangle me with what she perceives as my blasted nobility."

"You did not, then, wed Sabrina out of duty, lad? Nobility, if you will?"

Phillip was silent for a moment. He said, finally, "There are rules, sir, codes of behavior that must govern society, else we might well find ourselves back in trees and caves, wearing animal skins. I suppose that in the beginning my offer of marriage to Sabrina was motivated by a sense of duty. She refused me upon several occasions. As you are undoubtedly aware, it was her imminent ruin in London society that finally forced her to wed me. It was an honorable offer, sir, and one I have not regretted."

"An honorable offer," the earl mused aloud. "In short, a marriage of convenience, forced upon the both of you by the rules of society. How can you have such a marriage, my lord, if there is naught else to support it?"

"Your granddaughter is a stubborn little fool, sir. She refuses to believe anything else."

"I am not certain that you gave her any opportunity to believe anything else. Sabrina has a man's pride, a man's code of ethics, if you will. I begin to think, lad, that it is you who are the stubborn fool."

"If you will. In my opinion, such a quality makes us well suited."

"I do not believe, my lord, that Sabrina will consent to return with you if you are still bound to your original . . . business arrangement."

Phillip rose. "Sabrina did me the great disservice of leaving London before I could speak with her. It is true that we have not dealt well together since our marriage. However, it is my intention to assure that she will never again have the opportunity to misconstrue my feelings. Now, if you will tell me where I may find her."

"And if she refuses to speak with you?"

A singularly gentle smile touched the viscount's hazel eyes. "Then I shall simply have to tie her down, won't I, my lord?"

"It is likely that you will find her either in the orchard or in the stables."

"I thank you, sir." Phillip took the earl's hands once again into his and pressed them slightly. He turned at the door to see the old man gazing after him, his eyes reflective.

"Please do not worry, sir. I will contrive that Sabrina dismisses once and for all her absurd notions about my duty and nobility."

"Perhaps you will," the earl said slowly.

"I bid you good-bye, sir, for both your granddaughter and myself. We shall come—together—in a couple of weeks to see you again."

"Good-bye, my lord," the earl said, and Phillip let himself out of the room. He found Ribble downstairs at his post near the great oak front doors. He had already left instructions with the butler for the immediate packing of Sabrina's portmanteau, as he had no intention of spending even one night under the same roof with her dissolute cousin. He secured directions to the Monmouth orchard on the chance that Sabrina would not be at the stables.

When he stepped inside the warm, hay-scented stable, he was immediately approached by a short, balding little man who had all the appearance of one beyond his depth.

"Ye be his lordship?" Elbert, the master of the stables, asked. "Lady Sabrina's husband?"

"Yes. What the devil is going on here? Where is Lady Sabrina?"

Elbert tugged furiously on the one long clump of gray hair that hung over his forehead. "Lady Sabrina ain't here, m'lord. She told me to give ye a message."

"Well, what is it, man?"

"She said, m'lord, to tell ye that she's left the Hall and that she won't be back until ye take yer leave."

"Did she tell you where she was going?" Phillip asked, his voice furiously calm.

"Nay, m'lord," Elbert said quickly, too quickly for Phillip's taste.

"Did she take a horse?"

"Aye, m'lord, her brown mare."

"I see." Phillip turned away from Elbert and gazed a moment around the dim-lit stable. In a darkened corner, he saw a boy wrapping a blanket about himself. He realized he was likely in the midst of a conspiracy, as the servants would be loyal to Sabrina rather than to him. He called to the boy. "Come here, lad, I would speak to you."

" 'Tis Tim, my lord," Elbert said by way of introduction.

"Tim," the viscount repeated, his eyes running over the boy, "would you tell me why you are wearing a blanket?"

Tim sent an agonized glance toward Elbert. Phillip shook his head. Sabrina would not be so foolish as to dress herself in a boy's clothes. Still, he asked, "Did Lady Sabrina borrow your clothes, Tim?"

The boy lowered his gaze to the viscount's hessians and nodded his head.

"I see. Her ladyship has shown great ingenuity. Now, my good man," the viscount continued, turning back to Elbert, "you will tell me the direction Lady Sabrina has taken."

Elbert felt himself in a quandary. He did not at all approve of Lady Sabrina's dressing up like a boy and riding away from Monmouth Hall alone, and he had told her so. Still, she had seemed so frantic.

Phillip said quietly, "You know that she cannot be safe. Indeed, if she is discovered to be a woman, there are men who would delight in taking advantage of her. Dammit man, I have no intention of harming her!"

Elbert looked up into the viscount's face. He nodded slowly. " 'Tis east she's gone, my lord, toward the village of Iskerville."

"Thank you, Elbert." Phillip turned and quickly strode back to the Hall. Sabrina's portmanteau stood packed near the front door and Phillip himself fastened it to the boot of his curricle. As he whipped his horses forward, he tried to calm his anxiety, knowing that she could not be more than an hour ahead of him.

It was nearly dark when he reached the Flying Goose Inn in the small village of Iskerville. He questioned the landlord, then searched every nook and cranny of the public taproom. She was not there.

Nor did he find her at the Grape Arbor in the next village of Chirpenham. His fear for her safety grew as he tooled his grays down the pitted country lanes toward Turpendale.

The White Feather stood on the outskirts of the village, surrounded by naked-branched elm trees that bowed and dipped eerily in the night wind.

"A scruffy little lad, my lord?" the thin, stooped landlord inquired, gazing in some awe at the elegant gentleman in his front parlor.

A slight smile touched the viscount's lips. "Yes, I believe the scruffy little lad will do quite nicely."

The landlord shook his grizzled head dubiously. " 'E's a fair pitiful bit of a lad, my lord."

"Nevertheless, you will tell me where I may find him."

" 'E's in the taproom last time I saw him, my lord. Paid me for 'is dinner, 'e did, so I let 'im stay."

"No, you needn't accompany me," Phillip said quickly, staying the landlord.

He strode down the dim-lit corridor and pushed open the door to the taproom. Though there were few men present, his nostrils twitched at the heavy smell of cheap ale and sweat. The scruffy little lad he was searching for was curled up in a small ball on a brick ledge near the roaring fireplace. Her arms were wrapped about her knees and her face was pillowed on her thighs. A thick woolen cap covered her hair and a patched, faded cloak encased her from neck to toe. She appeared to him to be fast asleep.

He stood wondering for a moment just how the devil he would get her out of the inn without someone recognizing her as the Earl of Monmouth's granddaughter. An idea came to him and he smiled.

"So there you are, you damned little thief!"

There was a sudden hush in the room, all heads turned toward the irate gentleman who was purposefully making his way toward the sleeping boy by the fireplace.

"You steal my horse, do you, my boy! Little beggar, it's full price you'll pay for your impudence this time!" Phillip laid a heavy hand on her shoulder and shook her. "Wake up, you damned urchin!"

Sabrina's eyes flew open and she gazed open-mouthed up into her husband's angry face.

"Well, boy, what have you to say for yourself?" the viscount demanded, jerking her to her feet, his hands supporting her under her arms.

"Phillip," she whispered, trying to pull her scattered wits together.

His grip tightened about her rib cage. "You'll pay the piper this time, you thieving little cove. You've near to broken your mother's heart with your thieving ways."

A red-bearded man said in a loud voice, "So, he's got a mother and still he's a tippling little lout."

Phillip nodded, apparently approving of this opinion. "You'll get no support here, lad," he said sternly, looking back at his pale, wild-eyed wife.

"To do that to 'is mother," a stooped old man said, shaking his head. "Thievin' little bastard." He spit toward the hearth.

"You can't make me go with you, Phillip," Sabrina muttered finally between clenched teeth.

"We'll see about that, you foul-smelling little brat!" The viscount jerked her off her feet and threw her over his shoulder, careful not to dislodge the woolen cap.

She cried in a high, squeaking voice, "Let me down! Won't someone help me! I have done nothing!"

"Little bugger," the red-bearded man said, and turned back to his ale.

"Thank you for your assistance," Phillip called over his shoulder to the landlord, and carried the furiously struggling Sabrina out into the cold winter night.

He tossed her unceremoniously into the curricle and ordered the ostler to bring out her mare. After the man had tied her horse to the back of the curricle, Phillip threw a coin to him and gracefully jumped up beside Sabrina.

She huddled into a small, miserable ball as he whipped the grays out of the inn's courtyard.

"How did you find me?"

"Lord, you do smell foul! Find you, my dear wife? I persuaded your cohorts that by remaining silent, they were placing you in danger. Also, I just happened to see poor Tim wrapping himself in a blanket. Now I have a question for you, Sabrina. Just what is it you intended to do, dressed as an urchin and galloping about the country-side?"

"I assume that Elbert gave you my message. I would have stayed in the inn until you had left."

He gazed thoughtfully at her for a moment, then reached over and pulled off the woolen cap. Her hair cascaded down her back and over her shoulders.

"You bloody little fool," he said angrily, remembering his fear for her. "Just what do you think would have happened had it been discovered that a girl lay beneath those wretched clothes?"

"Undoubtedly, I would have received better treatment than I have from you, my lord!"

He frowned at her profile, then turned his attention to his tired horses. "We will stop at the inn in the next village. In the meantime, you will try to do something with that mop of hair. I am not such an ogre as to make you change your clothes in an open curricle in the dead of winter, but you will take off those breeches, for they show below your cloak. I have brought your clothes, so at least tomorrow you may appear as a lady."

Sabrina sat rigid and unspeaking for the several miles to the village of Danby.

A slight smile touched the viscount's mouth as they neared the inn. "Look, my dear, the inn is marvelously named the St. George. Fitting, don't you think?"

"Go to the devil."

A mobile brow shot up a good inch. "Careful, Bree, else I'll contrive to make your bottom more sore than it already is. Now, take off those breeches, else I'll do it for you."

Sabrina growled in frustration and slowly wriggled out of the breeches.

Phillip drew his weary grays to a halt in front of the shingled inn, and called for an ostler. A rotund little man encased in a huge white apron emerged from the ivy-covered building. "Keep your mouth shut, Bree, else it will be the worse for you." He added in an undervoice, "Contrive to stay downwind from our landlord, you are most offensive to the nose."

"My lord!" the landlord exclaimed, recognizing Quality as he drew closer to the curricle. He called over his shoulder, "Will, out here, boy! The gentleman's horses need the stables!"

Phillip nodded politely. "My wife and I are in need of your best bedchamber. We have lost our way and require the fine services of your inn for the night."

"Certainly, my lord, certainly. If you will deign to follow me. I'll have my other boy fetch up your luggage."

The viscount lifted his wife down from the curricle. "My wife is quite fatigued and is need of a hot bath," he continued smoothly, shielding Sabrina from the landlord.

If the landlord thought the gentleman's wife looked like a veritable ragamuffin, he made no comment, particularly after the viscount pressed a shining guinea into his palm.

Not many minutes later, Sabrina faced her husband

across the expanse of a large, airy bedchamber on the second floor of the St. George.

"Our luggage has arrived, no doubt," Phillip said as he moved to answer the tap on the door. Sabrina walked to the shadowed corner and waited silently until the viscount had given the boy orders for dinner.

"A hot bath and dinner will be coming shortly," he said, walking toward her. "If you don't mind, my dear wife, I would that you bathe first, else I might lose my appetite for dinner."

"Very well," she said, turning away from him. In truth, she was finding Tim's clothes unbearable.

She walked to the fireplace and sat down on the wooden floor, her arms wrapped about her knees.

"You are singularly untalkative, Bree," the viscount said as he sat down in a chair opposite her. "Are you not overly warm in that heavy cloak?"

"You forget, Phillip, that you made me take off my breeches."

"Then the removal of your cloak would give me great pleasure."

"Your pleasure, my lord, is of no concern whatsoever to me!"

"How quickly you have changed your attitude," he said, grinning at her. "As I recall you were most interested several days ago, to the point of nearly unmanning me."

She felt a tight knot of anger grow in her stomach. "I do not wish to discuss the matter."

"It would seem to me, my dear, that you are forcibly reminded of the incident each time you sit down."

She flushed, thinking of the several excruciating hours she had spent being jostled about on her mare's back.

A loud knock came at the door.

"Ah, your bath has arrived, Bree." As he rose to answer the door, he saw her gaze fleetingly toward the window. "We are on the second floor. Please do not try what you are thinking. A wife with a broken leg would be a deuced nuisance."

She tossed her head and said no more until after a

large copper tub accompanied by a huge bar of soap and several fluffy towels had been piled by the landlord's large, raw-boned son next to the fireplace.

"Thank ye, m' lord," she heard the boy say.

"There is no screen," she said flatly as Phillip walked back to her.

"I recall no screen the first time I bathed you. However, I do not wish to offend your maidenly sensibilities, even though you are my wife."

"I am your wife in name only, my lord!"

He paused, an arrested gleam in his eyes. He said gently, "I shall leave you now. I trust you will find fifteen minutes adequate time. I do have a great dislike of having my wife smell like she just mucked out the stables."

After Phillip left their room, Sabrina stripped off Tim's smelly clothes and eased herself into the tub. She quickly lathered herself, then sank back, allowing the water to reach her chin.

She had only just finished slipping on her dressing gown when she heard a light tap on the door. She sashed the waist tightly. "Come in."

"I have brought our dinner. Are you through with your bath and tub?"

She nodded and stepped back into the shadows as the landlord's son placed covered dishes on the table and hauled away the tub.

"Come and eat your dinner, Bree."

She slipped into the chair he held for her and looked down at a plate of roasted chicken and vegetables.

They ate in silence for some minutes, until Phillip, after one bite from the mound of overcooked beans, grimaced, and laid down his fork. He folded his arms across his chest and watched her finish her chicken.

Sabrina looked up to see her husband regarding her, a serious expression on his face.

"What is the matter, Phillip, have I spilled gravy on my chin?"

"No. And, I might add, you smell and look quite like yourself again."

He continued to gaze at her steadily. Finally, unable to

help herself, she burst out, "Why did you come after me?"

"Which time, my dear?"

She said sharply, "I asked you most sincerely not to let your . . . pride get the better of you."

"Yes, I suppose you did mention something about that. But then again, there was quite a bit of drivel in your letter to me."

"I meant every word I wrote, my lord."

"Yes, Sabrina, I know." She started at the curiously gentle tone of his voice. He added in a pensive voice, "I do wish that you had not dashed off. Poor Greybar was green with anxiety by the time I returned home. It was most unfair of you, Sabrina."

"Unfair of me! Your fury at me, my lord, was most evident! I saw no point in continuing our farce of a marriage."

"That is what I told your grandfather."

She felt a wave of misery wash over her. "Then why did you come after me, my lord?"

"Because like you, Sabrina, I no longer wished to continue with a marriage of convenience, or a business arrangement, as you expressed it. I could not tell you that unless I did come after you."

"You could have written to me," she said in a low voice.

"No, my dear, I think not."

She reared back her head at his softly spoken words. "I have made my intentions perfectly clear, Phillip. I intend to stay with my grandfather, here in Yorkshire."

"After tonight, I hope that will not remain your intention."

She suddenly realized that they were alone and that she was clothed only in a dressing gown. She quickly squirmed out of her chair and walked to the fireplace, putting the distance of half a room between them.

He swiveled about in his chair. "What is this, Sabrina?" he asked softly. "Are you afraid of me . . . your husband?"

"Of course I am not afraid of you, my lord! I tell you,

Phillip, I will not be seduced, even though it would please your male pride to have me." She slowed and drew a deep breath. "I will not be just another mistress to you, wife or no."

"But I have no mistress."

Her mouth dropped open and she stared at him. "But why?" she asked helplessly.

He looked at her long and thoughtfully, as if he were forming his words more for himself than for her. "I discovered, my dear, that keeping a mistress brought me no more pleasure."

"But your . . . freedom. It is so very important to you. I am not so witless as not to understand that."

"I suppose," he said slowly, "that my desire for freedom was a comforting aberration that kept me from making a fool out of myself for another woman such as Elaine. I think, Sabrina, that thirty years of freedom is enough for any man. It all seems rather foolish now, if you would know the truth."

She turned away and looked down at the glowing flame in the fireplace. "You scarcely know me, Phillip. You told me the evening of our wedding that you had had no choices since the morning you found me in Eppingham Forest. You cannot deny that, Phillip."

"Nor would I attempt to, Sabrina. As I told your grandfather, you and I have managed in our short time together to deal continually at cross-purposes. It must stop."

"But you are a rake, my lord, indeed, you have told me so many times. Yet, you did not even attempt to make. . . ." She ground to an embarrassed halt.

"You are normally not at a loss for words, my dear. I would that you would not be missish now. What is it that I did not attempt to do?"

"I am not being missish!" she snapped. "You did not even try to make . . . love to me on our wedding night."

"I misjudged your feelings, Sabrina! If you will recall, during our memorable interview at the Cavendish Hotel you appeared appalled at the mere thought of lovemaking. I am not a complete bounder, you know."

"Yes," she said in a low voice. "I thought as much. That is why I decided to seduce you."

"You what?"

She frowned at him, remembering her anger. "The second night of our marriage. I had decided that you were being noble. I came to your room, my lord, very late." Her voice rose harshly. "You reeked of a woman's rose fragrance!"

"Good lord! I suppose I should be grateful that you did not murder me in my bed!"

She bristled at the amusement in his voice and said stiffly, "I had a very good mind to, if you must know the truth."

"Did I wound your pride so much, Sabrina?"

She frowned a moment at his question, and looked away from him. "No, 'twas not so much my pride. If you would know, my lord, I felt that you had betrayed me, that you had not even given me a chance."

"A chance at what, my love?"

She started at the caressing tone of his voice and whirled about to face him. "I am not your love," she exploded. "Indeed, my lord, you made that clear from the very beginning!"

"I was wrong."

She stared at him, unwilling to accept his words for fear that she was mistaken in his intent. She did not at first notice that Phillip's gaze had dropped from her face.

"God, you're beautiful."

She suddenly felt a certain coolness touch her skin and looked down to see her dressing gown parted and her breasts bare to his eyes. She whirled about, mortified, and feverishly pulled the material back together.

Phillip made no move toward her. "Do you know, my love, that you have never kissed me?"

She nodded, dumbly.

"Before I allow you to do so, wife, I think it only fair that I know your intentions toward me."

"You are outrageous, my lord! I refuse to be made mock of, do you hear?"

He rose slowly from his chair and walked to her. He

placed his thumb and forefinger under her chin and forced her to look up at him.

"I do not mock you, Sabrina. I simply want to know if you return my regard. I do love you, you know."

"But I'm skinny," she blurted out. "I know that you do not admire skinny women."

"I would not say that that is precisely true," he said wolfishly, gazing down at her pointedly.

"I have seen you naked too, Phillip," she said foolishly.

" 'Tis most unchivalrous of you to remind me, madam. Now, Sabrina, I would like an answer from you. Would you be willing to spend say the next fifty or so years with me?"

"Would you go into a decline, my lord, were I to refuse?"

"Most likely I should become a dissolute, lecherous rakehell."

"Fifty years seems an exceedingly long time, my lord," she temporized, her hands unconsciously moving to his shoulders.

"Are you trifling with my affections, madam?" he asked, his hands moving naturally to her back.

"No, my lord," she whispered.

"In that case, my love, you may kiss me." He leaned down and let his lips touch hers, featherlight and undemanding.

Sabrina wound her arms tentatively about his neck to pull his mouth more firmly to hers. She felt his tongue probe gently against her mouth and with no more encouragement, moaned softly and parted her lips.

He grinned down at her and kissed the tip of her upturned nose. "My lady wife is thus far pleased?"

"I think I much like kissing you, Phillip."

"I trust there is much more you will enjoy, Sabrina. Now, dear one, I will allow you to seduce me, but only if you promise not to toss me aside like an old boot after you've taken your pleasure with me."

His arms tightened about her back and she nestled her cheek against his shoulder. "I most assuredly promise both the former and the latter, my husband."